I0638560

KEEP THE WIND
IN YOUR FACE

Books by John D. Nesbitt

For the Norden Boys
Lonesome Range
Black Hat Butte
Red Wind Crossing
Rancho Alegre
Raven Springs
Coyote Trail
Black Diamond Rendezvous
Man from Wolf River
Not a Rustler
West of Rock River
North of Cheyenne
Poacher's Moon
Adventures of the Ramrod Rider
A Good Man to Have in Camp
Keep the Wind in Your Face
Shadows on the Plain
Field Work
Blue Horse Mesa: Western Stories
Antelope Sky: Stories of the Modern West
Seasons in the Fields: Stories of a Golden West

Two Novellas:
"Dead for the Last Time"
"Trouble in the Labor Camp"

KEEP THE WIND IN YOUR FACE

John D. Nesbitt

SPEAKING VOLUMES, LLC
NAPLES, FLORIDA
2017

KEEP THE WIND IN YOUR FACE

Copyright © 1998 by John D. Nesbitt

All rights reserved. No part of this book may be reproduced or transmitted in any form or by any means without written permission.

ISBN 978-1-62815-705-5

For my brother Sandy

Chapter One

The lawyer from Omaha hadn't figured into the original plan of things, but when the party of four from Ohio canceled a week before the season opened, Del had to fill in his schedule on short order. He knew that most of the hunters on his waiting list would have gotten guides by now or decided to do without, so he would have to settle for latecomers. There were always those who called a few days before the season, and Del usually didn't mind turning them down. This time he took on two insurance agents from a small town in Illinois. The one who did the talking, Roger, was apologetic and grateful.

Then the lawyer from Omaha called. His name was Vince Furtino. He had just found out he could get away, he said, as he had had an important court case re-scheduled. What he would really like would be to hunt antelope, deer, and elk, all three.

Del explained that he was all booked up for deer and elk, and it was just a matter of chance that he had an opening for antelope—usually he didn't, he said, but he had an opening for two hunters.

"I'll take it."

"For two hunters?"

"Yes. Two of us."

"Do you have permits for area 35?"

"I will when I get there."

"Do you want to know my rates?"

"I have your brochure."

"O.K. I usually ask for a deposit, but there's not time for that right now. You'd get here as soon as the mail would. Shall I expect you here on Tuesday afternoon? Season opens Wednesday morning."

"Expect me there on Tuesday. I'll bring another hunter."

"You know what-all you need to bring. Just your personal things and your rifles. I've got a complete camp set-up."

"Yeah. That's in your brochure."

"Good enough, then, Mr. Furtino. We'll see you on Tuesday." As Del hung up, he thought the lawyer had sounded almost too confident. Del was still not sure he had a full slate of hunters, and he was glad to keep the Ohio party's deposit.

* * * * *

The lawyer's wife hadn't figured into any of the plans either, but she was driving the sparkling new maroon-colored Suburban when it pulled into Del's yard. The lawyer was reading a set of hunting regulations spread out like a road map against the dashboard. He folded it up and stepped out of the vehicle as Del walked out to meet them.

"Del Watters?"

"Sure am."

"Vince Furtino." He gave a forceful handshake.

Del took in a full first impression—tall, high-chested, and athletic, with dark hair receding on top and greying at the temples, a thick, straight beard neatly trimmed, dark eyes

2

behind tinted glasses, and chest hair curling out of the open neck of his flannel shirt.

Del did not like or dislike him; in his business, he didn't have to do either one. At least this one wasn't wearing a suede hat with a blaze of pheasant feathers on the front.

The lady walked around the front of the vehicle as the lawyer spoke. "This is my wife, Sylvia," he said.

"Pleased to meet you," Del said. "Are you the other hunter?"

"Yes I am," she answered, offering her hand. "And I'm pleased to meet you."

Del took a quick glance as they shook hands. He didn't like to look too long at another man's wife, but he liked her smile and the shine in her eyes. Del sensed it right there—the spark, or maybe better called a ripple, of magnetism that comes up at the first instant of mutual attraction. "I'm glad to have you both," he said. "Come on into my little office here and we'll get you checked in."

Once inside the office, a converted garage, Vince and Sylvia sat in the captain's chairs. Del sat at the desk and rummaged through one stack of papers.

"Come through Cheyenne?" he asked.

"Yes, we did."

"What kind of permits did you get?"

"Two permits for any antelope, area 35."

"Any trouble getting them?"

"No, they said they had plenty."

"That's good. They weren't selling that many in 35 to begin with."

3

"How does it look for us?"

"They move in and out of the country we'll be hunting, but in the last couple of weeks I've seen a few nice-looking bucks. I take it you'd like to get a buck, both of you."

Furtino smiled. "That's what we came for." He looked at his wife, and she smiled, too.

Del took another look at her, quick but absorbing. He liked her smile better than her husband's. Then he found the folder he was looking for. "Well," he said, "we should be able to tumble up a couple for you."

Furtino lit a cigarette. "The success ratio is pretty high, I understand."

Del pushed an ashtray to him. "Oh, yeah. Just about everyone gets one if they try. You'll get plenty of shots if you need to, and if you get tired of hunting horns, you can always fill your tag on a doe or fawn."

"That doesn't seem very sporting."

Del shrugged. "Some people hunt meat."

"Yes, I guess they'd have to, if they had one of those doe-or-fawn-only tags." The lawyer raised his eyebrows and flicked the ashes from his cigarette. "But you think we should do all right."

"Oh, I think so. I wouldn't expect to make it into the record book, but you should fill out in a few days. Most people do. The main problem they have is with shooting these longer distances, but like I say, you'll get plenty of shots."

Mrs. Furtino had stood up and was observing the photographs on the office wall. "Do you take the pictures?"

Del appreciated her profile as he answered. "When folks don't mind. And some hunters forget to bring along a camera."

"This lady has a beautiful deer in this picture."

"Yeah, that was a nice one. Big fat alfalfa thief. It was her first hunt. Yours too?" He caught a view of her. She was five or six years younger than her husband, maybe a shade over thirty, with a nice figure trimmed out in blue jeans and a windbreaker. Her hair was the color of wheat straw, he decided as he looked away.

"Yes," she answered. "This is my first time out. But Vince has hunted before."

"Not antelope, though." Del glanced at the woman and then at her husband.

"No, not antelope," Vince answered.

"Well, that should all change tomorrow." Del nodded, practicing his businesslike smile. "Now for the paperwork. This is a standard contract stating terms and rates, releasing me from liability for game violations on the part of the hunter . . . well, I guess you're familiar enough with this sort of thing. Go ahead and look it over."

After the Furtinos had looked over the papers, signed, and then paid Del with traveler's cheques, Vince was ready to go.

"I guess we should head on out this afternoon," he said, "to do a little scouting."

Del never knew, at first, who was going to be trouble and who wasn't, but Vince smelled like it already. Something in the way he proposed to do a little scouting suggested to Del that the lawyer was one of those hunters who wouldn't mind getting his animal the evening before the season opened. At the very least he was pushy, looking to get the edge on any proposition.

Del would have liked to say, "When you hunt with me, we do things my way until you get the gun in your hands and the season opens." Instead he was content to say, "I'm still waiting for the other two hunters, two fellows from Illinois. When I've got them checked in, we can go to camp."

"Where is camp?"

"About twenty miles southeast of here."

"Back the way we came?"

"Sort of, but off the highway, back in the rolling plains country where all you'll see for miles is windmills, jack rabbits, beef cows, and antelope."

"Will we be taking separate vehicles?"

"That usually works out best. That way, people can leave as they fill out. Meanwhile, if someone wants to take an animal in to the meat locker or the taxidermist, they can go right in. But we'll hunt in my outfit. That box there has the taxidermist's cards in it."

Vince leaned forward in his chair, pulled out a card, 3½ x 8½, and scanned the prices. "Seems reasonable," he said. "Is he the only one around?"

"No, but he's just starting out, been at it a couple of years, and he'll get a good job done for you at a good price, without waiting forever."

"Looks like he takes care of the shipping."

"Oh, yeah. That's standard. I imagine you've given some thought to what you'd like to have mounted and what you'd be happy just to have in a picture."

"I've decided I'll mount anything that goes fifteen or better." Vince turned to Sylvia, who was seated at his right. "But we can mount anything of yours that you like."

Sylvia smiled. She apparently knew her husband pretty well. "What's fifteen?"

Vince took the opportunity to show he had done his homework. "Fifteen inches from the base of the horn to the tip, going up over the curve on the outside," he said, in a matter-of-fact tone. "You learn to estimate through your scope."

Sylvia turned her eyes to Del, who said, "That's right."

"Well," she said, in what seemed to be a mild mockery of her husband's expertise and expectations, "should I hold out for a fifteen?"

Del smiled back. It wasn't good business, in the long run, to try to keep hunters on for an extra day or two. "Fourteen is pretty good for the country we'll be in. But you should suit yourself. Decide what you think looks good enough to keep."

"Sure," Vince said, lighting another cigarette. "We'll see what you get, and then we'll play it from there."

"That's a good idea," Del added. "This is your first time, both of you. You're hunting for success. Think about shooting an animal you'll be satisfied with, and think about making a good shot. If you don't get a wall hanger this year, there's always another year."

"Del's right," Vince said. "Think about the shot itself. Remember what I told you about rehearsing the whole sequence and being prepared." He flicked his cigarette ash into the tray, rose from his chair, and moved across the room to study the photographs. Sylvia remained seated, looking over the taxidermist's list of rates and services.

Del put the contracts back into the folder and the traveler's cheques into his cash box, which held no cash. "Those other two hunters should be rolling in pretty soon," he announced, "but if you two need to run downtown for anything, you've got time."

Sylvia put the taxidermist's card in her purse. "Is there anything we should be thinking about that you won't have in camp?"

"I've got a pretty complete set-up, right down to the candy bars and yogurt, but if you need cigarettes or camera film or snake-bite medicine—" he met Sylvia's quizzical look— "there's a pretty good liquor store at the second stoplight."

She smiled. "I think we're pretty well fixed for camera film and snake-bite medicine."

"Some folks forget. Especially the camera film."

Vince moved to the window. "Looks like your two hunters from Illinois just showed up. Maybe we will take a run downtown. Should we come back in half an hour?"

"That should be about right." As he spoke, Del raised from his chair and looked out the window. A light-blue, late-model Ford pickup with a camper shell and Illinois plates had come to a stop in the yard.

The two insurance agents were in their middle to late forties, maybe ten years older than Vince Furtino but not as well preserved. While Vince had the look of a man who worked out regularly, perhaps at competitive sports like racquetball and tennis, these two looked as if their most strenuous exertions would be playing a round of golf on Saturday afternoon or hefting a large can of tomato juice for Bloody Marys on Sunday morning. The taller one, Mel, had his jacket zipped part-way up, as people do to cover a drinker's liver. He had a well-developed case of broken blood vessels on either cheek, spreading beneath the eyes and over the nose, like a purple raccoon mask. He stubbed out his cigarette, sat down to sign the contract, and fell into a coughing fit. Acting as if it were a matter of course, he pushed himself up from the captain's chair with his left hand and, hacking and wheezing into his right hand, moved to the window.

Meanwhile his partner, Roger, filled out his own paperwork. When he finished, he peeled off a small stack of twenties, slid the money clip back onto the still respectable fold of bills, and stuck the wad into his shirt pocket. He shook out a cigarette, lit it with a monogrammed lighter, and turned to Mel, who was finishing his cough. "You gonna live?" he called in a cheerful tone.

"Oh, hell yes, I'm gonna live. I'll live longer than you." Mel lifted his glasses to wipe his watering eyes, and then he blew his nose with the same handkerchief. He cleared his throat again and added, "Hell, yes, I'm going to live. Someone has got to show you how to shoot all them antelope."

9

"We'll see who shoots what," Roger bantered back. By way of explanation, he said to Del, "we got one of them extra permits, doe-or-fawn-only. Whoever shoots his first one with the fewest shots gets to shoot the extra one."

"I'd think you'd shoot the additional antelope first, for practice," Del suggested. "By the way, whose permit is it?"

Mel spoke up. "It's in Roger's name."

Del flicked his eyebrows. "According to the law, that's who should shoot it."

Roger blew out a stream of smoke. "What does it matter as long as it's tagged legal?"

Del shrugged. "In some ways, not at all. I can't keep someone from pulling the trigger. And if I don't see something, I don't know it. But it's in my best interests not to sponsor game violations right under my nose. Even something small like party hunting."

"Party hunting?"

"That's what it's called when you fill one another's permits. I mention it just so you'd know."

"Just seems more sporting this way," Mel answered, clearing his throat again. He leaned out the door and spit into the flower bed, then stood up straight, squared his shoulders and took a deep breath, lit a cigarette, and said, "Loser pays for the extra tag."

Del, who had been waggling a pencil by its sharpened tip, dropped the pencil on his desk pad and closed his folder. "That's one way of doing it," he said, as he locked up his desk.

Chapter Two

Del, alone in his pickup, led the small caravan from his place through town and on out to the ranch country. The Furtinos were behind him, with Mel and Roger behind them. Del looked in the rear-view mirror and saw the maroon Suburban. Vince was driving, perhaps pleased in a small way to be in front of the insurance agents, who in turn were probably happy to be in back, having a beer and preferring not to have a lawyer on their ass. Del smiled and shook his head.

The camp where they were headed was all set up. The day before, Del had towed out the camp trailers, set them up, and leveled them. That morning he had set up his tent and gear, and now he was hauling the ice chests with groceries and refreshments. Everything was ready for the hunters to get settled in while Del went ahead with the next part of his work, which would be putting out a meal.

He looked in the rear view again, and he saw Vince and Sylvia both. He looked away, in the way he would make himself not look at another woman when he was with Rita.

Better to think of Rita, he thought, nodding. Lately when he wanted to think about life when it went well, he thought about the camping trip he and Rita had taken during the summer. It was a good thought, and it brought a smile every time—the right kind of smile.

On that trip, which wasn't work, he would look in the rear-view mirror and see the brown horse trailer snugged up behind the pickup. He would look across the cab, and instead of a bag of bread he would see Rita, dark hair touching her shoulders, dark eyes shining as she picked out music for the tape player and sang with the songs. Rita was fun to be with, not fun in a rowdy barroom sort of way, but the kind of fun a fellow could have when he found plump ripe chokecherries and then drank clear cold water, or when he caught the dark smell of cedar trees after a rain. As they drove, Del could nod at a flock of antelope, or later in the mountains, at a deer, and Rita would smile and nod back.

Del remembered the dry smell of dust and pines as they had driven up into the mountains, the smell of tarweed as he let the horses out of the trailer.

The midsummer sun was warm on dry grass as he saddled the horses, draped the panniers over the saddles, and laid out the camp gear. Rita, who had lived on a farm when she was a girl, knew how to move around the horses without spooking them. She helped Del as he hefted and sorted the items into piles—two equally weighted piles for each horse. She handed him the items as he loaded the horses. The panniers were warm to the touch, and so were the sleeping bags, pads, and tent canvas as he tied off the loads.

Up the first steep grade, breathing hard from the climb, they stopped to catch their wind and let the breeze cool them. Rita had tied her hair back, but a few loose strands blew in the soft wind. As she squinted into the afternoon, Del saw the crow's foot at the corner of her left eye. He put his arm around her waist and kissed her. She turned and kissed him back, a full kiss, as they stood on the ridge holding lead ropes to the two horses.

Down a longer, slower grade and across a timbered knoll, Del brought them to a flat grassy area. The creek flowed back eastward, to their left as they faced it. After Del unloaded the horses, stripped them and picketed them, he and Rita laid out the tent and set it up.

A tent was a nice thing, keeping out the sun or wind or rain when a person wanted things that way, but not keeping out the chuckle of the creek or the sighing of the wind in the pines. A tent was a clean, breathing place. It had a warm afternoon smell of canvas and dust as they rolled out the foam rubber pads and zipped the sleeping bags together. Del made pillows by putting jackets into the cloth bags that the sleeping bags had been in. Then, standing next to Rita, he raised his eyebrows, and she reached up and lifted his straw hat from his head. She tossed the hat onto the far corner of the bedding and turned to Del, whose hands moved down to her buttocks as he drew her closer.

A little while later, as they lay in the soft dim afternoon, Del saw that Rita had fallen asleep. He leaned to the foot of the bed and rummaged in the gear until he found a cotton sarape blanket, which he spread out and pulled over them. As he did so, he admired her dark hair spread out against the camp pillow, and the soft beige of her skin where the sun rarely touched it. Some women were fish-belly white in those places, and when they were like Rita, well into their thirties and had had a kid or two, they took on a pudgy, marbled look.

It was nothing to hold against a woman, but the contrast made him appreciate Rita even more. She had soft, smooth skin, its color somewhere between vanilla ice cream and weathered canvas, like the part of a sun tan that stayed through the winter. Hers was a natural pigment, pleasing to Del's sense of what seemed good. It went well with her dark hair, with the tent wall moving with the breath of the afternoon, with the sound of the horses clumping and grazing several yards away.

The evening air cooled quickly in the canyon where they were camped. Del gathered twigs and branches, straightened out the rocks that served as a campfire pit from one year to the next, and got a small blaze going. He rolled and dragged a stump close by so that he and Rita could lean against it. Then he tossed on a good load of firewood, to make a bed of coals to cook the steaks.

Now it was the cocktail hour on Horseshoe Creek, that time when the sky grew dark and the firewood burned toward coals. On a trip like this one, there was usually ice for drinks on the first day only, so Del made the best of it, serving bourbon and water in cold tin cups. He put on a quilted flannel overshirt and sat down next to Rita, who was wearing a lined denim jacket. Her dark hair and eyes were shiny in the firelight as she pursed her lips against the rim of the tin cup.

After the steaks, when the fire had blazed back up and then burned down to ashes, Del used his pocket flashlight to find their way into the tent and into the flannel-lined double sleeping bag, the kind the catalogs described as Adam and Eve.

In the morning, he heated water on his one-burner gas stove, using the bail-handled stainless steel kettle that also served as water bucket and dishpan. When the water was warm, he took it to the tent for Rita. He laid out a clean wash cloth and the plastic soap caddy and then went outside to make coffee.

The morning air was clear and fresh. It seemed all one with the cold creek water as he washed his hands and face, the cold water dripping from the small coffee pot onto the dust, the chatter of a squirrel carrying across the stream, the shift of the horses' hooves as they grazed. As Del stood in the cool clean morning, he had the same sense of harmony he had felt the afternoon before, while Rita was napping. He stood between the tent and the creek, and he knew that part of what he felt in that mountain air was the presence of Rita, coming through the tent walls like a pretty song and joining with the other beauties of the morning.

Time flowed and the shadows moved. When the sun was high and there was little shade in camp, Del saddled the horses and packed the saddlebags. He and Rita had planned to take a ride farther back in, eat lunch up on top, and then laze their way back.

The trail was narrow coming up out of the canyon, but it turned broad and sunny as it went up the side and onto the back of the mountain. At one point they crossed paths with wild turkeys coming back from water, and at another they pushed deer from the edge of the timber farther back in.

The grass was lush green as they moved higher up. The growing season was shorter here than on the plains, thawing out later and freezing up earlier. Del liked the high country in all seasons, but it was friendliest now. All the colors were rich and pure—the green meadow grass, the blue sky, the white puffy clouds, and then the royal blue lake nestled just below timberline.

They rode to the north side of the lake, to a spot a little ways uphill where the carpet of grass met the timber. When he had the horses unloaded and staked out, Del rolled out the picnic blanket, an eight-foot-square piece of canvas that he used for packing camp gear. They ate their lunch in the shade, washing it down with cool water from the blue-capped plastic quart bottles.

After lunch, they set things aside and dragged the canvas out onto the grass in the full sun. The horses paid no attention. For Del, and as he imagined it was for Rita, it was like being on a magic carpet on top of the world, above the blue lake, with green grass and darker green timbered mountains falling away to all sides, blue sky all above them, and a shining sun that warmed the canvas and the skin.

* * * * *

Del smiled. It had been a good trip, all right. There had been more to it than that, of course—good conversations with Rita, joking with her, slapping mosquitoes, wading in the creek, and all of that—but when he thought about the trip, there was a set of impressions that always came first and brought a smile. A trip like that was the part of a good life that made some of the rest of it worth putting up with.

Del slowed the pickup a half-mile from the turn-off. In the rear view, he saw Vince gain on him and then slow down. Del put on his left turn signal, saw Vince's go on, and then Mel's. He slowed, pressed the brakes, turned onto the gravel, rumbled across the iron pipes of the cattle guard, and rolled onto the quiet road. He smiled again as he thought of Rita. Then he looked in the left rear-view mirror and saw the maroon vehicle coming across the cattle guard and the light blue pickup turning off the pavement. No, he thought, this was different. It was work.

Chapter Three

Well before dawn on opening morning, Del slipped out of his sleeping bag and into his clothes. He expected frost on the ground this morning, but the weather had not yet turned cold. Later in the season, as his work took him into colder weather and higher country, he would sleep in long underwear and a stocking cap, with his pants and shirts folded up and stuffed inside the sleeping bag by the zipper seam. This morning he crawled out of the warm bag and slipped into his cool clothes, shutting off the hammer of the wind-up alarm before it had a chance to batter the twin bells. It would be warm enough later in the day; his task of the moment was to get moving around in the crisp morning air and to get some coffee going. Mel and Roger, who were shaping up to be real slob hunters, would need it.

Del stoop-stepped out of the canvas wall tent, the same tent he and Rita had shared. It was the kind that some people called a sheepherder's tent, and on trips like this one it served as his separate lodging. Things worked better that way. In his divided role as boss and servant, he preferred to keep his distance. If the hunters wanted to argue, talk over their heads, or stay up late drinking, Del would not be troubled. For the antelope hunting, he had set his camp in a grove of cotton-woods, with the two camper trailers parked in an "L" formation against the direction of prevailing winds. The Furtinos occupied one trailer, and the insurance agents had the other. The trailers provided propane heat and light for the lodgers. Although each trailer could sleep four people if necessary, they were comfortable accommodating two hunters along with their duffel and hunting gear. Either trailer could serve as a kitchen in bad weather, but for the present, both acted only as sleeping quarters. Their doors opened to the leeward side, facing Del's open-air kitchen, a canopied affair that stood as a front porch to his tent. He cooked and served meals under the canvas fly. It was not his custom to deliver the meals in the style of room service, but hunters were welcome to take their meals back into their suites.

Del's first step out of his own quarters, then, took him into the kitchen, where he fired the large coffee pot he'd prepared the night before. Then he took a quick trip to the cottonwoods, returned to wash his hands and face, and lit a lantern. He liked his kitchen in the pre-dawn, before any light showed behind the trailer curtains. His three-burner propane stove sat on a fold-out but solid table, under which two utility boxes held cooking utensils, tableware, canned goods, and spices. To one side, a large army surplus trunk held the general camp kit including ash trays, toothpicks, playing cards, shoelaces, bandages, a sewing kit, safety pins, a hatchet, sharpening stones, two extra sheath knives, extra gloves and knit caps, blaze-orange vests, hunting regulations, field guides to wildlife and plants, a pocket-size Bible, and a paperback dictionary. Right inside the tent he stowed the ice chests, which he brought out at mealtimes.

Del had refined his skill at planning a menu for strangers. He kept a good balance between pre-packaged food and fresh meat, vegetables, fruit, and breakfast food. The plan was to feed his guests the finest on the first night and morning, before any hunters filled their permits and left. After that, he would go through food that might spoil or get stale, and he would save the canned goods and junk food for short order and bad weather.

The evening before, as the Furtinos sipped chilled rosé and watched Mel and Roger demolish a bag of party ice with a quart of Lord Calvert, Del had laid out a fine spread of pork chops, mashed potatoes and gravy, green salad, and corn on the cob. They had been a cheery group, Del included, moving their camp chairs around the fire pit as the smoke shifted, tossing the pork chop bones and corn cobs into the flames. Mel and Roger were happy, nonchalant drinkers, not given to excessive brooding about what sort of trophy they might hold out for. They did not bring up the topic of who was to shoot the extra antelope. Roger seemed fascinated by the amount of sky he could see as he leaned back in his chair. The firelight played on his throat as he muttered, time and again, that you never saw anything like that in Decatur. Del sipped on a glass of their whiskey, agreed that it was a great life, and in between comments chatted with the Furtinos, mainly Vince, on the subject of the next day's weather, the last year's hunt, the present tending of the fire.

There had been one awkward moment, but it didn't last. Mel, learning that the Furtinos both had jobs and no children, had said, "Oh, dinks." Then, in response to the puzzled looks on their faces, he had said, "DINKS. Double income, no kids."

Sylvia smiled politely, but her husband took a moment to master the disdain that flashed across his face.

In the course of the previous evening, Del had derived a menu for this morning. In the glow of the lantern, as the coffee started to plunk, he hauled the ice chests out of the tent and took out the sausage, eggs, cheese, bread, butter, donuts, juice, and milk. He set up the camp chairs, which he had put away for the night, and in their midst he set one of the utility boxes for a serving table. After putting the sausage on to cook, he glanced at the two trailers and saw that they were both still dark.

As he walked to Mel and Roger's trailer, it occurred to him that they were the kind of hunters who would use an antelope guide on future trips, to do the camp work, the field dressing, and the skinning. Most hunters would see soon enough that there was very little about antelope hunting that they couldn't do themselves, once they knew what it entailed. Vince would be the self-sufficient type, but not these two. Del rapped on their door and called out, not too loud to disturb the mood of the morning. "Breakfast is cookin', fellas."

Right away he heard their muttering, then the trailer creaking on its jacks, as he moved to the other trailer. Before he finished his knuckle rap, he heard Vince call out, "We're already up. We'll be right out."

In the kitchen again, Del got breakfast into full swing. In a few minutes, he was joined by Sylvia, who warmed her hands at the stove, and Vince, who laced his boots by lantern light.

"Didn't see any need to burn the lights in the trailer," Vince said, leaning in his chair. "Would you pour me a cup of coffee there, dear?"

"I'll get it," Del said. "Both of you?"

"Please," she answered.

"Anything in it?"

"Both of us take it black." She took the two mugs, set her husband's on the utility box, and sat down in the chair at his left. She held the mug in her hands, and Del had the awareness that it was his—one of those old, tan, thick-lipped truck-stop mugs, the kind that, if a person ever broke one, turned out to be double-walled. Sylvia cupped the mug, blew steam across the top, and took a sip.

Del returned to his cooking and said, to no one in particular, "Scrambled eggs was all right with everyone, wasn't it?"

"It carried the vote," Vince said. "Damn, that coffee's hot. Good, though."

Del heard the other trailer door squeak open and closed, then open and closed again. He poured two more cups of coffee, scattered the grated cheese across the top of the dozen eggs bubbling like soup, and turned down the flame beneath the sausage.

"Smells like real food cooking," Roger chirped. "This coffee mine?"

"Either one," Del answered. "There's milk in the green ice chest and donuts on the end of the table."

"This is just fine." Roger moved to a chair and sat down, exhaling a long "Ahhh" of relaxation, as if to invite all present to share in his comforts and discomforts. At present it was his comfort, as he stretched his legs, hunched his shoulders, yawned almost in silence, and then shook out a cigarette and lit it.

Del was forking the sausage links into a napkin-lined pie tin when he heard Mel go into an early morning coughing fit, somewhere beyond the trailers. It was the type of coughing that failed to satisfy a listener—hacking, building up, and then stopping in a gag—and Del could visualize the clouded, contorted face as its owner tried to get the cycle going again and bring it to completion. Del wanted to clear his own throat and spit, but he made do with a mild "eh-hem" and said, "Here's sausage. Eggs coming up. Help yourself to the milk and juice." He set the tin of sausage on the table.

"One thing I forgot to mention last night, Del."

"What would that be, Roger?"

"Ketchup. I'm partial to ketchup on my scrambled eggs. Sounds terrible, doesn't it?"

"No. Lots of people like it. I go through quite a bit of it."

"I know a guy," Vince joined in, "who eats about half a bottle of that stuff with every meal. Carries it around with him, for Pete's sake."

"Oh, I'm not that bad." Roger turned to start his day-long banter with Mel, who had come into the lamplight. "You damn near missed breakfast."

Mel had a surly tone as he picked up his coffee. "Well, I didn't."

"I'll dish up the eggs," Del said. "Help yourselves to everything else. Ketchup is in the green ice chest."

"I was just telling these people how fond I was of ketchup on my eggs."

"Well, they must have been very interested."

"Vince was."

"Yes, I was," Vince put in, with a contentious note in his voice.

With the eggs portioned out, accompanied by sausage and bread, conversation died. The most audible sound was the clack of metal forks on melmac plates.

"Superb breakfast," Roger declared.

"Get enough ketchup?" Mel was becoming amiable again.

"Just right. And my compliments to the chef on his secret blend of coffee."

"There's more in the pot."

"I'll get it," Sylvia said. "I'm done." She went to set her plate down, and then she looked at Del.

"I let the dishes soak during the day," he said. "You can just set 'em in the dishpan there."

She kept her gaze on him. "The one you used last night."

He nodded back. "That one."

"Shall I take yours, too, Vince?"

Del glanced at Vince, who nodded, then rocked his coffee cup. Sylvia took her husband's plate and fork, set the tableware in the large enamel basin, and brought back the coffee pot. Del found himself watching her movements.

As she poured coffee, Vince spoke. "Sylvia and I talked it over, and we'd like to wait to fill our permits. Let you fellows do yours first."

"Oh, we're not in any big hurry," Roger answered. "Are we, Mel?"

"No, not at all. Taking turns would be fine with me."

Vince pushed a little more, in what seemed like his mildest courtroom manner. "We'd rather you fellows went first. We talked it over."

Sylvia had sat back down, out of the line of conversation. Del met her glance, and they both looked away. Del looked back at the other hunters.

Roger got up and fetched the box of buttermilk donuts, which he offered around to the others. Mel took one. Roger took one for himself and sat down. "Well, it's all right with me," he said, "but we don't want to seem greedy or anything. What do you think, Del?"

It seemed to Del that Vince wanted to get rid of the men from Illinois, partly so the Furtinos could have the undivided services of the guide, and partly so they could have the leisure to hunt for a trophy. "Whatever you folks decide among yourselves is fine with me," he answered. "That's better than elbowing and arguing every time a set of horns pops up."

"Well," Roger answered, "I hate to crowd in at the front of the line—"

"You're already there," Vince assured him. "We'd rather wait."

"O.K. with me, then. How about you, Mel?" Roger looked at his partner, who was brushing donut crumbs off his vest and studying the operation with his chin tucked down to his collarbone.

"Fine with me," Mel said. "We have three permits, though. You want us to do all three?"

"Sure," said Vince. "The last one is doe-and-fawn-only, so that shouldn't take much longer."

"We gotta shoot the first two first," Mel said, resuming the banter from the day before. "Roger might hang us up."

"That reminds me," Del said. "These antelope haven't been shot at since last year, so our first few shots might be nice and close. If we don't bungle it, we can make some nice quick kills. But the more we chase and shoot at them, the farther out we'll have to shoot to reach them. Just something to think about." Del turned off the lamp, and the morning outside the kitchen seemed lighter. "I'll put together a lunch box, and you-all can get your weapons. Season opens in about fifteen minutes."

A short while later, as the group gathered at the tailgate of the pickup, the world around them began to take shape in the grey morning. Every time Del gave his policy-and-procedure talk, he recalled the Alaskan bush plane pilot who had taken him and three others out on a salmon fishing trip. The pilot had shouted out his orders, long and loud above the droning of the engine, explaining how to vomit in the coffee can and how not to mash mosquitoes on the upholstery. Remembering the man who had seemed the caricature of a guide, Del tried to be congenial, matter-of-fact, but definite.

"Mel and Roger, you can ride in the back here, since you'll be shooting first. If you see something, don't bang on the cab or holler. Just talk to me through the sliding window. I'll keep it open. Vince and Sylvia can ride in front with me.

26

Everyone make sure, every time you get back in the vehicle, that your rifle doesn't have a live one in the chamber. If I ask you to make sure, don't take offense. It's a habit of mine." Everybody nodded comprehension. "And one more thing. If you see something you want to shoot at, wait till you get out of the vehicle. Then put a live shell in, get a rest on a fence-post or fender or bumper, and take your shot. But don't shoot from the vehicle. Oh, and when you get out, you have a better chance of not spooking them if you get out on the off side of the pickup. Like I said, if we don't get them too stirred up, they should give us some pretty easy shots, at least to begin with. And don't shoot any cows. O.K.?"

"O.K." was the answer all around.

Vince said, "Sun's coming up."

"Hot dog," Roger said, "let's go kill some annalope. I'm startin' to get excited."

Mel lit a cigarette and shot out a puff of smoke. "Don't let it spoil your aim," he said.

Chapter Four

The prairie grass lay white and curly and coarse in the early morning frost as Del drove the pickup out of the campsite and into the open plains. The sun was beginning to crest the eastern hills, causing the pre-dawn greys to give way to pinks. In less than half an hour, there would be full sunlight, bathing the vast, rippling grasslands in gradual warmth. Right now, at sunrise, was the coldest time of the morning, especially to newcomers.

Del scanned the country as he drove. In first light, the flash of white on an antelope's belly and rump would stand out against the expanse of tawny grass. "You're liable to see them anywhere," he said to the Furtinos. "Over the next hill, around the next bend—sometimes they seem to just pop up out of nowhere. They usually stay in the open, so the easiest way to find them is to drive along from pasture to pasture, windmill to windmill, and see what you meet."

The hunting party followed a vehicle trail for several minutes, and then Vince spoke up. "How much land do we have access to?"

"We've got permission to hunt eighteen sections here," Del answered. "That's three miles wide at this end, and then it widens to four miles. We're camped in the middle of the first section, and the ranch goes back five miles."

"All to ourselves?"

"For the first three days, if we need that long. Then starting on the weekend, this rancher will let in other folks. Here's our first gate."

Del watched as Vince got out, mastered the lever-and-chain device on the barbed-wire gate, let the gate loose, dragged it out of the way, and let the pickup drive through. Conscious of the silent woman beside him, Del watched in the rear-view mirror as Vince snugged the gate back into place, having first stepped through the gateway so he wouldn't have to crawl through the strands. When Vince was in the cab again, Del turned left and followed the vehicle ruts along the fence.

"That's a pretty clever gizmo he's got to pull that gate tight," the lawyer observed.

"Yeah, there's all kinds of them to figure out. Some fellas don't bother with them, some do. This old boy likes to keep his gates as tight as he can, it seems. Two rules in cattle country: always close a gate behind you if you found it that way, and always stay on the trails unless you have to pick up an animal."

"Erosion?"

"Bad. You'll see, in some places, how deep the ruts have gotten. You don't want to start any new ones unless you have to."

"Those sound like pretty good rules, then."

"Well, I guess there are others, that anyone except a fool ought to know better than do, like don't shoot cows and don't start grassfires."

"There's lots of quick fuel here," Vince agreed.

"You haven't seen the wind blow yet. With a little luck we—look over there." He let off the gas pedal and pointed with his left arm, then leaned back to speak through the sliding window. "O.K., boys, don't get excited. There's four antelope off to our left, up ahead about a quarter of a mile. I'll drive a little farther and then stop. Get out on the right side, and you can shoot across the—no, wait. I'll stop at that fence brace. You can use it. But still get out on the right side."

Del stopped at the fence brace and left the engine running. "Be calm," he said, leaning toward the rear window. Mel, with two cigarettes in his mouth, was holding both rifles, and Roger was easing over the side of the pickup bed. Del spoke softly but clearly, not in a whisper. "Take your time. They're not spooked. Come around the back." Roger crept to the driver's window for more instructions. "That second one is a buck. Get a good rest on that fence brace, and if you like him, take him. If he goes to move, wait for him to stop. He won't go very far yet."

"How far?"

"Oh, maybe twenty or thirty yards."

"No, I mean how far are they?"

"About a hundred and fifty yards. Nice shot for you. Take your time."

"O.K." Roger worked the bolt on his gun, got a shell into the chamber, set the safety, wiped his hands one by one on his pants, and crept to the cross-brace.

The antelope picked up and sauntered away at an angle, rumps bouncing and flashing. "Don't shoot 'em in the ass," Del said. "See if he'll give you a broadside."

Roger followed them with his scope, and when they stopped and turned to look back, he gave a lurch. "Shit," he muttered. He flicked his safety, settled back into position, and touched off a shot. The explosion ripped through the early morning air, and the buck dropped to the ground, flailing his legs and flashing his white belly. The other three antelope wheeled to the left and took off, leaving a plume of dust in their wake.

"Good shot," Del said. "I think he'll stay down, but get ready in case he doesn't."

Roger jacked a new shell into the chamber as Del stepped out of the pickup. "I think I got him right in the front quarter," the hunter said.

The buck lay on the ground, kicking. "I think so, too," Del answered, still in a low voice. "Here's how we'll do it. You hand me the gun and crawl through the fence, then you take your gun and work your way up to him. Meanwhile, I'll drive up the fence till we're across from him, and I'll come help you drag him to the truck."

"O.K. And if he gets up I'll drill him."

"Sure. But I think you hit him pretty good."

"I think so."

As Del handed the rifle to Roger, he had another thought. "One more thing."

"What's that?"

"Don't cut his throat."

"No? Why not?"

31

John D. Nesbitt

"You might want to have him mounted, and you don't want to ruin anything. He'll have bled to death by the time you get there."

"O.K."

The guide looked around at Mel, who had gotten rid of one of the cigarettes and had the other in his mouth. Smoke was curling up around his squinted left eye as he kneeled and watched the buck through his rifle scope. "Looks like he's going to stay put."

"Yeah, looks like it," Del said. "We'll drive up the road a ways, and if you feel like it, you can go over with me to help Roger with his animal."

"Sure." Mel lowered his rifle.

Back in the cab, Del looked at his other two hunters. "Well, how's that for a little action right off the bat?" He put the truck into gear and rolled forward.

"Ten minutes into the hunt," Vince answered.

"I don't expect them all to be that easy," Sylvia added.

"No," the guide agreed, "I don't, either. That was a nice bit of luck. But Roger made a good shot. That's a good start to the day."

"Do you want us to stay in the pickup?"

"Whatever you want. We'll drag it back to work on it, so you won't miss anything." Del stopped the pickup. "We'll just be a few minutes."

Roger was standing over his kill as the guide and second hunter made their way across the pasture. "I'll bet he's excited," Mel said. "I got buck fever just watching."

32

"Uh-huh," Del said. Something caught his eye, and he stopped. Pointing, he said, "Those other three antelope stopped on the next hill there. See 'em?"

"Oh, yeah. Roger doesn't see 'em."

"Those three will probably just stand and watch us. That's the way they are. Now would be a good time for Roger to fill that extra tag."

"We were going to wait."

"All the same to me. His tag."

When they arrived at the kill, Roger was still standing, studying the animal that lay on its side, teeth bared and eyes already glazing over. "They sure got skinny legs," he said.

"Hey, Roger," Mel spoke up. "Del says we ought to shoot one of them there. What do you think? They're just standing there."

"Well, we were going to wait and see, weren't we? See who took the least shots?"

"I doubt that I can get one with less than one shot. Go ahead."

"You think so, Del?"

"It's your permit. I don't pull the trigger for you. But they're just standing there. They're a little farther off than he was, maybe a little better than two hundred yards."

"Well, hell." Roger shrugged. "If you guys think so, what the hell. I'll see how I am at that range." He knelt down to take aim, and Del could see the rifle tip making little figure eights. The rifle went off, and a spout of dust shot up on the hillside in front of the antelope. The animals took off in high gear, and Roger kicked up two more puffs of dust behind them. He worked the gun again and clicked the trigger on an empty chamber.

"They're hard to hit when they're running," Del said. "But that's O.K. You got a nice one here."

Roger turned. "Yeah. What do you think? Is he good enough to have stuffed?"

"He won't make the record book, but he's a good looker. Horns are even and have a nice wide curve to them. And those ivory tips are an extra."

"Are they rare?" Roger ran a finger across one of the yellowish tips.

"Oh, maybe one in ten that I see has those tips."

Roger turned and looked in the direction of the three fugitive antelope, which had stopped on yet another rise. "Yeah," he said. "Let's save the head. But I feel like a dumb ass missing those others."

"How many were you shooting at?" Mel teased.

"Once they started running, all of them." Roger laughed.

"There'll be lots more," Del said. "Let's get this guy back to the truck. If one of you will grab the other horn, we'll drag him on his hips and not spoil the cape."

Mel took the other horn. "I'll get it. How are you doing, Roger?"

"I'm just a little bit bushed, actually. That took a lot out of me."

"Get a pretty good rush, did you?" Mel spoke over his shoulder as Roger trudged behind.

"Yeah, right after I shot him. I was calm up until then."

Back at the pickup, Del got a quick snapshot and then set up the skinning hoist while Mel snapped half a roll of film from his own camera.

Vince took interest in the hoist. "That's a smart idea. Mounts right onto your back bumper."

"Uh-huh. An easy one-man job." Del hooked the gambrel onto the winch cable and pulled out enough slack to reach the ground. He spoke to the insurance agents. "Shall I dress him?" They nodded, so he grabbed a hind leg and dragged the buck beneath the hoist. He skinned the two rear hocks, cut and snapped off the lower legs, poked the gambrel tips through the membrane windows on the hamstring tendons, and winched the body upwards. Before it cleared the ground, he cut off the front forelegs, and then he hoisted it free.

As the four hunters drank coffee and watched, the guide rolled up his sleeves, wiped the skinning knife on his pants leg, and went to work. It was better this way, to have a one-man job of it. No one got in the way, and the work got done neater and cleaner. All he needed was someone to pour water when he wanted to rinse his hands, and Roger was happy to have that part in the process.

Del did not take long to separate the antelope into three main parts: a gut pile, a cape and head, and a clean hanging carcass. As he put his knife in its sheath, he noticed that frost still lay in the shade of the pickup. "Well, Roger," he said, "if you get your tag punched out and signed, we'll get this fellow bagged up and we'll be ready to roll. The morning is still young."

"Tie the tag around his horn?"

"That works pretty well—"

"What if it's a doe or fawn?" Vince cut in.

Del thought, that was just like Vince, to push at the small details. He imagined the lawyer timing him from the time he took out his knife till the time he put it away. Del answered, "I was gonna say, that works pretty well until you got 'em skinned. Then, most people tie the tag around a leg."

"Oh," Vince said.

Del turned to Roger. "If we don't get you fellows your second buck by noon time, we'll go back to camp anyway, so you can take yours to the taxidermist."

When the group was under way again, Del made conversation with Sylvia and Vince. "Some people just field dress the animals and do the skinning later." He rested his glance on Sylvia and added, "Field dressing would be just the gutting part, before you'd do any skinning."

"I see. That would be quicker."

"Sort of. But when you've got the animal right at the vehicle, you can get the skinning done and not have to worry about it later."

"Your way is neater, too," Vince put in.

"Yes, it is. You get less hair on the meat—and antelope hair is bad. Plus the meat cools quicker."

"That's a handy set-up you've got."

Del was enjoying Vince's apparent flattery. He imagined that the lawyer saw himself already a step closer to exclusive proprietorship of the guide and was on the lookout to make the relationship a friendly one. "It is," he answered. "It makes my job easier." He glanced at the instrument panel, and in rotating his forearm, he saw a splotch of blood he had missed. One down and four to go, he thought, and no telling what the rest would be like. The hunters might make a clean go of it, and they might botch things terribly. There wasn't much he could do to control the details, but for his part, it mostly washed off.

About a mile from the first kill, he turned the pickup west again, following a trail that cut through a large pasture. There were no fences visible in three directions, and only one windmill showed to the southwest. Del knew that the present road would take them there. Half a mile later, the road topped a little swell, and off to their left he saw a herd of a half-dozen antelope. "Up ahead," he called through the window.

"We see them."

"That one looks like a buck. I think I can get a little closer." The antelope were still between a quarter- and a half-mile off, so Del drove on. When he came within three hundred yards, the animals set off in a trot, parallel to the road. "They want to play," he called out. "How's that buck look to you, Mel?"

"I'd like to give him a try."

"O.K. They'll probably pace us for a while and then cross over in front of us." Del watched the rumps and heads bobbing along ahead, in no apparent hurry, so he kept an even pace. The speedometer registered just under fifteen miles per hour. "There they go," he said, as the animals veered across the road, maybe two hundred yards ahead. "When I stop, get out on the left side."

The antelope angled off to the right, and when the pickup stopped, they stopped. The guide heard Mel clamber over the side of the pickup bed, jack a shell into the chamber, and click the safety. Del shut off the engine. "You can shoot right across the hood," he said in a quiet voice. "About two hundred yards or maybe a little more."

The antelope were lined out in single file, and they began to walk. The buck was last in line. Mel picked him up, let out a breath as he flicked the safety, and squeezed the trigger. Sylvia had her ears plugged, and Vince was watching through his binoculars, as the buck lurched and then broke into a run. Mel kicked up three quick shots behind the buck, which was still in the rear of the bunch but running strong. "Son-of-a-bitch," he said, fumbling in his left pocket of shells. "I should have got him. Damn me."

"I'm pretty sure you hit him," Del said.

"I'm sure you did," Vince called out. "I saw him hunch up, and he was running different from the others. You hit him."

"Not enough to knock him down."

"Well, get in," Del said, "We'll try to catch up with him. We don't want to lose him now."

Mel handed his rifle to Roger and climbed into the pickup. "Four shots at the sonofabitch," he said to Roger. "Four shots. Now we're even, as far as shots go."

"Did you get a pretty good rush?"

"When he took off."

Roger laughed. Del looked back to see Roger lighting a cigarette and Mel pushing new shells into his rifle.

The road curved to the southwest, following a low swell on the right. Del was doing twenty-five now and gaining on the antelope. All in an instant, the animals cut in a right turn and pushed on up and over the crest.

"They're through playing," Del said through the window. "We'll have to try to sneak up on them on foot. This'll work best with both of you."

Del parked the pickup on a level spot. Sending Roger off to the right and Mel to the left, he crept up the slope between them. He paused, crouched on all fours, waiting for Mel to peek over. Mel looked, then pulled back and signaled to the guide, who dropped back down the slope far enough to scurry over. Mel's face was flushed, but he seemed calm. "That buck is just standing there," he whispered, "about the same distance as before."

"I doubt you'll get any closer."

"Probably not." Mel turned and went into a sneak, stooping. At the rise, he settled into a kneeling position, brought up his rifle, and fired. Del came up behind him as the second shot crumpled the buck.

"Good work. I'll bring the pickup down to him. Just wait for me there."

The second buck was a little more of a mess than the first one. Mel's first shot had clipped the front of the stomach, and his last shot had shattered both front shoulders. But the cape was not spoiled, and Mel was satisfied with the horns, so Del took care as he skinned it. He opened it up and found the gut-shot mess, a smelly mass of half-digested sagebrush soaking in a purple soup of blood. He opened up the rib cage all the way to the neck and slashed the throat open lengthwise. With

Mel pouring, he used two gallons of water to get the animal near clean.

After the carcass had aired out and dripped somewhat dry, it went into the game bag with the first one, which had already spread a bloody stain on the white muslin. The guide washed his hands and dried them on the clean end of the bag. He noticed that the second carcass was tagged, so they were ready to go.

"Two of 'em in the bag, and it's only 9:30," Roger announced. "That's pretty damn good."

"From here we can do one of two things," Del answered. "We can hunt till we fill your third tag, or we can go back to camp and let you fellows take the heads to the taxidermist and the meat to the locker. Meanwhile we can hunt Vince and Sylvia a little bit, and pick up your third one when you get back."

Roger and Mel nodded. "Let's take these in and get the third one later," Roger said.

Vince looked at Sylvia, who said, "Sure."

Vince nodded, then added, "We'll hunt on the way back to camp, of course."

As Mel climbed into the truck, he fell into one of his coughing fits. He didn't gag and stop this time, but followed through and brought up enough phlegm to spit over the side of the pickup bed. Then in a cheerful tone he said to Roger, "I guess the third one is still yours."

Chapter Five

The lawyer from Omaha made his debut in antelope killing at high noon, shortly after an early lunch. His was a lone buck, standing at the base of a small sandstone bluff down in a draw and offering an obliging broadside at a little under two hundred yards. Del watched as Vince took slow and careful aim from a kneeling position, and he listened as the solid thud of bullet on body came back from the bluff. The hunter looked up from his scope in visible disbelief as the buck stood motionless for ten or fifteen seconds. Then it raised up on its hind legs, pirouetted half a turn, and collapsed. Vince let out a long breath of relief as Sylvia applauded and called out, "Good shot, honey."

"Thanks." He came back to the open cab and cradled his rifle in the gun rack. In a calm voice he said, "I'm going to step it off to see how far it was."

"I'll be right behind you," Del said. "We'll bring him back up here to work on him."

When Del reached the fallen animal, Vince announced the distance as a hundred and eighty yards. Del nodded, and each man grabbed a horn and started dragging.

It was a mild afternoon, sunny with a soft breeze. Del worked up a light sweat in dragging the animal to the pickup, and he could see a glisten on Vince's cheek and neck. By the time they were done with photographs, Del felt himself cooling down. Vince put on his jacket as Del, with his sleeves rolled up, went to work.

He dressed the animal in his neat and methodical way, never making a slip that would gash the meat or nick the hide. He had sharpened his knife at lunchtime, after the first two bucks had taken a little of the edge off of it, and even though this buck was a little older and the hide clung tougher, the knife made smooth cuts.

Vince watched, even more attentively since it was his animal, but he did not interfere or offer comments. He had no doubt gathered, correctly, that Del's hoist made the task a truly one-man job that went faster if only one man got his hands on it.

When Del had trimmed down around the brisket, shoulders, and neck and had removed the head and hide in one flawless piece, he laid it out on the crisp dry grass. "Well, what do you think?"

"I've decided to just mount the horns on this one. I'll wait for something a little better before I have the full head mount done." Vince lit a cigarette and kneeled down to study the head and horns as they lay perfect and unspoiled on the prairie grass, with the hide stretched out still intact—tube-skinned, as some called it—all the way back to the hind quarters.

Del found interest in the scene. Here was the lawyer from Omaha, in his tinted eye glasses, studying his nearly perfect work. The buck was not a trophy, but the horns were larger than on either of the other two heads that would now be cooling in the taxidermist's freezer. And even though Vince Furtino was a headhunter, not a meat hunter, he had made a clean shot. As Del opened the animal, he saw that the bullet had gone through the ribs right behind the front legs, cutting a furrow through the heart and spoiling only about a pound of rib meat. It was the best kill of the day, so far, and the lawyer was taking a nice long look at the remains of the head and cape before he tossed it aside like a trifle.

As Del washed up, Sylvia poured water from a gallon milk jug, just as Roger and Mel had done. Although he did not look straight at her, Del sensed her closeness and appreciated it. When his hands were scrubbed, he took out a clean muslin game bag, slipped it up around the hanging carcass, shouldered it off the gambrel, and, rolling it across his hip into the back of the pickup, was done with number three. He held out his hands and motioned to Sylvia, who uncapped the water and tipped the jug. Del rinsed his hands and wiped them on the end of the bag, then tucked the bag around the antelope's shanks. Sylvia set the jug on the tailgate and stepped away.

"If you want to keep those horns," Del said, "let's toss the whole works in the back, and we'll take 'em off back at camp."

"O.K." Vince had risen from his crouch and was drawing on the last of his cigarette, with the air of being in no hurry to dirty his hands, so Del stepped past him to pick up the head and hide. As he did so, he caught a whiff of the lawyer's cologne—Brut. He hadn't smelled it earlier, especially with Sylvia sitting between them, but he smelled it now. Maybe the light sweat had brought it out.

"One o'clock," Vince said.

"Our other two hunters ought to be back by now," Del answered. "Maybe we should pick them up and see about getting their last permit filled this afternoon."

When he had gotten the pickup turned around and was driving past the gut pile, Del noticed that it was already beginning to dry and wrinkle. The coyotes and magpies would be happy, and it wouldn't be a neat gut pile for long. A few minutes later, he scratched his index finger across the bottom of his nose, and he must have given an ugly look.

"What's the matter?" Sylvia asked.

"Boy, you get a strong antelope smell off the horns sometimes."

"Is that right?" Vince put his left hand to his nose. "Mine doesn't seem to smell, and I had hold of the other horn when we dragged him back. Oh, there's a little bit of it. But I washed my hands afterwards."

"Sometimes they'll keep that smell for quite a while. If you've got a pair hanging on the wall, sometimes you'll catch it just walking by."

Sylvia turned to Vince, who said in his nonchalant way, "I'll probably hang mine in the garage."

" 'Course a head smells that way, too," Del teased. "If Sylvia shoots a big one, she'll want to hang it right in the living room."

"We'll live with it," Vince said.

* * * * *

44

The two insurance agents had camouflaged any cologne or antelope smell with a couple of cans of Budweiser. They were sitting in the shade of the kitchen canopy, enjoying life to the brim as they best knew how.

"Any luck?" Roger sang out.

"Vince got a buck," Sylvia announced.

"Nice one?"

"Only about a fourteen," Vince answered, hitting the perfect tone between a boast and a sulk.

"That makes a good day of it," Mel said. "Are you folks ready for a cool one?"

"Sun's slipping over the yard arm," Roger chimed in.

Sylvia and Vince shook their heads.

"I could drink one," Del answered as he sat down.

The beer was cold and tasted good. When Del had drunk half of it, he realized Sylvia had gone to the trailer. Vince was still standing in the shade of the canopy. Del imagined he was hoping that Mel and Roger would kill their last antelope before sundown. Del didn't like to feel pushed, but it would probably work better if they did—and it would save a day's fee for Roger.

"Even though the sun *is* over the yardarm," Del said, taking another swallow, "there's a few hours of daylight left. Do you boys feel like going out for your last animal?" By his count, they had had only one beer each, and they did not show any impairment.

Mel looked at Roger, who wiggled his beer can and emptied it. "I guess we ought to," he said. "We can use the same bag we used this morning."

* * * * *

Roger rode in front, the guest of honor, while Vince sat on the fender well opposite Mel in back. Sylvia had stayed in the trailer, and Vince had come along for the ride. He had even left his rifle in camp. It was agreed all around that they were going out after one antelope, the first easy shot they came across, and then they would go back to camp to enjoy a leisurely evening meal.

Shortly beyond the spot where Roger had made the first kill of the day, at the place where they had earlier turned right, Del took a less-traveled fork to the left.

"New country?" Roger asked.

"There's some broken country off to the east here that seems to be better in the afternoon."

"Where did Vince get his?"

"Straight south of where Mel got his, maybe a mile and a half further."

"The wife didn't want to hunt any more, uh?"

"Sylvia? I think they wanted to save that for tomorrow."

"Probably a good idea. I hope she gets a nice one."

"I do too. I hope everyone does. Everyone else has."

"Oh, yeah. We're happy. Happy like two little pigs in shit." Roger lit a cigarette and blew out a cloud of smoke. "I can't get over it," he said. "We're damn near a mile above sea level, and you can see damn near to infinity in every direction. And there's not a power pole or fence post in sight. Man, this is some country."

"Sure is," Del said. "Big, wide, and open."

They drove on for several minutes without talking, and Del turned the pickup off the dirt road to follow a set of tire tracks in the grass.

"Someone out here ahead of us?" Roger asked.

"No, I made these tracks about a week ago, when I came out here scouting."

"Really?"

"Yep. Things change slow here. Except the antelope. They seem to bounce back pretty good."

"I bet we saw a hundred of them on our way into town and back."

"That's good." Del rolled the pickup to a stop. "O.K. This is the edge of it here, all along this little rim. It drops off and slopes away from here. You'll get a better idea when you look over."

"Will we go down in there?"

"You can do just as well if you walk along the edge and peek over once in a while, careful like."

"O.K., I get you. We'll be shooting down."

"Probably. You and Mel can go together. Just follow this rim out to the point there and on around. We'll cut across and meet you over there."

"O.K." Roger got out of the cab and took his rifle from the rack.

Knowing that the two insurance agents had had a couple of cool ones, Del watched Roger as he went through the motions of getting ready to hunt. He zipped up his blaze-orange vest, then felt in his pants pocket for extra shells. He took Mel's rifle and stood by as the larger man crawled over the tailgate. Then the two men walked away together, rifles slung upon their shoulders as their field boots made faint tracks in the dry grass.

Del did not think they needed two rifles, but he had already told them what he thought of party hunting, and he trusted that they would not shoot more than one antelope.

Vince had vaulted out of the bed of the pickup and now got into the cab. "I thought we might have seen something by now," he said.

"This spot should be pretty good. I saw about thirty of them just over the rim here last week."

"They only need one."

Del looked at his pocket watch. "We've got plenty of time yet. It's a little after three. This is about the time the antelope start moving again."

The two of them sat without speaking for about fifteen minutes until the two hunters had worked their way around the point. Del started the engine and put the pickup into a slow roll. "I told Roger we'd meet them over there, where you can see the cutbank." Vince, who had been cleaning his fingernails, put his knife away and nodded.

Del drove the pickup to the place he had in mind, then parked and shut off the engine. He put his hand on the door handle and said, "Don't slam the door. We'll get out and take a peek." Vince nodded.

Del and Vince set out on a slow walk across the grass toward the ledge. When they reached the rim, they were met with the collective stare of a dozen or more antelope, which had been working their way down the broad, dry wash and now came to a company halt. They were about three hundred yards away and a little to the left, on the way to Mel and Roger.

The guide and his patron stopped. "Let's just stand here," Del said in a soft voice. "Maybe they'll move on down to where our boys can see them and get a shot."

"That's a nice buck there," the lawyer said. "I bet he's at least a fourteen."

"Too bad Sylvia's not here."

"Yeah. Too bad."

Del interpreted the last comment to mean, as well, that Vince might think it was too bad he hadn't brought his own rifle. "Well," said the guide, "if these fellows don't shoot hell out of the whole herd, we can come by here tomorrow."

"Yeah. He's a nice one."

They stood still and watched the antelope for a few minutes, during which time Mel and Roger seemed to have gotten a hint and bellied down in the grass. A few of the antelope had dropped their heads to graze, but the buck had kept his gaze fixed on Del and Vince.

"Let's fall back out of sight," Del suggested. They backed up a few steps until the rim closed off the antelope from view. When the men inched forward again, Del saw that the buck was pushing the herd into a slow trot in the same direction the animals had been heading. Del waved Vince back again, and they watched the other two hunters. After a couple of minutes, Roger got set in his prone position and fired a shot.

John D. Nesbitt

Del and Vince moved in Roger's direction in a fast walk, and Del saw the other two men rise up and stand there, talking.

They must have hit one, Del thought. Otherwise, they would be firing willy-nilly at the whole flock. He saw Mel shrug his shoulders. Roger put his gun up to his shoulder and took it down. When Del and Vince reached the rim where the others stood, Mel gave a look of dismay as Roger raised his rifle again. Del saw in a flash what was causing the confusion: the buck antelope had been shot in the hind quarters and was dragging himself down the wash, a hundred and fifty yards away. When Roger touched off his second shot, Del saw a puff of hair blow off the antelope's head, and the antelope snapped to the ground with one horn flopped over.

Roger turned around with his rifle lowered. After a moment's silence, he said, "I'm sorry. I don't know what to say." His voice sounded lonely. "I just lost my head for a minute."

Mel took the live shell out of his own rifle and spit on the ground. "That was a real shit-head thing to do."

"I don't know what I was thinking. I guess I wasn't thinking at all."

Mel wasn't through. "What the hell were you going to do with it, anyway? You know you got to have a tag to give the taxidermist, and fill out all that silly-ass paperwork. And now you ruined the horns anyway. What the hell were you thinking?"

"I don't know."

"I guess not."

Roger turned to Del. "What do we do now?"

"I guess we go get your antelope."

"But I can't take it in."

"You weren't going to anyway, were you?"

"I don't know. I guess if it was a doe, we were."

"What's this 'wee' shit?" Mel snapped.

"Let's calm down a minute," the guide said. "Let's think about it. You already have your two heads at the taxidermist. And you have your two carcasses at the locker. What are you having done with them?"

Roger did the answering. "The locker is making them into jerky and sausage, and shipping it to us."

"I suppose they're expecting a third one."

"More or less. Well, yes, I said we'd have another one."

Del looked down at the antelope sprawled in the draw. "I doubt you can pass him off as a doe or a fawn, and technically, you're supposed to show evidence of sex. But we're not leaving it here."

"Oh, no," Roger bounced back.

Del took a deep breath. Shooting the wrong animal was a violation, but not his. Leaving meat to waste was a violation, too, and not treated kindly. He didn't want a part of that one. "Then I guess we skin it here, leave the head and hide, and you guys take the meat with you in the morning."

"Will it keep?"

"It'll cool out pretty good tonight. You can take it to a meat locker when you get back, or better yet, cut it up yourself or have someone help you. Just hang on to the tag, of course."

"Sure. Do we punch it out?"

"Oh, yeah. That'll show some good faith, at least."

As Del walked down through the yucca and sagebrush toward the ruined buck, he wondered if the carcass would get to Illinois. *It's not my job to wonder,* he said to himself. As long as they used up their tag and got the hell out of there, and took this thing with them, Del would have done his job. By rights he should turn them in, he thought, but he'd rather just get rid of them. He grabbed a hind leg and shook it, and it flopped at the thigh. The hindquarters would be bone-splintered and bloodshot. And the head was wasted. *Some people,* he thought. There were two main reasons to kill an animal—for the head and for the meat—and Roger had made a mess out of both.

Del started dragging, and Mel grabbed the other hind leg and fell in. Roger trailed behind, carrying the two rifles. Del picked out the way as they climbed the slope, zigzagging around yucca and sagebrush and cactus.

Roger was wheezing almost as much as Mel when the group dropped the antelope next to the pickup. From the air about them, the guide caught the sweet and sour smell that emanated from boozy sweat and breath. Vince, who had stayed topside, had the hoist set up and was sitting on the tailgate enjoying a cigarette. Whatever hostility he might have felt toward his fellow hunters at breakfast seemed to have mellowed into disgusted tolerance. He might even be pleased, for all that the guide could tell.

This was what the job came to, Del thought, as he slashed his way through the task. Everyone wanted to pull the trigger, then stand back and watch the hired man clean up the mess. Take away the photographs and the elated talk afterwards, and all you had was a dead stinking animal hanging upside down, bloodshot gamy meat that averaged about twenty dollars a pound. For his own part, Del had the satisfaction of knowing that he brought out people like this, year after year, to ruin the things he loved the best. And he couldn't blame it on them.

When Del had the animal skinned, he opened up the body and tumbled the guts out. He plunged both hands into the blood-filled chest cavity, groped around until he'd gotten a good purchase on the heart and lungs, and pulled as hard as he could. A gush of blood shot up and out of the cavity, pumped by the heart he squeezed in his hands. It drenched his right pant leg below the knee. Then the heart and lungs gave way, came ripping up out of the cavity with a sucking sound, and the curdled blood sputtered down through the open throat and onto the ground.

Sometimes, he thought, *sometimes, it gets tedious—blood up to your elbows, blood on your clothes, the smell of every-one's stinking prairie goats stuck in your nose and throat.* He looked into the cavity and at the front of the carcass, then took his knife and scraped a few loose hairs off the inside of the hams. *Well, this one's done*, he thought. *Now for the evidence.*

He took the tubular hide and turned it right-side-out, and as the three hunters watched him, he scooched the gut pile into the hide, using it as a garbage bag. After drawing a breath, he dragged the pouch-like burden to the rim and swung it over.

Back at the pickup, he found the stiff, blood-stained game bag they had used earlier in the day. He pulled it up over the carcass, put his shoulder under the hind quarters, and lifted the carcass off the gambrel. No one had spoken a word since they had come up with the antelope.

As he washed his hands, assisted again by Roger, Del said, "Well, that little job is done. Suppose we go back to camp, have a drink, say the hell with it, and enjoy supper."

Chapter Six

Del thought the evening meal was almost enjoyable, despite the hangdog attitude that came and went with the two insurance agents. Vince had conveyed the news to Sylvia as soon as the group returned to camp, so there weren't any uncomfortable questions or answers. Del hung the antelope near Vince's in the cottonwoods, having made sure beforehand that the doe-or-fawn-only tag was punched out, signed, dated, and tied to a shank. The antelope hung in the periphery of their vision, so that it was almost out of sight and out of mind.

Del cut up two chickens, floured and seasoned the pieces, and set them to frying in two skillets. In a third, he fried a big batch of sliced potatoes and onions. As a general rule, he preferred not to serve red meat like beefsteak after everyone had been wallowing in something similar all day long. While the three skillets sizzled and crackled, Del put together a green salad, set out bread and butter and salad dressing, and put an apple pie on display. Camp life was shaping up happy again, assisted by a fresh bottle of Lord Calvert. The Furtinos drank highballs with Roger and Mel, who had regained some of their jovial demeanor.

"Go easy on the water," Mel scolded, as Roger poured drinks. "Del's got only so much of it."

"He uses about a gallon per antelope, it seemed to me," Roger answered, "and two when they're gutshot." Then he fell silent.

Mel picked it up again. "The dangerous thing, the thing to avoid at all costs, would be to run out of ice. I don't mind a highball that's low on water, but I don't like a warm one."

"You ready for another one, Del?" Roger's face had regained its beaming, hospitable expression.

"I could drink one."

Mel's voice came up. "Remember what I told you about the water, now."

On the fringe of the merry chatter, Del thought they resembled a happy family—the kind of family that has drinks and animated conversation, making things bearable for the one among them who just got caught sleeping around or who just came home from jail.

At last it was supper time, and all hands fell to the meal.

"Did you bake the pie?" Roger asked.

"No, that one is store-bought. But I know how."

"I bet you do. You seem to like to cook."

"I do."

"Damn good chicken," Mel proclaimed, tossing a drumstick bone end-over-end into the coals.

"Very good all the way around," Roger said. He stood up and shook his plate scraps into the fire. "Can I get you another drink, Del?"

"No, thanks. I'm fine."

"Anyone else?"

"Hate to see you drink alone," Mel offered.

"Not much danger of that, I'd say," Roger answered.

Everyone agreed that the pie was good, considering it was store-bought. They agreed, furthermore, that if the opportunity ever presented itself, they'd like to try one of Del's. Meanwhile, the guide and camp cook had put on a pot of coffee, which, despite its boiling over while they picked their chicken bones, met with round approval. Yes, they were a happy family, Del thought, as he left the fireside to tend to the dishes.

Washing dishes in camp was always enjoyable. In addition to getting everything in order, it warmed a fellow's hands and left them clean. When all the washing was done, Del scrubbed his arms in the warm soapy water before he pitched it. Then he rinsed the dishes, set them to dry on the table, and returned to the campfire.

Now that the family was together again, Roger had a little more to say. "I guess I really screwed things up this afternoon. I know it was a stupid thing to do. I just wasn't thinking, I guess. I'm sorry if I put a damper on anybody's fun."

Sylvia smiled as if to say it was all right.

Her husband was in a convenient position to be indulgent. "It's O.K.," he said. "No harm done to us. We were through hunting for the day, anyway."

"I know," Roger resumed, "but I still feel like I peed on everybody's picnic."

"Don't worry about us," Vince assured him.

"I still feel like a jerk. I feel like I brought Mel into it, too."

"Oh, I'm all right," Mel said.

Del spoke up. "Well, it's done. It wasn't a good thing to do, and it's not the type of thing I like to have happen. But it's done and taken care of, and you shouldn't have any more trouble with it. You might want to call the meat locker here in town when you get back home, just to let them know you don't have a third animal for them."

"I'll do that," Roger said. "You know, Del, I appreciate your . . . your understanding in this."

"I've seen quite a few people go through their first hunt. Sometimes it gets to them—the wide open spaces, the novelty of the antelope, the sheer numbers of them. Sometimes people just lose their bearings."

"I guess that's what happened to me. Worse than a kid in a candy store. But I appreciate how you've taken it, Del."

"It's all right, Roger."

Mel cleared his throat and said, "I hope this doesn't make you not want to have us again some time."

Del poked the fire with a stick. "Well, you were a little late this year. Usually I'm booked up well ahead of time. If you want a guide next year or whenever, call earlier in the year to get one lined up. I'll send you a list of guides that you could call."

"What time of year is the best to get a hold of you?" Roger asked.

"I'll send you a list of guys that I think could fit you in."

"Oh." Roger was quiet for a moment, and then he half-asked, "No hard feelings."

"No, no hard feelings at all. I just think it would be better that way. Everyone's entitled to a mistake, and this way it won't be hanging between you and your guide."

"You're probably right." Roger reached into his inside jacket pocket and took out an envelope. Leaning forward in his chair, he handed it across the corner of the fire to Del. "I wanted to give this to you this evening, in case we don't get up for breakfast."

"Well, thank you," Del said, opening the unglued flap and peeking in. Thumbing the bills, he counted an extra fifty dollars. He was used to tips, but just to be sure, he said, "This more than evens us up, Roger. You overpaid me a little."

"I wanted to. Not for what happened this afternoon, but because everything went so well this morning. Mel and I talked about it on the way into town. We were both real happy about how things went. We still are. We both got our animals, and you did all the work."

The guide glanced at Mel, who looked contented as he sat with his drink in his lap. The campfire reflected in his glasses as he nodded.

"Well, thank you," Del said. "I'll accept it as a gesture of appreciation, and I'm glad you got a couple of nice wall mounts."

"So are we," Roger said, and Mel nodded again.

After the insurance agents had retired to their trailer, where they had enough ice to do justice to the remaining Lord Calvert, Vince invited the guide to the Furtinos' trailer to look over a map. When the three of them were seated inside at the little table, out of the breeze, and in the warm glow of the propane lamp, Vince replenished their highballs with a bottle of Canadian Club. He took off his glasses and cleaned them with a Kleenex.

"I liked the way you handled those two guys," he said.

Del shrugged. "They're all right."

The lawyer didn't answer as he put on his glasses and unfolded a map onto the table. "I need to know about deer and elk hunting," he said. "Where are you going to be?"

The guide traced his finger on the map. "I'll be right in here for deer season, and I'll be over here in the mountains for elk. But that shouldn't make much difference to you. Where do you plan to hunt, or do you have permits yet?" He turned to Sylvia, who had been paying attention to his directions. "Are you hunting deer and elk, too?"

Vince answered for her. "No, she's just hunting antelope. But I'd like you to guide me for deer and elk."

Del was pretty sure he'd told the lawyer over the phone that he was booked for deer and elk, but he told him again.

The lawyer pushed a little. "I like the way you do things. I thought maybe you could fit me in."

"Let me explain, Vince. I'm a small-time outfitter. I run only one camp at a time. The way I have things set up—with the agreement I have with the ranchers, with my camp set-up, and really, just with the number of hunters I can handle—I couldn't in all fairness take on another hunter. It wouldn't be fair to all the people I already have arrangements with."

"What if we both came? Would two hunters make it more worthwhile?"

Del paused as he let the question sink in. He liked the idea of having Sylvia come back, but he didn't like Vince's pushing, and he didn't like the way Vince seemed to be using his wife. "I'm afraid that would be even more out of the question."

Del expected the lawyer to go into a mild pout, but instead he said, "Well, you've got to run things the way that works best for you. Why don't you show me again where you'll be, and tell me what you know about the country."

Del showed him again, and he gave a general rundown on the types of terrain a fellow might hunt in, where he might get access to private land, where he would have to hunt on the National Forest, and where he might find a place to stay. Sylvia seemed to take an interest in all of it, too.

* * * * *

In his tent, as he lay in the sleeping bag and listened to the tic-tic of the wind-up alarm clock, Del could hear a low murmur from the Furtinos' trailer. At times the murmur rose and dropped, as if Vince needed to make some of his thoughts more emphatic. The guide was glad not to have room for Vince, even if it would have meant having Sylvia along. He didn't need to get mixed up with either of them. Let alone both. The lawyer was bad medicine; for all Del knew, the wife could be, too. Sylvia was an attractive woman, and he enjoyed her presence. There seemed to be a spark in the air when her eyes met his, just as there had seemed to be a spark when they had crossed paths one time outside the firelight. But there was not any good reason to get mixed up, and there were lots of good reasons not to.

The murmuring seemed to have stopped, and Del heard the squeak and shift of the trailer. It sounded as if the Furtinos were going to bed. When there were no more sounds than the night breeze riffling the kitchen canopy, Del sat up, unzipped the window flap, and saw that the lights were out in both trailers. He zipped the flap shut again and lay back down.

After lying in the sleeping bag for quite a while, Del realized that he wasn't asleep yet. He had been flitting in and out of sleep, but now he was awake, hearing the wind-up alarm clock ticking on. The fluorescent hands read twenty past eleven. There was something wrong. He unzipped the front flap of the tent and peeked out. Both trailers were dark and still in the cool breeze, and beyond them the moulting cotton-woods whispered. A quarter moon hung in the sky, and in the subdued light he could see the two game bags hanging like cattle thieves in the cottonwoods. There was nothing wrong outside.

As he lay in his bedding again, he went back to the last conscious thoughts he remembered having, and he let his thoughts drift, montage-like, through the events of the day. Vince kept coming back on the screen with his narrow scrutiny, a look somewhere between an inspection and a challenge. There it was.

Del realized that he himself had been doing something unconsciously. He was opening and closing his right fist, as he had been doing before he came back fully awake. Something about the lawyer—or maybe the lawyer and his wife—had Del wound up tight. Beneath all of Vince Furtino's manners and polite attention, there lurked the taunt of judgment. The lawyer had been studying him, assessing him, and he had found him a small enough threat to be worth buying.

On top of that, he was using his wife as a bargaining chip. It reminded Del of the way Vince had been with the head and cape of his antelope; he didn't mind belittling what he was proud to possess. But this was a woman and not some part of a dead animal, and the lawyer's arrogance rubbed against Del's grain. Vince was sure he was in control, confident he could use his wife and then act as if he hadn't. That meant he expected Del to rise to the temptation and then sit back down, like a dog, when it was taken away. That was pretty damn smug, if Vince thought he could work them both that way.

Having stopped with his fist closed, Del opened it, stretched and flexed it, wiped the palm on his undershirt, and reached for the plastic quart bottle. The water was neither cold nor warm to the taste. He could have drunk half the quart, but he didn't like waking up between midnight and sunup and having to decide whether he should go on a moonlight stroll. He took a small drink.

It didn't do any good to double his fist. He'd learned that. Some people learned not to go into business for themselves; some learned not to have a drink before five or after ten; some learned not to be getting their hands into the wrong pair of pants. Del had learned not to double his fist in anger. And like those other things that some people learned, not always the right people and not always enough of them, it was something learned that he knew he had to renew, reinforce.

He knew he could hit another hundred men as hard as he had hit that one, and do no more harm than knocking someone out. But once, just that once, he had brought his work-strong arm upwards in an uppercut, his knuckles hitting the point of a chin that snapped a man's head back onto cervical vertebrae that no one had known were flawed. The autopsy had brought out the finest details, that the man had cracked his head on the pool table and again on the bar-room floor, but that he had already been finished when his head snapped back.

The two years that had followed that night were now a measured unit, a duration marked off and circumscribed. Life had been fine before that, and life had gotten better again, but that interval was like a long, serious illness. It was time lost but not forgotten, something he had survived and recovered from. Some people said of their tough times that it made them stronger, more fit for what would come next. Those two years were not like that; they were something he'd gotten through but hadn't gotten much from except the knowledge that he couldn't double his fist.

After the first wave of fear and bewilderment, as he sat in the San Diego County Jail on what he thought was a charge of first-degree murder, had come the gradual changes. At his arraignment, he learned he had been charged with first-degree manslaughter, which had been reduced to involuntary man-slaughter. From that point, his lawyer managed a series of postponements so that he could, as he said, gather more information.

Del had a good lawyer, which was to say he paid as much as a man of his means could be expected to pay. The first thing to go was the new Monte Carlo, then the house. Between the legal conferences and the court appearances, he had less day-to-day contact with his business, and he found himself doing business in a way he despised. He let go jobs he had bid, he strung out jobs he had started, and he subbed out jobs to the shoe-string contractors who traded on his good name.

By the time a year had elapsed, Del saw the lay of the land clearly enough to sell his business while it was still worth something. A less prosperous lawyer, but one who called himself an attorney nevertheless, settled that paperwork for him. Gone were the trucks, the backhoe tractors, the cement mixers, the wheelbarrows, and on down to the picks, shovels, sledgehammers, levels, and trowels. Eight years of effort were summed up in a check for forty-three thousand dollars, which in turn was consumed by the defense lawyer and the Internal Revenue System.

Finally Del's defense lawyer got the criminal case dismissed, shortly before it was to go to trial. His investigations into the background of the case, plus his delays, seemed to have some effect on the D.A.'s enthusiasm to bring the case before a jury. All of a sudden, there was a void. All the tension and anticipation, all the buildup, had dropped flat.

Now Del's life was empty. He was out of trouble and out of work, and his social life was a wasteland. He had spent years building a business, thinking he would move into marriage and a family when he was set up. When he had gotten tangled up with a married woman, he did not realize he had been marking dead time, but he saw it now when the dust had cleared.

Then came the lawsuit, Ellen suing him for wrongful death. Del read the document with disbelief, and he gave a bitter laugh when he came to the part about "loss of companionship." Ellen had not felt much of a loss for the year and a half before that night, and if she ever did feel at a lack, she had found Del soon enough. Del couldn't believe she was suing him, when he had as much as answered her prayers. She'd gotten her marital problems settled without a divorce, and with the life insurance, she had had a plump windfall shaken into her lap as well.

She apologized to Del when he called on the phone, told him she felt terrible but her lawyer made her do it—after all, she said, it was just like those cases where one insurance company was suing another. It was nothing personal.

Del told her he would come and restore the companionship once a week or so, just like before, which was more than she was likely to get otherwise, as far as money went, because there was nothing left.

She was sorry, she said, that he'd had to hock everything, and she was sure this was just a formality the lawyer had to follow up. She thanked Del for his offer, explaining that her attorney (the word she used when she shoveled the greatest blame his way) had advised her to keep things platonic. She agreed that they should just remain friends, and after all that had happened, didn't Del think so too?

That was Southern Cal for you. Everyone wanted to settle there when they got out of the service. Everyone wanted to cut the fat hog in the ass, get in on the good money of building houses for one another to live in, building shopping malls where they could spend the easy money they'd made in the building. Buy a house for fifty grand and sell it for eighty. Trade up. Get a place with a pool. Put in a decorative waterfall. Improve the value. Trade up. Then, when everybody was rolling in money that had been born out of money, sue the shit out of the next guy.

Fortunately for Del, at that point he still had a little money left from selling his business. He hired the same defense lawyer, who was able to get the wrongful death suit dismissed. But it took time and money. By then, Del had lost all his financial assets, plus two years out of the prime of his life.

It had been a good time to leave, just before the oil prices jumped and the real estate prices leveled off. The money wasn't as easy as it had been, and he would have had a long ways to bounce back. With some satisfaction, he imagined the whole damn works tumbling into the ocean as it was prophesied to do, taking with it an avalanche of decorative fountains and retainer walls installed by Watters Masonry, free estimates.

It had been a good time to leave, to go back where he had started, to do what he had done before he went into the Navy. The pay was better than it was before he went away, and he didn't mind having the money trickle back through insurance agents and lawyers at the rate of a hundred dollars a day, with an occasional fifty-dollar tip. He had lost everything once, and now he was building back up, trying to hang on to the little bit he'd put together, trying to enjoy the parts of life that still mattered. Starting over, he was content to get by with less, to have simple needs and simple means. But it all took effort, investment of life-energy, all of which was at stake if, in closing his fist, he lost his grasp.

Before he dropped off to sleep, Del thought of luckless Duane Bentley lying dead with a Budweiser light swaying over him, and then Ellen on the other end of the line wanting to be friends. That made two good reasons not to ever double his fists again.

Chapter Seven

Del woke up feeling all right in the quiet of pre-dawn. The tent seemed like a good place, as it had when he and Rita were setting it up—a snug shelter, keeping out the bite of the elements but not walling out the world around. As he lay in his sleeping bag, Del developed a feeling for the clear tranquil morning that was taking shape outside. This was a good part of the day, all his, before the hunters got up.

On some mornings he dressed without lighting the lantern, but this morning he needed the light so he could dig out clean clothes. He went for a full change, even trading in the blaze-orange cap for his deer-grey, sweat-stained everyday Stetson. The law called for some item of blaze orange, so he broiught out a lightweight vest. Also by lantern light he uncased his rifle and laid it on his bedding, along with his cartridges and antelope permit.

After shutting off the small propane lantern inside the tent, he ducked outside to start breakfast. In the lingering moonlight he started the coffee, took a stroll, rinsed his face and hands, and set out the grocery chests. Roger's parting words the evening before were that he and Mel would join the others for breakfast, so there was a full meal to lay out. Del put a pound of bacon to fry in the cast-iron skillet, skidding the strips apart with the spatula as the pan warmed up. He laid out the other provisions as he had done the morning before, working now by stovelight as well. When the coffee was plunking steadily and the bacon was sizzling, he went to wake his hunters. Remembering the previous morning, he rapped on Vince and Sylvia's door first, then moved on to the other trailer. In the kitchen area again, he turned on the double-mantle lantern, pushing down on a state of-the-art ignition device that sparked the propane into a bright suffusion.

Roger's spirits were on the rise with the new day, and Mel was less surly than a person might have imagined. They expressed an interest in seeing Mount Rushmore on the way back. They wondered if the antelope would keep, and Del assured them it had cooled pretty well overnight and should make the trip all right. He also told them they could keep the game bag for future hunts.

Vince and Sylvia likewise were well-humored, as well they might be, now that they had the guide and more than ten thousand acres all to themselves. If the lawyer harbored anything less than good will toward his wife or toward his guide, it didn't show.

Sylvia took notice of Del's hat, it seemed to him, but she said nothing. As she poured coffee and moved around the breakfast area in the lantern light, Del noticed she had put on clean clothes, too. He made a successful effort not to let his eyes follow her, but through half-glances and mild whiffs he had a pleasing sense of laundered denims, a clean flannel shirt, and mild herbal soap. He was sure that, had he sat closer to the lawyer, he would have detected a fresh application of Brut, even though the man had not shaved around the edges of his neatly kept beard.

When breakfast was over and the insurance agents had set the day's first clouds of road-dust curling into the air, Del noticed that both Vince and Sylvia had rifles ready for the day's hunt. He ducked into the tent and brought out his own rifle, which seemed to surprise Vince.

"Are you going to hunt today, too?" he asked, as he took his cigarette from his mouth.

"I thought I might, if Sylvia fills out without much trouble. Looks like there'll be three of us hunting today."

Vince looked at his cigarette, which had burned over halfway down. "I'm just bringing mine along in case I need to back her up. I didn't realize you had an antelope license."

"Oh, yeah. I'm not one of your eat-nothing-but-beef natives."

"I take it you're not a hard-core headhunter, then, either." Vince took a drag on his cigarette.

"Not seriously. I guess I'll put my gun in the gun rack, and one of you can carry your gun, whichever one sits by the door."

"That will be me," Vince said. He dropped the cigarette on the ground and stepped on it.

Del wanted to say something to the effect that since it was Sylvia's hunt today, she should be first out of the gate, but it all paid the same and he rather liked having her ride next to him.

As the hunters rolled along in the pickup, the morning was a replica of the previous one. They saw their first antelope while the sky was still pink. Three antelope flashed and bolted, half a mile away. Del stopped.

"Probably the same three Roger shot at yesterday morning," Vince stated, bringing down the binoculars. "No horns in that bunch."

Del sensed an air of authority in Vince's actions, and he wondered if the man had laid out the limits of how modest a head his wife could take. Sylvia did not seem very troubled by Vince's proprietary manner, though Del wished she would. Every few minutes the lawyer would pat his wife's leg, now and then adding a comment like "You're all set, now," or "You've got it all mapped out in your mind, now."

Sylvia nodded each time. It seemed to Del that she had learned to treat a comment politely even when it sounded like a command.

Del turned left onto the road that led to the broken country, scene of yesterday's fiasco.

Vince spoke up. "You think there might be any bucks out here? There weren't any other horns worth mentioning in that herd."

"We won't go all the way there. We'll turn right again in a little while and head southwest, sort of in a diagonal between the place where Roger shot that one and the spot where you killed yours."

"Oh." Vince patted Sylvia's knee again and said, "Ready to shoot the big one?"

"Sure thing," she said. "Right through the boiler."

Del smiled to himself. He was pretty sure Sylvia had her own sense of humor.

Del shifted into third and drove on. The road they followed to the southwest meandered through rolling plains country, landscape such as they had hunted the morning before. It was the type of country that looked flat and uneventful from a distance; but once a person got into it, it was full of swells, low hills and ridges. A newcomer on foot could get easily disoriented, thinking that a distance to some given point was much shorter than it was, thinking that there couldn't have been so many dips and rises. To cover this country on foot, for hunting or for any other purpose, would not give a person the feeling of getting anywhere. In a pickup, though, or on horseback, it was easier to gain on the country, to see it at a rate at which it made sense.

The element of surprise still lay in the land. The undulations were subtle enough that animals came into view without a great change in the landscape—maybe the pickup climbed a barely distinguishable rise or took a gentle curve in the road, and in an instant, enough intervening land had receded to bring animals into view. Antelope were always a pleasant surprise, seeming, as they did, to materialize out of the land they moved across with so little effort.

The second band of antelope they saw made that sort of phantasmal appearance. The party in the pickup could see there was a windmill up ahead, with the road leading to it. When the windmill came into full view, it did so all at once, and Del stopped. A little over two hundred yards away, at the base of the opposite hill, the water tank sat in the midst of a dark, hoof-beaten area. Cattle, and lots of them, had worn trails to this spot and had worked it up in wet weather. Thirty yards to the left of the watertank, where the grass grew, there

73

John D. Nesbitt

lounged perhaps a dozen antelope—some grazing, some sitting in a placid cud-chewing pose, and some watching.

Vince had his field glasses up as soon as the pickup stopped. "Oh, yeah," he said.

"The one with his hind end to us," Del added.

"Yeah. Get ready, Sylvia."

The antelope loitered ahead on the left, across the corner of the hood from where Del sat. He shut off the engine and, with his eyes on the antelope, said, "Just ease out the door and keep low. Sylvia, you should be able to shoot from the front bumper, kneeling. This hood is probably too high for you." He looked at her, and her eyes met his. She nodded and took the rifle as he lifted it up and out of the gun rack.

Del heard Vince mutter, "Take a good shot. I'll be backing you up." Del glanced at the antelope and then at Sylvia again. Through the open door, he saw her nod to her husband, crouch, and move to the right front corner of the pickup. Del lost sight of Vince until a rifle barrel poked into the view of the left rear-view mirror.

Del focused his gaze on the antelope again. This was the antsy part. It always seemed to take forever when someone else was getting set. The antelope had all perked up, and those on the ground were pushing up onto their stick legs. The buck turned to offer a broadside. Then came a shot from Sylvia, nearly simultaneous with a puff of dust on the hill. The shot had gone over the buck's shoulder. The animal just stood there, turning his head toward the hill and then toward the pickup. Sylvia put another shot over the shoulder, and a second later, Vince's gun roared from the back fender. The buck dropped to his front knees scrambling, as if he were trying to dig into the ground. Then he slumped over.

Sylvia stood up straight and called to Del, "Did I hit it?"

"No," he said.

"Who did? Oh."

Vince was coming around to the passenger side. "I was backing you up," he said.

"Did I hit it?"

"I think you gutshot him. He was just standing there, like they do when they're gutshot."

"Did I hit him, really?" She looked at Del. "Did I, do you think?"

"We'll see," he answered, "but it didn't look like it to me. I think both of your shots went right over his shoulder."

"Why didn't he take off, then?" Vince's voice carried more uncertainty than challenge.

"He was up against a hill," Del said. "Sometimes it fools them, the shot slapping into the hill like that, maybe the echo too, and he doesn't know which way it's coming from. It throws him off. I've had them run right straight at us after a shot like that."

"Why did he just stand there?"

"He was probably studying it. And it had been a year since he'd seen anyone doing anything but check cows. But we'll see. Make sure your guns are unloaded, and we'll drive on over."

As she climbed in, Sylvia looked at Del as if she were searching for an answer and not finding one. As Vince climbed in and pulled the door shut, he said, "I'm goin' to feel like hell if I'm the only one who shot that sonofabitch."

Sylvia patted his leg and said, "Don't worry."

Vince fired up a cigarette.

Just for a moment, Del wished Vince had been present when the subject of party hunting had come up with Mel and Roger. Then he thought, no, they had both carried rifles later anyway, and he would be rid of these two soon enough. All he had to do was take care of the animal.

The buck was an average mature animal, comparable to the two that the men from Illinois had taken to town. A selective head hunter might see a dozen a day such as this, waiting for the real prize. He was a handsome buck, but at this point in the trip, he was common business--or common enough that no one took out a camera or thought to pose. Then again, there was the necropsy to tend to, to see how many holes would be found on the inside left rib cage.

As Del skinned, separating the hide from the carcass in neat, methodical motions, Vince and Sylvia watched. Del brought the hide down around the haunches, then worked on down around the belly, around the ribs, and to the brisket. They found a hole where one slug had entered, but amidst all the bloodshot and swollen tissue, it was hard to see if there was another hole.

Del worked the hide down beyond the shoulders, pulled the legs free and clean, trimmed down to the neck, and cut the exposed throat. He cut through the neck bone, detaching the head and hide as before. As was his practice, he drew the hide right-side-out and laid the unit on the grass.

As soon as he opened the cavity, he was sure it was not gut- shot. It smelled too good, just the warm, watery smell of viscera. "This one's fat," he said, pointing at the lace-like layer of fat on the swelling stomach. "You won't often see fat like that on an antelope." He reached down in, trimmed loose the liver, cut through the diaphragm to the heart and lungs, and hauled out the whole mess. There was not a speck of gut-shot confetti in the cavity. "Pretty clean," he said. Inside, he saw one hole where the bullet came in and another where it exited on the other side, two ribs ahead. Glancing at the pile, Del saw the lungs clouded and splotched in purple. "Looks like one shot did it," he said. "Right through the lungs." Having brought the evidence to presentable form, he stepped back to allow Vince and Sylvia, the jurors, to study the exhibit.

"Looks like I'm the only one who hit it," Vince conceded. He turned to his wife, who had also taken a quick but squeamish look at the evidence. "I don't know what to say," he went on. "I thought I was just backing you up, but it looks like I went ahead and used your ticket." The lawyer sounded discouraged.

"It's O.K., honey," she said, laying her hand on his forearm, "I know you were just trying to help."

For that brief interlude, seeing the husband's penitence and the wife's tender forgiveness, Del was touched by the simple exchange. For a moment, Vince was humble and human, almost likeable.

Vince said, "By the way, you should go ahead and fill out your tag." As Sylvia turned to tend to the details of her permit,

Vince regained his larger character. "At least we didn't make a mess of it," he announced, as if trying to find some consolation, something positive, in the way things had worked out.

Del did not miss the hint that Vince was making an effort to put a moral distance between what he had done this morning and what Roger had done the afternoon before. "That's right," Del said. "You made a nice clean kill."

He himself had stayed pretty clean on this one, he thought, as he ran his right forefingernail beneath his other nails, dislodging little curds of fat that had been packed in. Then with the lawyer pouring water, he scrubbed the dried blood from his hands and forearms.

When they had the antelope bagged up and were on their way again, Del observed to himself that Sylvia was being a good sport about the way things had gone. Even so, she seemed to be subdued by her husband, first by his barging in for the kill and then by his making it seem all right. He had even poured the water, a task he had let her perform the day before. Del felt himself wanting to touch her—if not physically, at least with a sense of feeling or understanding.

"I think you were shooting a little high," he said.

"I think so, too," she answered. "I should have hit him. He just stood there for me."

"I bet you'd like to try again."

"Oh, I can't have those shots over, that's for sure. But there'll be other times." She looked at her husband. "Too bad we don't have an extra tag like Roger and Mel did."

"You can't shoot horns on one of those," Vince said. "Or you shouldn't."

Del felt a ripple inside. He had an awareness that she would be leaving before long, and he wanted her to carry away a good feeling about him. With something of a teasing tone, he said, "Really, do you think you could hit one, horns or no horns, if you had it to do over?"

"I don't know. I'd like to think I could." She looked at him with a quizzical expression. "Why?"

"Well, I've been sitting here thinking. I've still got my permit. We could let you have another try at it, and if you do all right, you can have what you shoot and I'll take that nice clean piece of table meat that Vince got for us a little while ago."

"Are you serious?"

"I wouldn't have offered if I wasn't." Now Del was glad Vince hadn't been there when the subject of party hunting had come up with Mel and Roger.

"Gosh, Del, that's really a nice offer," she said. "I don't know if I'd feel right."

"It's perfectly all right with me. I want you to have a good hunt. That's not why I carry a permit, but if it works that way and you have a good hunt, then we'll all be happy." He looked her in the eyes. "I mean it."

"But then you won't get to hunt," she said.

"Oh, I've hunted plenty, and I'll hunt plenty more."

"You're serious. You mean it."

"I mean it," he said, as their eyes met again.

Vince joined in. "That's awfully damn nice of you, Del. But we hate to take your hunting away from you."

Del looked across at Vince. "It's not a big deal to me. I've shot plenty of antelope, on my tags and on other people's— some of them for my own hunters, as far as that goes. Not entirely legal, but it has happened. I want Sylvia to get an antelope."

"Well, so do I." Vince patted his wife's leg. "That makes three of us, doesn't it?"

Del sensed the lawyer's gratitude at being let off the hook. He thought that later on, each of the Furtinos would realize that he had given the tag to Sylvia when he could have given it to Vince earlier and let her hang on to hers. It would not please Vince when he perceived things that way, but for the time being, Del could see that the lawyer was contented with his acquittal and clean slate.

Del thought, he did want her to get an antelope. But he knew he also wanted her to appreciate him, to respond to a level of feeling she wouldn't get from her husband. In his attraction for this woman, he had let himself be drawn in to compete for her attention, or affection, and he knew even as he did it that he was competing. It had caused him to let down his own guard, but he told himself that even with one more antelope, he would be done with these people soon enough.

The guide and his hunters puttered on, twice taking roads off to dead end in the east and then returning to the main road, which was little more than a path itself. They were in among cattle more often now, coming upon cows and calves that lumbered out of their way and then paused, drooling, to watch the pickup rattle by.

At about 11:30, they parked at the top of one of the higher rises in the vicinity. The day was warming up towards sixty degrees, and there was a breath of wind. Their picnic spot offered a broad view of the landscape as the guide let down the tailgate and spread out sandwich makings, snack bars, fruit, and donuts. The group had a peaceful meal, with no one saying much at all. The land stretched out for miles in every direction, and nowhere was the glint of a vehicle to be seen. The only sound to be heard was the click of a knife blade on the lip of the mayonnaise jar, the rustle of the bread wrapper, the crunch of an apple.

There came the whisper of movement in the grass, the soft tread of heavy feet on dry ground. Within a minute, they were in the company of a small semicircle of cattle, some red and some black, and all with white faces.

"We've got company," Sylvia said.

"They get used to following a pickup in the winter," Del said, crunching his apple.

"Do you think I could pet one?" Sylvia asked. "One of the calves?"

"I doubt they'll let you get that close. These range cattle aren't that gentle if you try to get near."

"It's just as well," Vince said. "They weren't meant to be pets. They were meant for the meat hook and cutting block."

"They look like they have a good life in the meanwhile," Sylvia countered.

"Until they go to the feed lot." Vince got off the tailgate, poured himself a cup of water from the plastic jug, and took a drink. Shaking out the tin cup, he moved his arm in a slow wave to take in the cattle, which seemed to serve as the lawyer's mute audience. "They have no sense of their own fate," he went on. "Look at them. Little more than hamburger on the hoof. No sense of their own mortality."

Furthermore, the cattle showed no sense of being rebuked. Del, with no great wish to come to their defense, said, "Nice warm sun today. If Mel and Roger were here, they could tell us when it slipped over the yardarm."

Chapter Eight

The last antelope of the hunt was not an easy one to find. Four times the party came upon antelope, each time in a small herd of six or eight and each time accompanied by Vince's verdict, "No horns." Del understood that Sylvia didn't want to shoot at a doe or fawn. Other than Vince's announcements, his comments were few.

Del might have gotten bored except that he enjoyed having the woman sitting next to him, legs to one side of the gearshift that he had to work. Del was glad she had stayed around for a while longer. She was another man's woman, but she looked good and smelled good and, though he never touched her, she felt good.

Moreover, it seemed as if he felt good to her. There was nothing tangible, but if he moved his hand, she saw it. If he flicked his glance her way, she met it for a flicker. It was a bold feeling, waving outward and being fed back. If Vince sensed it, he didn't show it. Maybe he didn't want to recognize it, as if by not recognizing something he did not allow it to exist. Maybe he felt, as Del had felt earlier, that all of this would be over in a little while anyway. Maybe he didn't sense anything, but chances were that he did and chose not to acknowledge it with a response.

Vince's rifle was in the rack where Sylvia's had been. He carried hers, upright and butt down on the floorboard, the better to help Sylvia make her move on the destined antelope when it chose to present itself.

Well into the afternoon, shortly before four, the antelope offered himself. He did not spring up apparition-like; rather, the hunters saw him from a distance where he sat in the lee of a low hill. He and his three doe companions rose before the pickup came within a quarter of a mile.

"That's one," Vince spoke up.

"Yep," Dell answered. "Maybe he wants to play. We'll just poke along."

Sylvia shifted in her seat, then leaned forward with her right hand on the dashboard.

The antelope crossed the road ahead of them and turned to flash bright in the afternoon sun. As Del was thinking of rolling to a stop, the four animals flashed again and were off on a lope. Del geared down and kept driving. The antelope switched now to the right and now to the left, but they kept a course generally parallel with the pickup's.

"They're about the same distance," Del said. "I'll try to gain on them a little, and if they stop, we'll stop." As he picked up a little speed, the antelope veered off to the left and over a low hump. They were gone.

"Let's go on," Del said. "We might meet them up ahead."

They followed the road as it took the shape of a large question mark, going straight until it veered to the right and then curved left around the hill that the antelope had gone over.

And there, around the corner, the antelope were standing. When they saw the pickup, they bolted. Del stopped. Two hundred yards away, the animals sashayed and stopped. By then the lawyer had slid out of the cab and was crouched, handing the rifle to his wife, who slid out behind him. She snicked a shell into the chamber and crawled to the front of the pickup. Del heard her settle the gun on the bumper. The buck took three steps forward and stopped, then flopped over flailing as Sylvia's rifle shattered the afternoon stillness.

The buck scrambled to his feet, staggered, fell again, and rose on his front quarters. He must have been hit in the back, Del thought. "Hit him again!" he called out, aware at the same time that Vince's rifle was still in the rack. Sylvia's rifle click-clacked and then boomed, snapping the antelope over on his side, where he kicked his legs in soft motion. Sylvia stood up and came into view.

"He's down," Del said. "Let's go get him."

Vince took the rifle and helped her into the pickup. "Good shooting, honey! You got one!"

"Are you sure he's down?" she asked Del. She was breathing hard as she took her seat.

"Yeah. You hit him good the second time. He just doesn't die as easy as some of 'em do."

"Where did I hit him the first time?"

"Somewhere in the back. You have your camera ready, Vince?"

"Sure do." Vince shifted on the seat and closed the door.

"That gun's unloaded isn't it?" Del put the pickup into motion.

"Oh, yeah," Vince answered. "I checked it."

Del shook Sylvia's hand, then Vince's hand, and a moment later they were close enough to see that the buck had finished kicking.

After Vince had shot half a roll of film, including one of the guide, the killer, and the kill, Del brought out his camera. "It's always good to get another picture of a woman hunter for the wall." He snapped his routine shot and then had the impulse to take another. He could have said it was because he had a vested interest in the antelope, even if it was really because he liked his client. But he said nothing as he took a second picture of her kneeling by her antelope, rifle upright in her hand, blue eyes shining, wheat-straw hair playing in the breeze.

Bringing the camera down, he saw the other three antelope perched on a knoll about a quarter of a mile away, watching. He motioned toward them with his head, and Sylvia and Vince looked at them. "They're safe," Del said, and they all laughed. It wasn't really funny, he thought, but it must have been time to laugh.

As Del was setting up the hoist and gambrel for the skinning operation, Vince dragged the antelope around to the back of the pickup where Del was working.

"Del, what would you think if I tried my hand at one?"

"Huh?"

"How about if I skin this one and clean it?"

"Sounds fine by me. We've got all the time we could want."

The lawyer did a pretty neat job. It was not as flawless as Del would have expected, given the way Vince did everything else, but it was well done. He left a few nicks on the meat here and there, which would never matter once the meat was cut and trimmed, and he left some loose hair stuck on the meat. When he had the hide and head detached, he opened the abdomen. "I'm not sure what I do first here," he said.

Del, who had been enjoying his new role as spectator, slid off the tailgate, drew his knife, and helped with reaming out the colon and trimming out the bladder. "Smells like it might be shot up a little," he said.

The lawyer nodded and probed down into the cavity with both hands, bringing them out spattered with blood-soaked bits of chewed vegetation. Del poured water for Vince, who rubbed his hands clean enough to return to the task.

The guide stood by, watching and ready to help. "Be careful not to spill any more than you have to," he said. "The least little bit will leave a smell and a taste."

The lawyer nodded.

When the liver, heart, and lungs came out, Vince stood back to assess his work. "Not bad," he said, "but it needs a washing." As Del poured, first one gallon and then another, Vince picked at specks. When he was done, he washed his hands and arms, dried them on the game bag Del had laid out, and lit a cigarette.

"Boy," he said, "that's more work than it looks like."

"You did a nice job, honey," his wife said, kissing him.

At that moment, Del wondered whether the couple would spend the night at camp, and if so, whether the lawyer's arms would smell of antelope when he wrapped them around his wife. Then he rebuked himself. It was none of his business. It was his job to get animals into the sights of his hunters, and then, when meat was on the ground, it was his job to tend to it. So he put a bag on the animal, slipped the bundle off the gambrel, and heaved it into the pickup bed, while the lawyer smoked a cigarette and drummed his left fingers on his wife's hip.

Del had the makings of one more fresh-food supper, and after that, it would have been mix-and-match canned goods and cold cuts—all the things that would keep until deer season opened. Tonight's meal would consist of hamburgers, fried potatoes, salad, and a cherry pie, the latter coming from the same source as the apple pie the night before.

The lawyer and the guide each ate two cheeseburgers while the lady ate one. It was an enjoyable meal, with plenty of good satisfying food and only two guests to tend to. That meant, among other things, larger pieces of pie and a larger balance of conversation with Sylvia. Del learned a little more about her job that she had mentioned on the first night. It was a middle-management position for a chain of clothing stores in the Omaha-Lincoln area, a job that allowed her to take a trip such as this one.

"Are you going to stay here with Vince, while he hunts deer and elk?"

"We haven't decided yet. It depends on what openings he finds. I wouldn't mind, but I wouldn't mind going back, either. I do like my job."

"Well, you don't have to hunt everything all at once if it doesn't work out that way. There will be other years."

Vince rejoined the conversation. "How many hunters do you have for your deer season?"

"I hunt six the way I'm set up right now. They're on their own a little more than we are with the antelope, so I can handle a couple more." Del turned to Sylvia. "They field dress their own deer, for example. Then I come around to help pick up or pack out as we need to."

"Sounds like your numbers are sort of flexible," Vince offered.

Here comes the wedge, Del thought. He said, "I need to draw the line, though. Given the access I'll have and the set-up I have, six is my capacity."

The lawyer gave him a direct look through the tinted glasses. "I thought maybe you would have reconsidered, given it a little more thought."

Yes, Del thought, the man had sensed something, and his self-assurance showed he was still confident of keeping things under his control. Del pushed back. "I may have thought about it a little more, but I didn't change my mind."

"I thought you might."

Del took a sip on his coffee. Might as well, he told himself. "Apparently you don't follow my meaning. What I mean is I don't care to have you hunt with me again."

The lawyer took a moment to absorb the statement. "You mean you're brushing me off like you did those other guys?"

"You could look at it that way, if you see a parallel."

"That doesn't seem like good business." The lawyer was staying game.

"It's good business for me to be able to decide who's going to hunt with me and who isn't. It's not always a matter of whether I like or don't like someone. I'd appreciate it if you'd just accept it as I put it out. Nothing personal."

"Nothing personal." The lawyer's voice was deadpan.

"So why don't we enjoy our pie. It looks like we're ready for it."

"O.K.," Vince said. "But before it gets too late, I think we should square our accounts."

"We could do that in the morning, or are you thinking of pulling out tonight?" It seemed to Del that the conversation had taken a couple of quick turns in the past few minutes.

"We need a motel room and a shower before we take off, so we might as well go into town tonight."

"No hard feelings, I hope."

"No, none at all." The lawyer was hauling his wife away, but he was not going to seem like a bad sport at this point.

Neither was Sylvia. "We've had a great time, Del. Everything has been first-rate. And we appreciate what you did to help me get my antelope."

"I'm glad you got one. I'm glad Vince got one too, of course. I just want everyone to go away satisfied."

She had a very appealing look in her eyes when she said, "This will be a memorable trip. I'll have fond memories of it." She held out her hand, and he shook it.

When the Furtinos were gone and Del had the dishes done up, he mixed himself a drink and sat by the fire. Things were peaceful again, the way he liked it. He had a few minutes to think. The antelope hunting had come and gone like a whirlwind. He had done all right on the daily fees and on the board and room, although another day or two of income would have been welcome. They had killed six buck antelope in two days, which was not uncommon. Hunters who couldn't shoot well or who held out for bigger trophies tended to draw out the excursion, but this set of hunters had worked their way through it all rather efficiently. There had been a couple of botches, trigger-happy mistakes, but he had been through worse. And they hadn't lost any crippled or gutshot animals— that was a good aspect of this hunt. Everything had come out even, and he had a decent carcass hanging in the cottonwoods. It had worked out all right. A guide could do worse, had done worse, than Mel and Roger. The Furtinos were all right, too. They followed the rules, usually, and hadn't been that much trouble. Sylvia had even left a thank-you note in their trailer. All the same, Del was glad she and Vince were gone.

Chapter Nine

It was not hard work to a man who had spent years at digging trenches and shoveling gravel, but it gave a fellow a stiff back that needed occasional straightening. Del leaned on his shovel handle with his right hand, and with his left he took off his hat and dragged the cuff of his shirt across his forehead. The quick flurry of antelope hunting had left him a couple of days open, time when he could deliberate on details for deer hunting. Digging carrots was such a detail.

Whisker, so named for a tuft of white on his chin, and Little Tulip, for the blaze on her forehead, stared at him across the corral railing. Del felt a kinship with them. They were his horses, the ones that had gone to the mountains with him and Rita. They were good horses and would do their work without treats, as would Spud, the horse he leased for the season. But the carrots were a nice touch.

If it came right down to it, he could get by without the horses. In most places where anyone would drop a deer, he could get close in a pickup and then, with the help of a hunter or two, drag the deer the rest of the way. The horses, though, added a quality that the hunters liked. They could hunt on horseback, even when they didn't need to; they could take pony rides while they were waiting for their partners to fill out; and they could feed the horses carrots as part of the camp camaraderie.

Deer hunting camp would be a little more primitive, in some respects, than the antelope camp. At the ranch where Del had leased access for the past few years, there was an old ranch house that had been put up by homesteaders. The house was sixty or seventy years old, but it had been kept up even after headquarters had moved to the larger outfit that had absorbed the spread. The wooden shingles and batten-and-board siding were weathered and in some places cracked, and a few window sills and door jambs let in drafts, but the house stood well against the weather. The wooden floor was still solid, even if it creaked a little here and gave a little there. Overall, it was a serviceable hunting cabin in the fall as well as a refuge from bad weather any other time of the year. For Del's purposes, it had the rugged attraction of not having electricity or running water. It had a hand pump in the kitchen, which still brought up water, and it had a stone fireplace that put out the heat. The camping trailers would not be part of this layout, but Del would pitch his tent between the cabin and the horse corral.

He was getting things into good order for the camp, right down to the carrots. Not being rushed as he sometimes was between the antelope and deer excursions, he had had time to cut and wrap his meat and to get the antelope pictures developed. Usually he waited till the end of the entire hunting season and had them all done together, but he had gotten to the end of a roll, had time to get it done, and was curious to see how the snapshots had come out.

Both Mel and Roger had taken good pictures. Roger's face was happy, flushed from a combination of festivity the night before and good fortune on opening morning. Del, remembering the dismay on Roger's face when he blundered later on, was glad to have caught the earlier exuberance. Mel's expression was more stolid, nearly expressionless, but inoffensive.

Vince's face, by contrast, had a glint of arrogance that verged on antagonism. Del remembered the coolness with which the lawyer had received his less-than-trophy buck, and he wondered how much he imposed his own interpretation on the restrained, smiling face of Vince Furtino.

The expression on Sylvia's face stayed with him the best. As he interpreted it, at least, it was radiance and happiness, uncomplicated joy from a small victory. He couldn't help thinking that the smile was for him, the smile that stayed with him as he dug carrots, straightened his back, clucked to Whisker and Little Tulip, and dragged his shirt sleeve across his brow.

When he had the two five-gallon buckets each about half-full of carrots, he set them on the floorboard of the pickup cab. He would have to make a preliminary trip to camp, to set things up, and the carrots would go on this first trip. He would set them soaking in water when he got there.

He loaded sleeping pads, extra sleeping bags and blankets, his tent, the camp boxes, his large propane stove and a smaller one, lanterns, propane bottles and hoses, an ax and a shovel, tarps, ropes, and meat processing gear. He also included the camp chairs, which would work indoors as well as outdoors. Next he loaded all the horse gear—feed buckets, a sack of grain, halters, bridles, saddles, blankets and pads, scabbards, saddlebags, and panniers. That gave him a full pickup load, so he tarped it down. He hitched up the horse trailer, loaded up his two horses, and was on his way.

He was back from camp by evening, with just enough daylight left to load hay and firewood. Tomorrow he would haul Spud, the groceries, and his personal gear when he led his hunters to camp. A small voice within him said he should wait around the phone this evening in case somebody canceled, but another small voice said hell with it, let the person talk to the answering machine. After a quick dinner, he gave Rita a call, got cleaned up, and headed into town.

As Del saw things, Rita was the same person in town as she was in the mountains, except that now she had more of her daily life wrapped around her. She had been raised in the country but now lived in town and worked at the bank. That meant she dressed nice, at least five days out of seven. Sometimes she went out on weekends, usually with Del. She liked to drink, but not too much. She liked to dance but not get sweaty. She liked to cook but nothing fancy. She liked to watch television and video movies. Having married young, she had kids who grew up and married young, all but the one who was just starting high school. She had also had two husbands who had never grown up and so were no longer a bother. At thirty-eight she was a handsome, well-kept single woman without a great deal complicating her life. She liked to spend soft quiet hours between the sheets with Del, but not when her youngest son was around.

Tonight was a school night, so the lad was at home watching a horror movie when Del arrived. That was O.K. Rita had to work the next day, and so did Del.

The boy, whose name was Mickey, was at the stage where he tapped the top of every door frame he went through, hiking a foot as if he were doing a miniature lay-up. He expressed interest in four-wheel-drive pickups, didn't seem to care much for hunting, and probably harbored ideas about the girls at school. No amount of teasing from his mom would bring it out, though, and his favorite pose was to sit slumped in the armchair, sprawling his legs out as if to display his untied high-topped gym shoes. He was working on his belching, which fit in with his pose and was promoted by the can of Coca-Cola that he usually had balanced on his knee or thigh. Perhaps his hardest task was to ignore his mother as she sat on the couch with Del, the two of them making eyes, holding hands, nudging, and carrying on other covert maneuvers. The belching facilitated his nonchalance, and he had the tact not to over-do it.

Rita and Del sat on the couch, each with a seven-and-seven in a light-green bumpy glass. "I swear I don't know why they make some of these movies," she said. "There's not a speck of sense in some of them."

"There's nothing else on," the boy said. It was evident that he didn't want to confess an interest in the movie but didn't want his mother to change the channel, either.

Rita turned to Del, patting his leg. "So things start up for you again tomorrow."

"Yep."

"How many hunters do you have coming in?"

"Six all together. Three pairs."

"All new?"

"All new to me. But not any beginners, as I understood it."

"Oh." She yawned and looked at the television, then watched her hand as it did a spider-walk on Del's leg. "How come they start a hunting season in the middle of the week, anyway?"

"They start the seasons on the same day of the month every year—like this season, they always start it on the first of October, no matter where it falls in the week."

"They should start the seasons on weekends. A couple of the guys at work are real put out about it."

"It would be fairer to the guy who's got a normal job."

"It doesn't matter to your out-of-stater, though."

"Oh, no. Every day is Saturday to a dog."

"Huh?"

"They're going to be off work one way or the other."

"Oh. I see. It's all the same to them, you mean."

"That's right."

"Actually, they probably have a little of an advantage, then."

"Compared to the guys you work with, yes. Your friends have a legitimate gripe. The out-of-staters beat them to the game and spook what they don't shoot. But the locals should feel sorry for the non-residents."

"Really?"

"They get treated like tourists, which in a way they are. They have to pay for everything, and then they have to go back to those places where they came from."

"You got just the right amount of sarcastic in that," she said. "You sound like other people in the tourist trade. Like they say, love their money and hate their asses."

"I'm not quite that bad. But I wouldn't want to live where most of them come from."

Mickey belched.

"My lord," his mom said. "Do you do that around the girls at school?"

"It wouldn't matter. They couldn't hear it."

"Why?"

"They got their heads up their butts."

Rita and Del stared at each other, and Mickey kept his straight gaze on the television.

"You can see that things have changed a lot since we were in school," Rita said.

"They sure have," Del answered. "We used to tie our shoe laces."

Rita took a sip on her drink and tossed her hair back. It wasn't quite long enough to stay in back of her shoulders, so she had to toss it every once in a while.

"How long will you be out?" she asked.

"Probably a little less than a week. Then I'll be back for a few days to get things ready for elk."

"Busy boy, aren't you?"

"Well, it's a busy time of year."

"Got to make hay while the sun shines, I guess."

"Yep. Make hay now, roll in the hay later."

Rita poked him and frowned, making a small grimace in the direction of Mickey, who sat stone-faced.

Del went on as if there had been no answer. "Actually, I should be back in just about a week. After my hunters fill out, I'll want to hunt a day or two as well."

Rita rested her head on his shoulder. "It will be nice when winter's here, when the snow is on the ground."

"Uh-huh. We can get snowed in."

They sat awhile in silence, watching the movie and sipping on their drinks. Del was just beginning to get the drift of the movie when it ended. He finished his drink as the ice cubes were beginning to melt into smooth rounded pebbles. Rita asked him if he'd like another drink.

"No, thanks. I should be going. My day starts early tomorrow. If I sit here much longer, I'm likely to fall asleep."

Del found his hat and waited at the door while Rita took the glasses to the kitchen. Just as she was coming back, Mickey spoke up.

"Hey, Del, you want to know what we learned in biology?"

"Sure."

"A roll in the hay makes more D.N.A."

Del laughed. "That's a good one." Then he said to Rita, as she slipped her arm around his waist, "I think they might be learning more than we did. We didn't get past dominant and recessive genes."

She leaned her breast against him. "I think I had dropped out by then."

"You don't learn it all out of a book," he said, as he moved toward her to kiss her.

After the kiss, she drummed her fingers on his forearm. "You be careful, now."

"I will. And I'll be back to see you when we get all the deer killed."

"Jewel didn't leave me much," she said, "but he had one good saying about hunting."

"Oh?" Jewel was her first husband, the one before Mike, Mickey's father. She never mentioned Mike when the boy was around.

"Yeah. He'd tell you to keep the wind in your face."

"I'll do that." He kissed her again and whispered, "I'll see you when I get back."

On his way home, Del felt better than he had felt in a while. Being with Rita brought out good feelings. It wasn't just the excitement of a relationship still coming into bloom, although there was some of that, too. There were other good feelings as well, quieter-toned, the kind that seemed like they might last even if things got steady and serious.

Rita had been through marriage twice and had a certain amount of baggage, as people said. Del was at about the same place, even though he had passed up what would have been the blush of young love and new marriage. He thought he and Rita were well matched—old enough for a grown-up romance but not too old to enjoy it. That didn't seem too bad for a couple of kids sneaking up on forty.

On a broader scale, also, he and she seemed to go together well. As he saw it, the shape of her life fit with the shape of his, like soft bundles when he packed the horses. Maybe Rita dressed nice and didn't like to dance too hard, but when Del was with her, he didn't feel any sharp edges. She came close to him regardless of what she was wearing, and she wasn't afraid of rain, dirt, or blood. She had been as comfortable as he had been in the mountains. He remembered how he had felt that afternoon in the tent when he drew the blanket over them. Everything seemed to go together, the dark shades and quiet pleasures. It had seemed like her world as well as his. They weren't in the mountains any more, but the feeling was still there. What he liked seemed to match pretty well with what she liked—maybe not a perfect match like the Adam and Eve bags when they zipped together, but like Adam and Eve when they were rolled up and ready to go. They might squeeze together just fine.

* * * * *

The next day, after he had fetched Spud to his own corral, he bought groceries and packed the ice chests and boxes. Shortly after noon the first hunters showed up, a pair of brothers from California. One was an accountant and one was a carpenter, but they were both rugged, husky men in their early thirties. They had brown hair and reddish beards, both of them, and they smiled the same. Len was the accountant and Chick was the carpenter. Their last name was Becker. They had hunted together in Idaho and Colorado, and now they were trying Wyoming. Len had shot a six-pointer in Idaho the year before, a nice buck in the picture he showed Del.

"We'd like to try for four-pointers," he said, "but we'll see how things go."

"I've seen some good bucks out there during the summer, but it sounds like you've hunted enough to know that it's not the same as ordering from a catalogue."

Len laughed. "Oh, yeah. We know. Tell him about your last one, Chick."

Chick smiled. "After Len got his six-pointer, we hunted two full days. I passed up a three-pointer and a few forked horns and finally settled for a two-by-three. And all the time I worked on him, dressing him out and then dragging him down the draw, there was a picture-perfect four-pointer just standing there watching me."

Del chuckled as he knew he should. "Sounds like you'll fit right in," he said. He brought out the paper work, went through it with them, and made small talk about their drive from California. Both of the brothers liked to talk, and they let each other take turns. Len was finishing a description of a mobile home that had spilled on the interstate near Rawlins, when the second pair of hunters pulled into the driveway.

From the Iowa plates, Del knew that these would be Danny Castagnola and Ron Grosbaum, the two who hadn't hunted mule deer before but who had hunted lots of whitetail. They introduced themselves to the Becker brothers, with hearty handshaking all the way around. Danny was slender and dark-featured, while Ron was square-built along the lines of the Becker brothers, with fairer hair and no beard. Del figured them to be in their middle thirties, and there was a familiar shade to their sun tans, which made sense when he learned they were brick masons.

Tradesmen tanned differently according to the surfaces and substances they worked close to. Del always thought he could pick out a hot roofer in a dark barroom. Now he wondered if he himself still had the look of his former trade. He doubted it, and his yard gave no sign, either. His driveway was lined with loose field stone, and his wheelbarrow, which he used for carting firewood, had a steel-rimmed, spoked wheel and rusty handles.

Danny and Ron hit it off fine with the Becker brothers. They had all hunted before, and they bore the cheerful, chummy spirit of wishing the next fellow the best of luck but no doubt hoping that he didn't get to the big one first. The Beckers showed great interest in learning that their new pals had hunted whitetails with shotgun slugs. In turn, they were not slow in letting it be known that they had hunted blacktail and mule deer across the West. Del could see a genuine trade fair of hunting lore and intelligence beginning to take shape, and there was no telling what other information might be shared on the subject of gas mileage, stereo equipment, or medical coverage. He would not have to work to keep the conversational ball rolling.

Del's third pair of hunters, a father and a son, rolled into the yard a few minutes after the guide had finished the paperwork with Danny and Ron. The father introduced himself, Ken Kerr, and his son, Ken Junior. Ken was fair-haired and greying, well-groomed and fit. Before he sat down at the desk, he had it understood that they had driven straight

103

through from San Francisco—Burlingame, really—in their new Blazer, that his son, who went by Kenny, had taken time out of his first year of varsity football just for this trip, and that he, Ken, was manager of a small chain of steak houses in the Bay Area. The Becker brothers, who came from Fresno, had not heard of Ken's chain but accepted his assurance that it was "one of the nicer kind, along the lines of a Black Angus." While this exchange was going on, Kenny had shaken hands with the other hunters and was taking a seat.

When Del had finished with his last set of paperwork, he raised his voice enough to address everyone. "I guess we're all set. I need to load the horse and the groceries, and we can go. If you all take your own vehicles, you can drive in to the taxidermist if you need to, and you can leave when you're ready. But you won't have to drive once we get there. We'll hunt on horseback or from my outfit." He looked around as the men nodded. "If I could get each of you to take an ice chest, I can take the other groceries in my cab. Have you got room for an ice chest in each of your vehicles?"

There was a general rumble of agreement, after which Ken asked, "Did you say you're loading just one horse, Del?"

"At the moment. I've got two out at the camp already."

"Oh, O.K."

"We'll rarely have to use all three at once, anyway. But having three works out pretty good."

"Sounds great. Ready, son?" Ken put his left arm around Kenny and clamped his shoulder. "We're going to have one hell of a good time."

As Del took a lead rope out to the corral where Spud stood hip-shot, he was glad he had the set-up he did. He also appreciated Ken's concern that he was getting what he paid for. Ken wasn't pushy like Vince Furtino; he was just making sure that his boy was going to get a pony ride.

Chapter Ten

The ranch house faced west, and between the front porch and the hitching rail there was a fire pit for cook-outs. As the hunters settled into their lodge, Del got a fire going. He wanted to have a bed of coals suitable for grilling the T-bones. In this camp, unless there was a bad wind or a heavy snow, he barbecued steaks the first night out. It was a perfect touch for the hunters, who could sit in camp chairs on the porch, put their feet on the railing, have a drink, enjoy the isolation, and watch the fire flicker as the sun set over the ridge to the west.

Sometimes, when Del thought about the elaborate arrangements and expense that men like Ken Kerr went to, it seemed that their kind of hunting was a far cry from the original purpose of living by the hunt, providing for oneself and one's family. When Del thought of things that way, it all seemed like a large Easter egg hunt with pony rides—an extravaganza for the privileged paying guests, while their hired native soaked his elbows in blood and guts, then scraped venison fat from the hair on his arms.

But it didn't always seem that way. Once the guide and the hunters got the paperwork done and the vehicles parked out of the way, their enterprise settled down to the simpler terms that they were really here for—escape and freedom. Escaped from traffic, city noise, glaring lights, ringing phones, and the looming threat of crime, these men were free to enjoy the quiet land as it grew into reality around them. Tomorrow they would try the role that they would have lived if they had been born in another age. When a hunter stalked the ridges and the draws, it didn't matter if he was the dishwasher or the manager or the owner of the corporate chain. He put himself on terms with the land he hunted and with the game that took its living from it. There was escapism, no doubt, but into a world with its own real laws rather than into a playground.

As Del forked hay to the horses, he laughed at himself. He was the biggest escapist of all, and he had never kidded himself about it. If sometimes he lost his sense of exuberance and freedom, it was because he lived this life all the time. It wasn't a once-a-year excursion with the high point a glorious kill, as it was for his hunters. He saw a lot more of the killing, had a hand in it to the point of drudgery and sometimes even regret, and had less of the fun. It was a trade-off, being a servant for a short while so he could be free the rest of the time. When he thought about it, he acknowledged he was living a fair version of the great escape.

Leaning the pitchfork against the corral post, he crawled through the rails. He eased up to Little Tulip, asked her how she was, and massaged the base of her ears. Still munching hay from the feed bunk, she leaned her head into him, pushing. The mare was Rita's favorite. Del smiled. He damn sure was an escapist, and glad of it. He didn't have to go back and listen to the rattle of a cement mixer or the siren of a cop car. He'd stay right here with Whisker and Little Tulip, and when the snow was deep on the ground and mounded on the tops of the fence posts, he would brush the ice off his horses' backs and go back inside the house for venison stew. He came as close as he could, it seemed, to escaping the world at large and living the way he liked. The way things were shaping up with Rita, he might have someone to share it all with.

The thought of Rita brought a smile to his face again. He felt a flicker inside, and then the feeling brought another image to his mind. He saw hair the color of wheat straw, a pair of sparkling blue eyes, a trim figure in blue jeans, the pert shape of her breasts beneath a pullover sweater.

Del raised his eyebrows, remembering the attraction and realizing it hadn't gone away. He knew the feeling. It was the type of fascination that a guy was tempted to follow up on. It was another kind of escape—to go after something appealing, to forget about the risks and rules, to indulge in a little tumble while he was still at least technically free of commitments. He could see it as an adventure, something for the moment, without a clear view of anything beyond. Out here and away from it all, it seemed as if he could think about things like that and not really do any harm. It was something he could keep inside.

Del patted Little Tulip and turned away. He crawled out through the corral rails and headed for the house.

Back in the large front room of the ranch house, he saw that the hunters had gotten settled into their bunks and had their gear arranged. Danny and Ron had taken the two bunks on the west wall, and the other four hunters were on the east wall. Next to each bunk was a simple, two-shelved nightstand made of pine boards nailed together, and above each stand there were two hat-and-coat hooks mounted on the wall. Caps and coats hung on the wall hooks, shaving kits sat on the nightstands, boots poked their toes under the bunks, and duffel bags showed from under and between the bunks. On the north wall, the hunters had found the gun rack, where their rifles stood oiled and ready.

"Looks like everything is in good order," Del said. "What would we think about opening camp with a drink? It looks like a nice evening to sit on the porch."

At the other end of the large room, on either side of the fireplace, he had his kitchen and camp gear. He pulled out a bag of ice, a package of clear plastic highball glasses, and a liter-and-a-half bottle of Ancient Age, and set up seven glasses with ice. "Water is in the blue five-gallon can there, and Seven-Up is in the brown cooler. Help yourselves."

Outside, Del unfolded camp chairs and set them on the porch. Then he went to the fire pit and poked at the fire as the men found the chairs and the porch railing.

"Damn, this is nice," Ken announced. "Not another camp or cabin in sight. The whole place to ourselves." He turned to his son. "You're not going to find this in those hunting lodges where Jim Wilcox and his buddies go." Kenny nodded, and his dad went on. "They go up there to drink and play cards and probably play around with their camp whores." He turned to the Beckers. "You know the kind of place."

Len smiled. "Oh, yeah. They don't go to hunt. They just go to get away from their wives."

Chick joined in. "I think that in half of those high-price places, they have a guy around just to fill tags."

"To do what?" Kenny asked.

"To fill their tags," his dad explained. "To go out and kill their animals for them while they lay around the lodge. They just open their gun case to see if their wife left something in there to catch them on, like a love note or their only clean pair of socks."

Chick laughed. "Yeah, I've heard of that. I don't know how many people they really fool."

"Nah, they don't go to hunt," Len added.

"This is the way to do it," Ken said. "Get off by yourself and do the real thing. I'll tell you, it *is* quiet here. Isn't it?"

"Sure is," Chick answered. "When we were in Colorado the year before last, all you could hear all night long was the generators kicking in at the other camp sites."

"Is that right," Ken put in.

"Yeah," Chick went on, "they had their big motor homes parked in the camp site there, on the National Forest, you know, and every one of them seemed to have a gas generator that kicked in now and then to run the electricity."

"The hell," Ken answered.

"Not exactly our idea of getting away from it all," Len added. "We decided after that to get set up to hunt on private land."

"Those motor homes are all right," Ken said, "but I wouldn't want to take one hunting."

Danny spoke up. "Even a camper trailer. I think you want to give a second thought to how you'd ever use one of them."

Ron laughed. "Yeah, you gotta be careful who you take along."

Danny had his audience now, so he told his story. "A couple of guys we know back home came out this way to hunt in the Black Hills, and they pulled a camper trailer all the way. It was an older model but still pretty nice, about an eighteen-footer that sleeps four to six." He took a sip on his drink. "Well, they pulled it all the way out here, slept one night on the road in it, and got into the Black Hills just at dusk on the evening before the season opened. They shot a deer off the road and tossed him in the trailer, figuring to skin him when they got camped. When they opened up the door, that deer was back up on his feet and had kicked the hell out of the whole inside of the trailer and had bled all over."

Ken took advantage of the pause in the story to offer, "That sounds like a hell of a mess. How did they get him out?"

"They had to shoot him again. And then they had to clean him, clean the trailer, and sleep in it for the rest of the trip."

"You've got to make sure the deer is good and dead," Len Becker said, laughing. "Whether the deer is legal or otherwise. You hear all kinds of stories of how they get back up. I read one story about a buck that reared up and got his horns all tangled in a fellow's camera strap." He nodded at Ken. "The guy was hunting with his dad, and the dad was afraid to shoot the deer. I think, the way the story went, his dad finally got a clear shot."

Chick came in for his turn. "And then there's the one about the guy who was posing with his deer, with his rifle resting in the antlers, and the buck got up and ran off with the rifle." He paused for a sip. "I wasn't there, but I heard the

111

story from someone who said he was, and it could sure enough happen."

"Oh, yeah, no question," Ken agreed. With a look at his son he added, "You damn sure got to make sure they're dead."

Ron wasn't going to be left out. "Reminds me of a story I heard about a couple from the east, like New Jersey or New Hampshire, one of those places, who came out here on vacation—tourists you know, out here to see Mount Rushmore and Yellowstone and all that. They were driving through this part of the country, and they hit a dog. Well, they felt bad, so they put the dog in the back seat and drove on till they could come to a town that had a vet. Pretty soon it came to, and it started growlin' and snarlin' and they couldn't get it settled down, and it got worse and tried to bite the guy's old lady, until the guy had to bonk it on the head with a flashlight. You know, they thought maybe it had gone wacky gettin' hit."

"Oh, you bet they will," Ken said. "We had a dog when I was a kid, and he got hit out on the street and didn't seem to be hurt, but not too long after that he went cuckoo. We had to put him away."

"Well, that's what these people thought, and it made them feel like double hell, first hittin' this doggie and then havin' to put it down with a flashlight. When they got to a town with a vet, they right away offered to pay the bill and get the poor critter stitched up. I guess the vet gave it a knockout shot and fixed it all up and didn't say much. When these nice people paid the bill and thanked him, they said they guessed they'd leave it there. They asked the vet what would be the best way to get in touch with the owner, since it didn't have a tag. The vet said what do you mean, an owner? Well, they said, a dog like this has got to have an owner, and he'll probably be wonderin' about it. That old vet just laughed like hell and said this ain't no dog, it's a coyote!'"

As the other hunters broke into laugher, Ron and Danny joined in.

"That's a good story," Len said, "a good reminder not to pick up hitchhikers."

"Sure is," Chick agreed. "It's kind of got a little more suspense to it than the one about the deer in the trailer—no offense, that was a good story, too, but I like this one better. Here are these nice, well-meaning people babying an animal that would like to tear 'em to shreds."

"That's what it is," Len returned. "Yeah. It's not just about why you shouldn't pick up hitchhikers. It's about the hidden enemy." He opened his eyes wide and put on what seemed to be a diabolical grin. He drained the last of his drink, rattling the ice cubes against his upper teeth. "I guess it's a true story."

"I heard it as a true story," Ron answered. "Have you ever heard it before, Del?"

Del turned toward the porch. "No, but it could happen."

Ken, undaunted at having been taken in earlier, was back in the conversation. "That *is* a good story. I bet that old vet likes to tell it. You can bet he likes the part about getting paid before he told them what it was." He rattled the cubes in his own glass. "Say, Del, can I get you another drink?"

"Not yet, thanks. But you fellows help yourselves. It'll be a while yet till these coals are ready." Del nodded at the fire.

As the hunters clumped across the porch and bunched at the door going in, Len pecked his forefinger on his brother's chest. "Beware of the hidden enemy."

Chick raised his right forefinger in mock inspiration and answered, "The beast that lurks within."

Sundown as it fell brought coolness with the dusk, and the hunters gathered at the fire pit to enjoy their highballs. They had brought their chairs from the porch, and now they sat around the fire.

With his second drink, Kenny was coming out of his shell. "I don't care if I get a wall hanger," he declared. "I just want to have a good time and not go home empty-handed if I can help it."

"Have you shot many deer in the past?" Danny asked.

Ken Senior took over. "We've hunted the past two years on a ranch in the Coast Range, down by King City. But it's awfully tight there, hunting those coastal blacktail." He looked at the Becker brothers, who nodded, and he went on. "We do all right there in the winter, hunting wild pig, but so far we haven't gotten any blacktail bucks."

"I killed a big boar hog there," Kenny added. "They've got a meat house on the ranch there, and that boar weighed over three hundred pounds, field dressed."

"I've never hunted those wild pigs," Chick said.

"Me neither," Len added, "but I've heard they're hard to hunt."

"Hell, yes," Ken said. "They're as smart as a deer, and just as fast. You wouldn't think it till you hunted 'em."

"Well," Len continued, looking at Kenny, "if you've hunted feral pigs and blacktail deer, you shouldn't have any trouble with these mule deer."

"Yep," Chick added, "you should do fine." He turned to Del. "I suppose you have it all planned out how you're going to hunt us in the morning."

"I've got some general directions for you so you won't crowd one another. As you get to know the country, you'll form your own ideas on how to hunt it, but I'll get you started. I think I'll send you and your brother out along this pine ridge that runs to the north. That's usually good, especially early in the season." The brothers nodded, and the guide continued. "The deer come back from the hay fields to the east, and they shade up in the pines during the day. If you don't get one while they're coming back, you can work the top of the ridge later on, and try to push something out."

The top of the ridge was jagged and dark against an orange sunset, and the Beckers looked at it and nodded again.

"Dan and Ron," Del went on, "I'll send you up the road here where it follows the creek in sort of a pass through that ridge, and you can hunt down into the basin that falls off to the west. It's bigger country down in there than you'd think just sitting here."

"Any place you send us is fine with me," Dan said.

"Me too," Ron added.

"I'll be surprised if you don't find something there," Del continued. He turned to Kenny. "You and your dad and I will take the horses south and then west where the ridge peters out. Eventually we'll end up down in the bottom, where Danny and Ron are likely to end up, too. That means we'll have to leave camp a little ahead of the rest of them, or well before sunup, anyway. They can leave when they want, as far as that goes."

Ken raised a question, "What's our general procedure when we get one down?"

"You want to field dress him first, of course. If your partner shows up and you know you're near a road, you can drag him—the deer, not your partner—you can drag him to the road where we can get him with the pickup. Oh—and make sure you tag him when you dress him. We're on private land, but there are no locks on the gates and a game warden could come through. We wouldn't want to get chewed out or fined. Anyway, drag him to a road if it's handy to do it that way. If not, try to get him to a place where he'll be in the shade for quite a while, and set him so he'll drain if he's got any blood left in him. Let's see—what else? Oh. You probably already know not to cut his throat if you're sure he's down and dead, and you want to have the horns and cape mounted. Of course you've got to field dress him quick, then, so he doesn't jump up and steal your rifle or hook your camera strap."

Ron had a question. "Do we hunt all day or come back here for lunch?"

"We usually come back, but anyone who wants to stay out can pack along a lunch. We've got all kinds of take-along food, which I'll have set out. Usually it's a good idea to carry some kind of snack food, just in case you stay out longer than you think or in case you just run out of gas." Del turned to the Beckers. "You fellows know what I mean when I say you're at

116

a different altitude and climate than you're used to." He looked around at the rest of the hunters. "If you get winded, just stop and catch your breath. Be prepared. Weather can change really quick here, drop twenty or thirty degrees in a damn short while, and you can see right now that it cools off pretty fast when the sun goes down. You'll notice it in the draws and shady spots, too. I always carry a pair of gloves, and the standard practice is to dress in layers. That way you can take things off or put them on when the weather changes."

Len spoke up. "We all wear blaze-orange, right?"

"Right. Everyone has to have a cap or a vest or a jacket. I've got extra if anyone needs it. Let's see—what else. Directions. You have to try pretty hard to get lost on this place, but if a snowstorm blows up or if things just cloud over, it would be a good idea to keep your bearings or get them real quick before the curtain comes down. The best landmark here is that rock cliff on the ridge. It's straight west of camp here, and the road is right below it. Keep an eye on it for the first little while that you're out, and I don't think anyone should have any trouble getting back to camp."

Chick asked the next question. "Any special rules or places to stay off of, like touchy neighbors?"

"Just the regular rules. Don't shoot anything unless you or your partner is going to tag it. Don't shoot any cows. Don't leave candy wrappers or cigarette packs or soda pop cans on the ground, and don't start any grassfires. Anything else?"

"Would you like a bucket of water?" Chick asked.

Del was taken aback for an instant. "Do you mean right now?"

117

"Yeah. I always feel better if there's a bucket of water by the fire. I'll go get you one if you want."

"Sure. There's a bucket in the kitchen." Del poked at the coals with his iron rod. The hunters had drawn in around the fire, and the glare of the stoked coals lit up the circle for a moment.

As Chick turned to go for the bucket of water, his brother smiled, teeth shining in the firelight as he gazed at the ridge to the west. It was black against a slate-grey sky. "Yeah," Len said, in an abstracted sort of way, "it's nice to have a bucket of water in camp."

Chapter Eleven

Morning seemed to be still the middle of the night when Del reached over to shut off the clanging hammer of the alarm. He could hear the horses shifting in the corral outside his tent, and he had a sense of having been aware of them as he slept. He had a residual taste of last night's whiskey, and he had to take a leak, but other than that, he felt well rested. Today would be a busy day for him, a big day for some of his hunters. He thought first of Kenny. There had seemed to be a tacit agreement among the hunters that the young man should get the guided hunt on opening morning.

Del clucked to the horses as he came out of the tent. They snuffled back. After he had pitched them some hay, he crawled through the rails, and by the light of his pocket flashlight, he looked at their feet. There was a pleasing mixture of smells in the frosty air—dry hay, warm horse body, cold mud, steaming manure. Del spoke in a soft tone to the horses as he moved among them, and when he was satisfied that they were all in good shape for the day, he left them to munch their hay.

Trying to be both quick and quiet, he went to work on breakfast. Because the hunters would want to get started before sunrise, breakfast was not as leisurely as it was during antelope season, but he still had to lay out a full spread. He got a pot of coffee going and a pan of bacon sizzling, then set out the tableware. Next he took out a large stainless steel mixing bowl, cracked sixteen eggs into it, poured in milk, grated in some cheese, and flipped the bacon. He set out milk, orange juice, donuts, margarine, bread, and jam. Remembering Roger, he smiled and set out ketchup with the tabasco, salt, and pepper. He took out a second skillet, poured a thin layer of warm bacon grease into the bottom, and set the eggs to cooking. He lifted out the first set of bacon, drained the grease, and set the second batch to frying.

As he was setting out the snack foods for the men to take along on the hunt, the Becker brothers began to stir. Within a few minutes, all six hunters had their feet on the floor. That was good, he thought—he wouldn't have to wake anyone. The smell of bacon and coffee was no doubt a more welcome greeting.

When everyone was settled at the table and working on scrambled eggs and bacon, Del gave a brief review of who would go where. He pointed out the granola bars, snack bars (candy bars masquerading as health food), real candy bars, dried fruit, and cookies. He explained where the lunch food was, saying that they could pack a lunch or help themselves as they came back in. He told Ken and Kenny that they would be back at the cabin for lunch, but to fill their pockets just in case.

"Take your time with breakfast," he said to the whole table, "and toss your plates and silverware in the dishpan when you're done. I'm going out to saddle the horses."

"Do you need some help, Del?" Ken asked.

"Not really. Take your time. It will be a good half hour before anyone has to leave, and I can get things ready in that time. When you're finished and all set to go, you can come on out, but there's no hurry."

"O.K." Ken turned to his son. "Kenny, you'll probably want to watch some of this, to get an idea how it's done."

"No hurry," Del reassured him. "We'll be through it several times, so there's no need to get indigestion on opening morning. Oh, by the way—there's water heating in that basin on the stove if any of you want to shave or wash your face or whatever."

Del led the horses to the hitching rail one at a time as he saddled them. He worked with smooth motions as he brushed and saddled Whisker and then Little Tulip. He was tying Spud to the off side of the hitching rail when Kenny came out onto the porch.

"Anything I can do?"

The truth was that the job went smoother if he did it himself, but the procedures were important and interesting to some hunters. Saddling the horses was part of the total adventure that Ken had brought his son to experience. Ken, who was in many ways a high-school-aged kid himself, would probably have liked to watch too, but he sent the son out to have it by himself. So Del told a half-truth. "Oh, most of this goes all right as a one-man job, but you could give me a little help, I think. You been around horses any?"

"Not really. I've just gone riding a couple of times at stables. We didn't saddle them or anything."

"Well, O.K. That's fine. Come on over here to the front of the horse." Del slipped the bow knot he had just tied, and he coiled the lead rope so Kenny could hold it. The kid who smashed his way through bloodthirsty linebackers came pussyfooting over to take the rope Del handed him.

"Good," Del said. "Hold the rope with your right hand and pet him with your left there. In a minute you can move around to where I am, which is a more natural position. This horse's name is Spud."

"Hi, Spud."

"O.K. Move over here now. That's it, rope in the left hand and your right hand free. Yeah—scratch him on the jaw and underneath there, too. See, he likes it." Del moved to the horse's front quarter and rested his hand on the withers. "O.K. Now, a good way to get along with these critters is to be smooth and gentle. Talk to 'em and pat 'em while you work around 'em. Don't sneak up on one, and don't do anything jerky or sudden. When I can, I keep one hand on him, so he knows where I am and I know where he is. When you go around his back end, keep your hand or arm on him like this, and he won't worry about you. Lots of people who are new around horses, they want to take a big wide circle around the ass end, but that just makes him wonder what you're up to. When you walk away from him at his hind end, pat him on the rump. When you walk up to him there, talk to him and then pat him. O.K.?"

"Got it."

"We'll go through all this again in the daylight, so I won't pause on every little detail right now. But the first thing we do is brush him."

"Right."

"And it's a good idea to run your bare hand over him, to check for any burrs or scabs or sores."

"Uh-huh."

When Del had brushed the horse, he said, "I'm going over to get the pad and blanket and saddle."

"All right. Here, Spud. Good boy."

Back in a minute, Del held the saddle on his right thigh while he settled the pad and blanket on the horse. "You always check the pad and blanket for burrs and stickers. This country is terrible for that sort of thing. I checked these before I brought them over."

"O.K."

"And you check your cinches and your saddle, too, to see if they picked up anything. Then you set your saddle on— some people like to sling it on—and you come around to the other side here and let down the cinches and the stirrup."

"Why do some people sling it?"

"It's more cowboy. They grab the saddle horn and give the saddle a swing, and the horse braces himself because he's used to the stirrup and cinches coming down to slap him, and then they snug the saddle into place as it lands on his back." Del moved back to the horse's left front.

"Why is it more cowboy?"

"Some folks do the whole job with their right hand while they hold the reins or lead rope with the left. Maybe you're with a whole crew of fellas and there's not a hitching rail handy, or maybe you're out on the prairie and there's nothing to tie him to."

"We saw plenty of that kind of country on the way here."

"I imagine you did. O.K., the next thing is to reach under, grab the cinch, and pull it up. Then you run the latigo through, and through, and—unh—through again, if you can get it, and buckle it. Then you buckle the back cinch, just snug. The front cinch is the main one, so you always tighten it first and loosen it last. Don't leave the back cinch buckled by itself, or the saddle can slip around underneath the horse and cause all kinds of hell."

"O.K."

Del ducked under Spud's neck. "Now you take the breast collar, snap it on the bottom here—there's a little ring in the middle of the front cinch—then tighten it to the D-ring on the front of your saddle."

"What's the collar for?"

"If you're the Lone Ranger, or if you're in a parade, it's for show, and you get all kinds of fancy silver work done on it. But we use it to keep the saddle from slipping back when we have ol' Spud carry us or some big mule deer buck out of a canyon."

Kenny laughed. "That sounds like a good idea."

"Now we're ready for the bridle." Del fetched it.

"Usually we slip the halter off and put the bridle on, but for hunting, we'll put the bridle on over the halter and put the lead rope in the saddlebag. That way you can tie him up quick and easy, and he won't go breaking a nice leather headstall or set of reins." He draped his right arm up over the horse's head, eased the bit into his mouth, and settled the headstall around his ears. Leaving a little slack in the reins, he wound them around the pommel. "One more thing."

"What's that?"

"Pick his hooves." Del drew a hoof pick from his hip pocket and, bending down, lifted the hoof that Spud offered. "You clean out the underside here, so he doesn't have any rocks or junk in here to make him sore." Del worked his way around all four hooves and then straightened his back. "That should do it. Let's tie him up, and when your dad's ready to go, we'll hit the trail."

Back inside the ranch house, Del smiled at the Becker brothers, who had just finished washing and drying the breakfast dishes. Danny was giving a last-minute perusal to the hunting regulations while Ron and Ken were drinking coffee.

"All set?" Ken asked.

"Just about. We're saddled up. Those of you who are hunting on foot will probably want to take off pretty soon. Is anyone staying out all day, or are we all back here for lunch?"

"We plan to be back," Danny said.

"So do we," Chick added.

"O.K.," Del said. "No one's going to worry, of course, if any of you stay out longer than planned. Everyone is on his own. If you don't make it in by bed time, maybe we'll start to wonder."

After a round of everyone wishing the others good luck, the Beckers and the bricklayers were gone. Father and son picked up their rifles, father verified that son had his knife and his license, and they were ready to go. Del turned off the lantern and flicked on his flashlight, and the three of them went out into the cool morning.

"Kenny, you'll ride Whisker. He's the gelding with the white chin. You've got a scabbard on the southeast corner, right behind your right leg. Ken, you'll be on Spud, the horse that Kenny and I just saddled. I don't have a scabbard for you, but I gather you've hunted on horseback before and you have an idea of how you like to sling your rifle."

"It's been a while, but it'll come back."

"If you carry things in the saddlebags, either of you, try to keep even weight in the bags. If you want to stow a coat, you can tie it to the back of the saddle. I'm going to get my gear, then we'll get you two mounted and your stirrups adjusted, and we'll be on the way."

Del went into his tent and came out with his saddle gun and his panniers. He slipped the rifle into its scabbard and strapped it in.

"What's that you've got?" Kenny asked.

"Panniers. A set of bags, like a big set of saddlebags, for packing." He unrolled the set. "See, it drapes over the saddle, and each side can hold half a deer or a quarter of an elk."

"Sort of like a big pair of newspaper bags," Ken suggested, "like you'd put on the back of a motorbike."

"Same idea," Del said. "These are blaze-orange, which will be more obvious when the sun comes up." Del rolled up the panniers again and tied them onto the saddle. Then, leaving Little Tulip hitched to the rail, he pulled the bow knot on Spud's rope and let him around. "Ken, if you hand your rifle to Kenny, you can get aboard."

Del tightened the front cinch, ushered Ken into the saddle, took off the lead rope, and put it in the saddlebag. "When you

126

want to tie your horse, use this rope instead of the reins." Ken nodded. "Now, stand up in the stirrups. How much clearance have you got? You want about the width of your fist. O.K. You're fine. Now Kenny, hand your dad his rifle and hand me yours." Del brought Whisker around, tightened the cinch, took Kenny's rifle, and held the stirrup. When Kenny was planted in the saddle, Del unsnapped the lead rope and secured the rifle into the scabbard. "See this velcro strap? It goes over the outside of the rifle bolt, and that keeps it snug. If we go through thick brush or timber, sort of keep an eye on it." Kenny nodded. "O.K., stand up in your stirrups. Looks like we need to let them out a notch."

With that done, Del untied Little Tulip, snugged the cinch, stowed the lead rope, and swung aboard. He touched the stock of his rifle where it rode in the scabbard. "Ken," he said, "you'll find out that Spud there likes to keep about a head and neck ahead of these two, so let him have that much. We'll follow the trail that goes around the corral there. O.K., if we're all set, let's head out."

It was a still, crisp, quiet morning, just beginning to grey. The horses snorted and blew a couple of times each as the party rounded the corral and struck out on the trail. The horses settled into their *clip-clop, tlick-tlock* as their breaths puffed little clouds on the morning air. The saddle was firm but not very cold. Del leaned forward to pat Little Tulip on her neck, and she was warm to the touch. "Good girl," he said, and he caught the sweet smell of alfalfa on her breath. He pulled on a pair of cotton gloves, adjusted his reins, and re-seated himself in the saddle.

127

The image came to him of a woman rising from sleep—a light-featured woman in the soft glow of a bedroom. He blinked the image away and looked around, tuning himself back in to the world of men and horses, rifles and saddles, cold air and hard dirt.

On his left he could see Kenny in the greying morning. The lad seemed to be riding all right, and he had ridden enough to know how to keep the slack out of his reins. Looking ahead, Del could see Ken moving up and down in a bounce that was exaggerated by the rifle slung on his shoulder. After they had ridden half a mile, Ken lifted the sling off his right shoulder and slipped the sling up over his head and onto the left side of his collar, so that the rifle rode diagonally across his back.

Del took in the country as they rode on, still in silence. The ridge on their right began to take form in the first traces of dawn. The pastureland on their left and ahead of them began to show grey. Gradually the sky pinked in the east, and the world stretched out around them, a world of free and vast and silent possibilities.

Chapter Twelve

By the time it was light enough to shoot, the party had reached the large drainage that Del had planned for his two hunters. The three of them dismounted for a discussion. "The land falls away from here," Del said in a soft voice. "Not real fast, but for quite a ways. It'll seem like pretty big country, once we get down in there. We'll be glad we've got the horses."

"Will we ride them down in?" Ken asked.

"What I've got in mind is to let you two work a couple of these draws on foot, and I'll take the horses around and meet you on the bottom in about an hour. When you hit the creek bed, either turn right or stay there."

"Will the creek have water in it?" Ken asked.

"Probably not, but you'll know it's the creek bed. Your draw will end there in a wide gravelly bed."

Ken looked at his son and said, "That's easy enough."

Kenny nodded.

"I can pick you up down in the bottom, and we can ride up and out to the northwest and circle around north of where Len and Chick will be hunting."

Ken made a motion with his arm as he said, "Sort of a large circle back to camp, then."

"Yeah, only we hope we don't have to go all the way."

"Oh?"

"Yeah. We want you two to shoot something nice on the way down in there."

"Oh." Ken laughed. "Naturally. That's what we came for. But if by chance we don't shoot something, we'll meet you at the bottom."

"Right. Meanwhile, I'll keep my ear tuned and if I hear some action, I'll cut across and find you."

"So if we get something, we stay with it."

"Right. After you've got it dressed, one of you can stand out where I can see you. No need to make a bunch of noise with shouting or signal shots."

After Kenny had unsheathed his rifle, Del took out the lead ropes and hooked them to the two horses' halters. Next he loosened the front cinch on each of them. Then, leading the two horses on a slow poking walk, he rode back in a northerly direction to pick up the dirt road again. Once he turned in the saddle and saw father and son standing together at the rim of the basin, with the father pointing out their strategy.

Spud and Whisker were both well-behaved horses on a lead rope, and Little Tulip knew to stay on the road until told to do otherwise, so the three horses and lone rider moved together as the sun rose glinting on the frosted grass. A faint breeze stirred, bringing the blended smell of trail dust, grass, sagebrush, horse, and a trace of cedar and juniper. Deer hunting smelled different than antelope hunting, even before the bloodshed started, and the smell of the morning seemed right.

This was the part of his job he liked best, the time when he was away from camp and people and the pickup, when he could be solitary and unbothered. He had plenty of time to work his way around and down into the basin, so he let the horses poke along. Their slow, steady rhythm lulled him, as he wandered from one fleeting thought to the next, to try to fit together the words to "Little Joe the Wrangler." He had pieced in most of the first three verses and had gotten the herd of cattle to Red River, when Little Tulip stopped. Snapping out of his trance, Del saw that Spud and Whisker had stopped, too.

Del scanned the country ahead, sweeping the pasture, trail, and ridge with his gaze. He brought his gaze back in a figure-eight pattern, and then he saw it. Half a mile ahead, out in the pasture, with their whiteness shadowed by the rising sun, stood a small band of antelope. One, two, three, four.

Del clucked to Little Tulip. "Just goats," he said. "Let's move along." He nudged her with his heels, and she moved ahead, then stopped. "They're just silly antelope," he said, and clucked again. As the horses moved forward, the antelope flashed and broke into a run.

He found himself smiling, thinking of the hide-and-seek that antelope liked to play. Well, he wasn't playing today. The horses went back into their walk now, and he was still smiling. He realized he was thinking of Sylvia. She was in daylight now. He recalled her as she had looked in the photograph, smiling and shiny. He remembered how it had been to sit next to her in the pickup, taking in her mixed scent of face soap, perfume, dust, and laundered shirt. He recalled how easy but how impossible it would have been to touch her, what a slight,

131

subtle tension hung in the air as Vince, peering through the binoculars, absented himself. Del thought of how she moved around the campsite in her clean denims, clearing the table or pouring coffee. They had nearly brushed against each other a dozen times, with never a spoken acknowledgement.

He wondered how aware she was of another presence—if she was aware in the way that he was. He remembered the time they had crossed paths in the darkness, outside the firelight. Then he thought of the flickering glances and the full eye contact, how she had looked when she had said good-bye, and the simple note she had left, and he was pretty sure.

A vision of dark-haired Rita flashed through his mind, and he brushed it away. He was enjoying his thoughts of Sylvia and the moments that seemed to have grown together.

He could not think of Sylvia for very long without re-membering Vince. It was not pleasant to imagine, but the undeniable knowledge presented itself—she was not always the exquisite goddess, close enough to enrapture a man but out of reach. No, she was not untouchable. That airy presence had debased itself, time and again, to mash and mingle with the master, for that would be the role assumed by the lawyer from Omaha. Although Del knew it was bad manners to think about the intimate lives of people who had a license to privacy, he could not resist imagining how Vince would rule the goddess—not with a brief study and dismissal, as with the antelope he had brought to the ground, but with a recurrent possession and release. Del liked to think that when she was on her own again, she would return to her fuller self—ethereal, whole, unblemished as if she had never been touched. That was the essence he had felt as she had sat beside Del in the pickup, as she drifted past him in camp, as she wafted into his impressions of this early morning on the plains.

Back in Omaha, it would be an hour later. That's where she would be right now, probably on her way to work, wearing earrings, a jacket and skirt . . . *Ka-Blam!* The crash of a rifle shot broke the morning stillness like a sonic boom. Del flinched as the horses lurched. Then he recovered and drew back on the reins, transferring his reaction to Little Tulip, who shared it with the other two horses being led. As quickly as the little group had begun to bolt, it stopped. Del's "whoa" faded in the air, and the horses went still and silent. Del touched the stock of his rifle as he waited for more shots.

About a minute later, he heard two more shots. They didn't seem as loud as the first one, perhaps because he was expecting to hear them, perhaps because they came from a different gun or were fired in a different direction. In any event, all three shots came from somewhere pretty close. He estimated that he had left Ken and Kenny about fifteen to twenty minutes earlier, and from the gunshots, he guessed they hadn't gone down very far into the drainage. Picturing the lay of the land, he decided to go back the way he came. With a little maneuvering of reins and lead ropes, he got the three horses turned around. As they were now headed in the direction of camp, all he had to do was cluck, and they fell into a brisk walk.

The horses seemed surprised, but cooperative, when he took them down the ridge where he had left the Kerrs. The

133

ridge spread out wide at the top and narrowed as it went down. The draws on both sides had a sparse population of stunted cedar trees and juniper bushes, and a generous distribution of rocks. About a quarter of a mile down the ridge, he heard a whistle. Looking down to his left, he saw Kenny part way up the other side of the draw. He was waving his orange cap and pointing at a clump of trees. Del waved back and headed the horses down into the draw.

About fifty yards from the clump of trees, the horses started to balk, so Del dismounted and led them the rest of the way. When he arrived at the site, he was pleased to see the two hunters leaning over a good-sized deer.

"We got a nice one, Del," Ken called out.

"Good. I'll tie up these horses and be right with you."

When Del joined his hunters, he saw that the buck was a husky three-pointer. The rack was symmetrical, with long, graceful, polished tines. The deer's eyes had already clouded over blue, and in typical dead-deer fashion, its tongue was hanging out. Ken had cut off the musk glands from the hind legs, and he was beginning to open the abdomen. Kenny was holding up the opposite rear leg, exposing the cream-and-grey-colored underside.

"Who got him?" Del hoped it was the boy but sensed otherwise.

"Kenny got the first shot at him," Ken said, pushing himself to his feet and turning around. He pointed with his knife. "He came over the ridge there, and he didn't look hit at all. He came down to the bottom and stopped. I was following him with my scope, and when he stopped, I touched off a shot.

Boy, he just lurched up towards these trees, so I shot again, and I know I missed my second shot, so the first one must have done it."

"Where did you hit him?"

"Right behind his front left leg. He gave me a perfect broadside at a hundred yards."

Del turned to Kenny. "Well? Can you talk about it?"

"Oh, yeah." He grinned, then turned away to spit. "I got a bug in my mouth on the way over."

"I bet your mouth is a little dry, too."

"I got a drink from Dad." He looked at his father.

Ken said, "Got some left if you want a drink, Del."

"No, thanks. I've just been sittin' on my butt." He turned to Kenny again. "Tell me how you missed the big one."

"Well, he was walking up the draw on an angle, and he didn't see me. He'd stop, and I'd get the scope on him, and then he'd move on. I couldn't get it timed right, and I know I was wiggling, and I just missed him clean. That was all there was to it. He went on over to the other side, and Dad shot him."

"Well, you got a little action first thing this morning, and he didn't get away."

"Oh, no. It turned out great! I'm glad Dad got him. I had the jitters when he was coming up the draw, but I think I'll be steadier next time."

Ken had returned to the task of opening up the belly. "What do you think of this one, Del?"

"He's good-sized. Looks like you'll find some fat on him."

"He looks big to me," Ken said, "but we've been looking at those little coastal blacktail."

"Well, I'd say he's about average. He's not little, and he's not huge. He's good-sized and he's got a respectable rack on him. By the way, I should get a picture of you."

"Kenny already took some pictures."

"You made sure he was dead first."

Ken laughed. "Oh, yeah. I cut his throat."

"I see that. Let me go get my camera, and I'll get a picture anyway."

Ken did a neat job of field dressing the deer, explaining each step to his son as he did the work. Del stood by and watched, lending a hand when it came time to tip or move the deer. When Ken had gotten the bladder and colon lifted out and the liver and heart trimmed free of their neighbors and tossed back inside the cavity, he had his son pour a dribble of water on his hands. He seemed quite at home with the whole operation, and even though, the night before, he had seemed to know a little bit about playing around with the camp whores, he had the movements of a hunter who had always filled his own tag. As he rubbed the caked blood from his fingernails he spoke to Del.

"What do you think would be the best way of getting him out of here?"

Del felt that in the spirit of adventure he should pack the deer out on horseback, but there was a more expedient way. "I think the shortest, quickest way would be to drag him up over the top and leave him in the shade of a tree, where we can come by later in the pickup and get him."

"That makes sense." Ken looked at his son. "Are you ready to drag a little dead weight?"

Kenny, who looked as if he had hoped for a more entertaining proposition, shrugged his shoulders and said, "Sure."

Del intervened. "I think I can get one of these horses to do it for us."

"Really?" Ken's eagerness suggested a fondness for labor-saving devices.

"I think so. Let me get some nylon twine to lace up his belly, and we'll see what Spud says." Del went to his saddle-bag and took out a roll of white twine, from which he cut about a two-foot length. He cut a series of holes, like shoelace eyelets, along each side of the slit in the belly. He threaded each hole as he cut it, crossing the twine like shoe laces, and when he came to the hindquarter end of the gash, he snugged the laces and tied them off. "That should keep the big chunks out," he said.

"That's a good idea," Ken said.

"I always carry at least a little bit of twine. It's handy for other things, too, like tying the tag onto the horns. By the way, did you punch your tag?"

"Yeah, I did, right away."

"That's good. We can tie it on when we get him to the top."

Del took out a manila rope from his gear and looped it in a figure-eight around the buck's neck and then his horns. He brought Spud sashaying into place, tightened the front cinch, dallied the rope around the saddle horn, and beckoned to Ken. "Let's have you hold this lead rope for a minute." Bringing the other two horses around, he said, "Kenny, you can ride Whisker and lead Little Tulip. Just stay right ahead of us, and Spud will be more likely to want to follow. O.K.?"

"Sounds fine to me. Let me get my rifle."

Del brought the other two horses around and tightened Whisker's cinch. He got Kenny mounted and set, and then he turned to Ken. "Now, Ken, I think I'll lead him, and you can follow by the deer as he drags. If you want us to stop, just holler."

"Do you want me to steer him or hold up one leg or anything?"

"Nah. I think Spud is going to take this in little spurts and lurches, and it's not liable to be very smooth."

The pull to the top went, as Del had said, in a continuous series of jerks, so they were not very long getting there. They stowed the deer in the shade of a broad-based cedar, and Ken wrapped the permit around an antler beam and tied it.

"What next?" he asked.

"How about if you two go right back down and hunt to the bottom. You might bump into something else, especially down in the bottom. I'll go around like I started to before, and I'll meet you in, let's say, three-quarters of an hour."

As Del was coiling up the tow rope, a shot came rumbling from the north. He paused in his coiling. "Sounds like Danny and Ron."

Ken and Kenny nodded and stood listening. No shots followed.

Del finished coiling his rope and put his horses in motion. Holding the lead ropes with his right hand, he swung aboard

Little Tulip, keeping the lead ropes clear as he brought his right leg over the cantle and the tied-down pannier roll. He sorted his reins and his lead ropes, and he put his retinue into motion. "Good luck, boys. Hope you find his big brother."

"O.K. Del," Ken said. "We'll see you down below."

Another shot rumbled from the north. "Sounds like business," the guide said, turning in the saddle.

Ken raised his eyebrows and nodded.

Kenny waved and said, "Take it easy, Del. We'll see you in a little while."

Little Tulip stepped into a brisk walk, and after about a half-mile, Del found himself swayed back into the same rhythm he had been in an hour before, putting together the words to "Little Joe the Wrangler." He did not sing out loud, but as he listened to his own saddle creak along with the accompaniment of jingling bits and clip-clopping hooves, he could hear the song in his mind.

> Little Joe the Wrangler,
> He'll wrangle never more—
> His days with the remuda they are o'er.
> It was a year ago last April
> That he rode into our camp,
> Just a little Texas stray and all alone.
>
> He said he had to leave his home,
> His pa had married twice,
> And his new ma whipped him every day or two.
> So he saddled up old Chaw one night
> And lit a shuck this way,
> And now he's out to paddle his own canoe.

Del faked his way through the next two verses, where the trail boss took a liking to Little Joe and hired him on as wrangler. With the next verse, the song came back with clear wording.

> We had driven to Red River,
> The weather being fine,
> And were camped on the south side in a bend . . .

Chapter Thirteen

Del met the Kerrs in the creek bottom as planned. Neither of them had any adventures to share, so without much of a delay, they mounted up and fell into formation with Ken in the lead.

"Tell you what, Ken," Del said. "Originally I thought we'd climb out to the left here, but let's go up the creek a ways instead, and see if we bump into Danny and Ron."

"Good idea. I'm kind of curious, too."

Del looked back at Kenny, who nodded. The three of them followed the creek bed in silence, or at least without talking. The horse hooves swished and crunched in the gravel, clacking on the larger stones. The air was warming as the sun rose higher in the sky, and the sounds took on what seemed to be a duller tone. There wasn't much to watch except for the back side of the horse and rider ahead. Del watched Ken take out a snack bar, the kind with rice krispies on the inside and chocolate on the outside. Ken took his time eating it, then put the wrapper back into his jacket pocket and licked his fingers. Just watching the sequence made Del thirsty. *Wait a little while longer*, he thought. No need to start drinking water too early.

They had followed the creek bed for a little less than a mile when they heard a whistle from above on the right. About three hundred yards up a ridge on the left side of a draw, Ron sat against a rock. When the party in the creek bed stopped, Ron stood up and waved his hat.

"Guess we should go up," Del said.

When they were within speaking distance, Ron spoke first. "Sounds like you guys got the first one, uh?"

"I killed a nice little three-pointer," Ken answered. "How did you two do?"

"Danny got one. Three on one side, four on the other. Two little forks at the top."

Ken nodded.

"Where is he?" Del asked.

"Danny? Or the deer?"

"Either one."

"We drug the deer over to the road. It was mostly down-hill. Danny's loafing around back there, in the general vicinity. I came over here to watch for you for a little while."

"That road is less than a half mile, isn't it?" Del asked.

"I'd say so."

"I think maybe we'll drop back down to the creek bottom, follow it till it meets the road, then follow the road back till we meet you or Danny. How's that sound?"

"Sounds fine. I'll cut back the way I came." Ron shouldered his gun. "See you there."

When they came to the road, they drew rein for a few minutes. Del explained to Ken and Kenny how the road ran across the bottom and up the other side of the basin. "I think Danny and I should walk back to camp and get the truck, and he and I can pick up the two animals we've got down. Ron can take this horse and go with you two, if you don't mind. We can meet you back at camp around lunchtime."

"Are you sure you don't want me to go along with you?" Ken asked. "After all, I've filled my tag."

"No, I'm sure. Things will work out fine this way. You can skin your deer after lunch, if you like, and in the meanwhile you and Kenny can show Ron the lay of the land. You might scare up something, too. Take it slow, and if you see a little draw you want to detour into, go ahead. If you go to shoot, make sure you either tie up the horse good and snug or have someone holding him."

Ken took a look down the faint road they would be taking. "O.K. That all sounds manageable enough."

When they met up with Ron again, Del swung down from the saddle and explained his plan. He handed the reins toward Ron and stepped away from the horse.

Ron seemed pleased at the prospect of riding. He said he had taken riding lessons during the summer so he would be ready for the occasion. He took the reins and moved toward the horse with no hesitation. He measured the stirrup length as he had learned, laying the fender on his forearm and seeing where the stirrup touched his shoulder. He let the stirrups out one notch, climbed aboard, and was set to go. Then he swung down. "I might want my rifle."

"Good idea," Del said. "Let me get mine out of the bucket, and I'll take her reins." They got Ron's rifle secured, and the party on horseback clip-clopped away.

Danny seemed withdrawn and subdued for a man who had just shot his first mule deer. He led Del to the place where the

143

buck lay, blue-eyed and dirty-tongued in the shade of a wide-spread juniper. The antlers had blood smears on them, as did the white hunting permit that was wrapped and tied beneath one of the small forks of the four-point side. The throat was slashed, and the neck hair was matted with blackened blood.

"Nice buck," the guide said.

"Yeah," Danny breathed, "I'm really pleased. I thought he got away."

"Where did you hit him the first time?"

"Down in the lower neck, in front of the shoulders. When I came up on him for the second shot, I didn't take any chances. I got him right square in the front quarters."

Del leaned over to peek at the insides, to make sure it was cleaned out. As Danny reached over to hold up a hind leg, the guide caught the faint whiff of a scent he disentangled from the odors of buck musk, blood, dirt, juniper, and man-sweat. The scent was familiar but elusive, like a face without a name.

"Good job," he said. Danny smiled a relaxed, satisfied smile, and the guide put a name to the face. He guessed that the hunter had smoked a joint. Neither of them spoke another word as they returned to the road and started the hike back to camp. Del recalled Ron, who had not seemed thick-lidded at all but quite alert. So Danny must have smoked the joint alone, sitting on a rocky slope dotted with brittle sage and stunted trees, gazing at the wide-blue sky above and the dead deer at his feet.

Del's first impulse was to chew him out and tell him not to come back. But as he thought it over, he realized that if the man had smoked a joint, he had done so after he was through hunting. From Danny's point of view, it would seem like a harmless act and not in violation of any game laws. And after all, Del thought, other men had done worse things, and he had helped them out.

By the time they had made the long, gradual climb back to the ranch house, Danny's state had faded, and he had become conversational. He told how he had shot the deer, followed it, shot it again. He said his wife would be happy for him. He hoped Ron got a good deer, too. Really, he hoped everyone did, but especially Ron. You couldn't tell it from the way Ron acted, but he was really excited about this trip. He'd been reading articles for a year about this kind of hunting, and he'd taken horseback riding lessons and had even run bleachers after work. Naturally everyone wanted the kid to get a good buck, but he sure as hell hoped Ron got one, too. Damn, that would be nice.

They took turns at the kitchen sink, one working the pump as the other splashed and cleaned up. As they washed, Del decided he couldn't let the dope-smoking go entirely, but there was no reasonable way to come right out and mention it. He came at it sideways. "Did you put your gun away?"

"Oh, yeah."

"Did you check it to make sure it was unloaded?"

"Sure. Why?"

Del looked him in the eyes. "Sometimes a guy doesn't think too clear after he's killed an animal. Overlooks little things."

Danny returned the gaze, then looked into the towel as he dried his hands. "I was a little distracted," he said, "but I checked the rifle before I gutted the deer and again when we got back to camp."

"Uh-huh." Del pulled his collar back straight, looked at his own eyes in the mirror, put on his hat, and said, "We have just enough time before lunch to pick up those two deer. Shall we?"

The task of picking up the deer was routine and uneventful, made pleasant by small talk about Del's pickup, the baseball playoffs, and the world of difference between this and hunting whitetails along the tree lines and corn fields.

Del remembered to take a picture when they got back to camp, so he positioned Danny in a pose with a natural background.

When the photographing was done, Danny asked, "You take a picture of everyone you take hunting?"

"Just about."

"I saw you had a whole wall full of 'em in your office there."

"Oh, yeah. And if for some reason someone's film doesn't turn out, it's no problem for me to send a picture. Let's hang these deer in that lean-to on the east side of the house."

It would have been convenient for Del to set up his skinning hoist, but the lean-to suited their purposes. It was strong-timbered, and it caught the afternoon shade. Meat could hang there for a week, chilling in the night air and staying cool through the day.

The Becker brothers returned ahead of the horseback trio. They had hoofed it all morning and had seen three does and a small set of horns at a distance. They nodded in cheerful approval at the news of how the others had fared, and Len stated that they were going to hunt the same ridge that evening.

Chick carried the rifles inside, while Len sagged into a chair on the porch and unlaced his boots. He took out his pocket knife, picked a sticker from his left hand, and then finished the job of pulling off his boots and wool socks. He draped his socks over his boot tops, in a manner that suggested a long-ago lesson from scoutmaster or father. Chick came out onto the porch with two beady-cold cans of Seven-Up, sat in the chair between Len and Del, and exhaled. The brothers exchanged a set of glances that the guide could not decipher until Chick spoke out, "Well, how about my manners. Del, would you like a Seven-Up?"

Del laughed. "No, thanks. I'm fine. I'm just about ready to get lunch anyway." But before he did, he had the pleasure of watching Chick take off his boots and socks exactly as his brother had done.

Del laid out the cold cuts for lunch. He and the three hunters were working on the first round of sandwiches when they heard the horses crunching and clip-clopping in the graveled drive. Del put down his sandwich and went out to tend to the horses.

Ken dismounted in slow motion, showing stiffness from his hours in the saddle. "Saw a lot of country," he said, "and quite a bit of sign. But nothing to shoot at."

"Did you see anything at all?" Del snapped on Spud's lead rope and tied him to the rail.

"One little bunch of does and fawns, about half a dozen." Ken took the rifle off his back. "You got my deer brought in all right?"

"Sure did. It's hanging in the lean-to."

"I sure appreciate it."

"No trouble at all. Lunch is on the table." Del took the reins from the other two, who had been waiting. "Did you see any places that caught your interest for this afternoon?"

Ron answered. "We thought maybe the other side of the basin from the ridges we hunted this morning. We saw a couple of places that looked interesting."

"Are you both up to taking a ride out that way for the afternoon, then?"

"Oh, yeah," Ron said.

Kenny chimed in, "Sure. You bet."

"Good enough. I'll get these horses watered but leave them saddled. Go ahead and serve yourselves some lunch. We can get in a little siesta before we go back out."

Del slipped off the bridles and loosened the cinches, then gave each horse a short drink before hitching it to the rail. After lunch he would give them another short drink, and then another before they all went out again.

When he went into the house, Ken was doing the talking. "It had been quite a while, but I didn't really have any trouble, except trying to figure out what to do with that damn rifle. Carry it slung on one shoulder, and it wants to slip off. Carry it slung across your back, and it bites into your neck, plus it gives you a sore back riding uphill."

"It's a lot of trouble riding in timber that way, too," Len added.

"Didn't have much real timber to deal with, but I can imagine. So then I tried carrying it across the front of the saddle—"

"—the swells—" Chick offered.

"—yeah, the swells, but a heavy rifle like that just bounces. That makes the horse want to jog faster." Ken paused to smooth out the smear of mustard on the sandwich he was making. He worked the butter knife slick as a trowel, it seemed to Del, but neither of the bricklayers seemed to take notice. Ken continued, "So then you lay the gun on your thigh, sort of diagonally, and it bounces there, too."

"Did your horse pick out any deer for you?" Len asked.

"I don't know which horse saw them first, but all three stopped short when that little bunch of does and fawns showed up. That's another thing. It's hard to see through your scope, that way. Even when your horse is standing still, he's heaving or shifting."

"They don't stand still like a deer does," Chick put in.

"I guess not. So there I am, rifle in my right hand, reins and saddle horn in my left, trying to swing my leg over the saddlebags so I can get down. I finally get a good look at the deer, and they're all skinheads."

Ken folded his sandwich together and took a bite. He had a way about him, Del thought. He could corner the conversation and not bother anyone. It might wear thin at some point, but right now he was doing a good job in his role as the beleaguered tenderfoot.

149

Del finished eating the sandwich he had started earlier. After a quick glance at the inventory, he decided on a ham and Swiss on brown bread. That, with a dill pickle and potato chips, rounded out his lunch. One by one, the hunters finished eating and threw their paper plates and napkins into the fireplace. The Beckers stretched out on their bunks, and Danny took Ken out to show him where the deer were hanging. Down the table from Del, Ron ate an apple and seemed to be giving thoughtful observation to its change in shape and color. Across from him, Kenny cleaned his finger-nails with his clasp knife. Del was picking up the last of his potato chip fragments with moistened thumb and forefinger when Ron raised a question.

"Is it O.K. if I give this apple core to the horse?"

"Oh, yeah. If you feel like it, you can feed each of them some carrots out of those buckets on the porch. About two or three carrots each. I think they'd appreciate it."

Kenny paused in the middle of closing his knife. He looked at Ron, who motioned with his head, and the two of them got up and went out to take treats to the horses.

Del yawned and thought of his tent. This was the lazy part of the day, the time when it was warm and the flies came out to buzz around. It was also the time when yellow jackets showed up. All a fellow had to do was open a package of lunch meat, and there they were. There weren't any in the house at the moment, but he imagined that some had made their way to the hanging meat outside. He could hear Danny and Ken talking, and from their tone it seemed as if they had begun to skin their deer.

Del cleared the table and cleaned up the kitchen area. Two down and four to go, plus his own. This season lasted twelve days, and it was a full two weeks until elk season started. There was plenty of time and nothing to bother or hurry them. If they ran low on food or ice or even drinks, he could break the spell and go into town for supplies. Meanwhile things took their own pace, which at the moment was slow and agreeable. As he wiped off the table with the dishrag, still damp from the morning dishes, he glanced out the front window. Ron and Kenny were rationing carrots to the horses, gaining their favor in a language that all animals spoke.

The guide took light steps across the room, through the open doorway, across the porch, and down the steps into the warm, lazy sunlight. When he came to the hitching rail, he said, "If you could, when you get done feeding them, I'd appreciate it if you could take them over for a drink of water. Let them drink about a gallon or so each, and then tie them back up. No hurry, though. Take your time feeding them."

"O.K., Del," Ron said.

"Say, Del," Kenny began, "would you show me how to tie that knot?"

"Sure." The guide pulled Whisker's lead rope loose from its bow knot and went through the motions twice. Kenny nodded and duplicated the knot. "Thanks, fellas," Del said. "I've got to go in and take care of a few little chores."

On the way to the house, he decided he would peel potatoes for supper and leave them standing in water. He walked across the porch with soft steps, and as he crossed the threshold, he saw the Becker brothers, side by side on their backs with their hands folded on their stomachs. Each man lay nearly motionless on his bunk. Except for the slight rise and fall of the folded hands as the men breathed, they looked like twin generals lying in state.

Chapter Fourteen

Siesta time came to an end little by little. From where he sat dozing in his chair on the porch, Del heard the Beckers get up and stir around. Danny and Ken came in from skinning their deer. They sat at the table and talked at a normal volume, discussing the work they had done and arriving at an agreement that they deserved a beer. Del heard the beer cans pop, and he dozed again. He awoke to clear consciousness when he heard Ken calling to his son.

"You'd better be getting up, Kenny. Shadows are starting to move."

The guide rose from his chair and ambled over to the horses. He took them to the water trough and watered them by turns. He watched as one by one they dipped a chin in the trough and took in a pull of water, drawing it in faint eddies. He led them, chins dripping, back to the hitching rail, where he bridled them and snugged the cinches. As he waited for Ron and Kenny, he checked all the riggings, and then he remembered to adjust his stirrups. As Ron came out of the cabin carrying his rifle, Del spoke.

"Ron, I think we'll have you riding Spud this afternoon. I need to leave the scabbard on Little Tulip because my saddle gun doesn't have a sling on it. You can get by, can't you?"

"Oh, yeah." Ron slung the rifle on his shoulder and approached the gelding, patting him on the neck and muttering small talk. He adjusted his stirrups and checked his cinches, then led the horse away from the others before he swung aboard.

The guide was getting his own rifle snug in the scabbard when Kenny came stepping out of the house. In another minute, they were all in the saddle, ready to head out.

"Let's go the way you came back this morning," Del spoke out. "We'll get to the other side and hunt back this way."

"O.K.," Ron answered, giving Spud some rein.

Kenny pulled up alongside Del. "Are Len and Chick going back out to the same place?"

"That's what they said. I think they liked the looks of it."

"I hope they get something."

"Oh, I'm sure they'll do all right. They're the kind that'll hunt a couple of days just to decide how they want to do the serious hunting. That would be why they covered so much ground this morning, to look things over."

"They would pass up a little forked horn, then, wouldn't they?"

"Probably, at least for the first couple of days."

"I'm glad my dad got a buck right away."

"Oh, yeah."

"I think his hemorrhoids were starting to bother him."

"Maybe I shouldn't have made him feel like he had to go on that second half of the ride."

"Oh, that was O.K. He wanted to go. I could tell that. And they didn't start bothering him till we were almost home."

Ron turned halfway in the saddle and said, "I've heard cowboys have a bad time with hemorrhoids."

"I suppose so," Del answered, "but probably no worse than truck drivers and heavy equipment operators."

Kenny stood in his stirrups and sat down. "What do you do when you're not guiding or taking people on pack trips, Del?"

The guide smiled and said, "I cowboy." When the three of them had finished laughing, he added, "But I can still hang on to the saddle, even if I lose my stirrups."

They rode into the afternoon sun, warm but not hot. By the time they reached the other side of the basin, the shadows had begun to lengthen and to assume the classic tone of an afternoon hunt. This was the way it always was, the way it should be, the air quiet and still and thinning as it lost its heaviness when the sun slipped south.

They left Kenny at the head of a long draw that sloped toward the general direction of camp. It was agreed that he and Ron would take their time hunting to the bottom, where Del would meet them with the horses. After leaving Kenny, Del and Ron rode south along the rim for about half a mile until they came to another draw that ran parallel to Kenny's. Ron dismounted and handed his reins to Del.

"I'll loaf around on top here with the horses," Del said in a low, clear voice. "After a half hour or so I'll start down and take it pretty slow."

"O.K."

Del took the horses on about another half mile, coming to a stop in a grassy swale. He slipped bridles from Spud and Whisker, and he snapped on their lead ropes. Then he loosened their cinches and let them graze. Little Tulip, who took a hackamore rather than a mouth bit, grazed with the other two. Del wandered with the horses, keeping the lead ropes clear, listening to the dry munching sound as they put hooves and teeth to the brittle grass. The sun warmed him as he meandered backward, enjoying the idleness that the horses fell into with such ease.

When he judged that half an hour had passed, Del snugged Little Tulip's cinch and mounted up. He tugged on the lead ropes to get his party into motion, and the group made its way to the road that, as the horses also knew, led to the bottom and then on out the other side and back to camp. It was not a well-worn road. Except in some places where the ruts were deep, it was smooth and mostly grassy. The group made its way without much noise, dipping in and out of shadows. Little Tulip shied long enough to recognize a twisted stick for what it was, and then they all moved on.

Something in the cool shadowed smell of dust and grass and sagebrush reminded him of his earlier ride, that morning, when he was alone on the trail with the horses. Maybe it was the smell, maybe it was the saddle creak and the scuffle-clop of the horses' hooves, but he found himself visited again by impressions of Sylvia Furtino. In the spare, quiet reaches of the autumn rangeland, a time and place he liked to have to himself and the horses, he thought of Sylvia and whether she would care for this kind of setting. He smiled as he imagined her microwaving a low-calorie dinner right now, safe in her house with the door locked against the rest of Omaha.

Del's thoughts moved to Vince. The lawyer could be within a hundred miles of here, bringing the same fall afternoon beneath his critical gaze. *To hell with Vince*, Del thought. He was glad he hadn't had room for the fellow. This was a good-natured bunch he'd ended up with, and even though deer hunting had a more sustained intensity than antelope hunting did, there were times like this, even in the middle of the hunt, when life stretched out wide and open on all sides, hemmed in by nothing more than a grassed-over road and a dry creek bottom. A fellow could cut loose and drift out of himself, hover with the afternoon, and yet never leave himself or the attentive watch he kept on the land. It pleased him to imagine his hunters, at a liberal distance from him and from one another, taking in the rippled, shadowy world in quiet solitude.

Del thought again of Sylvia, and he felt a twinge of guilt. If he was going to be thinking of someone he'd like to have along at a time like this, he should be thinking of Rita. She was the one he should imagine seated on the horse at his right, near enough for him to flip the end of a rein and pat her above the knee with the tickle-tip of the leather. Still, the image of Sylvia kept coming back, and Del knew he wasn't trying very hard to block it out.

Del was rolling down his sleeves and buttoning his cuffs when Little Tulip stopped under him. Spud and Whisker had halted as well. Down the trail on the right, less than a hundred yards away, a three-point buck stood autumn-blue in the long shade of the rim. Del exhaled softly, his breath nearly whistling through his teeth and rounded lips. Little Tulip flickered her ears at the sound but held still. Del's gaze moved in a quick curlicue, taking in the antlers and the vital spot before resting on the eyes. The deer, standing broadside, had his head turned to stare straight at the man. Del relaxed in the saddle but kept his eyes matched with the deer's. Behind those eyes, behind the dark-haired skull plate, there worked a series of impressions. The deer would not know why two saddles were empty, why the man looked like a cowboy instead of a killer.

Spud let out a long, heavy breath, Whisker swished his tail, and still the buck stood frozen. The guide relaxed his gaze, and the buck turned to jog away. He moved into a bouncing trot, his antlers moving up and down, clearing the shadows and catching the afternoon sun.

"You're on your own," Del thought. The deer had been moving north before it stopped, and now it kept that direction. Depending on how Ron had moved, their paths might cross.

Del stepped down from his horse and led the way down the trail. He paused where the buck had crossed, scanning the ground for a bare spot that would show a hoofprint. He found one. It was always interesting to see the track and know which animal it came from. The buck had been average-sized, bigger than a doe, but from looking at the track just by itself, the guide would not have been able to say, with any certainty, whether a buck or doe had left it.

Del rose from his study and walked on, with Little Tulip on his right and the other two on his left. Every twenty or thirty yards, he stopped to listen. When the shot came, it was louder than he expected, first a crash and then an echo as it rippled across the cool air of early evening. The horses flinched and came to a standstill. Del waited with them, but no

158

more shots followed, so after a long minute or two of silence, he stepped into the saddle and moved them all north.

The guide and his horses took the little gullies and draws at a quick pace, clambering up the slopes and skittering down but never breaking into a full run. When Del came to the larger ridge that he imagined to be Ron's, he drew the horses to a halt and then poked along the spine of the ridge. First he went uphill a couple of hundred yards, and then, seeing nothing, he turned back and took the ridge downhill for a quarter of a mile.

He saw Ron down in a cleft of the big draw, tugging a deer into a position for field dressing. At the guide's whistle, the hunter looked up and waved, pointed at the kill, and bent to work again, pulling at the dead weight.

Ron had not yet put a knife to the buck when Del arrived with the horses. Ron had the deer laid out on the slope, belly downhill, and he was starting to roll up his sleeves. "I got a nice one," he said.

"Yep, that you did," the guide said, slipping out of the saddle. "What do you think about the head? Want to save it?"

Ron frowned and then relaxed his face. "No, I don't think so. He *is* a good looker, though. His horns are nicer proportioned than Danny's."

"I'd say so." The guide looked westward up the draw. "I think we have just enough daylight to get a picture if you want one."

Ron smiled. "That would be pretty good." He picked up his rifle from the grass, checked to see that it was unloaded, and knelt by the buck for his two poses.

Del was putting the camera back in its case when Kenny came walking down the slope from the north. "Got one, huh? I was hoping you did. Just one shot, huh?"

"It was almost self-defense," Ron answered. "I was hunting about halfway down this ridge, keeping from skylining myself, and I heard something trotting my way. I thought it was a horse until he came over. He couldn't have been seventy-five yards away when he stopped and looked down the draw, away from me. I shot him behind the left shoulder, and he staggered down this way a hundred yards and keeled over."

Kenny picked up a hind leg and held it so Ron could get at the abdomen. Del watched, and when he saw that Ron went about the task without any hesitation, he spoke up. "If you fellows have things under control, I think I'll ride back and get the pickup. I've driven most of the way up this draw before, and I think that would be the best way to get him back to camp this evening. Sound all right?"

"Sounds fine," Ron said, sloshing his hands in the blood-filled cavity.

Kenny nodded and said, "Sure," but he kept his gaze on Ron's movements.

"Good enough," Del said. "I'll leave your two horses here so I can make tracks to camp. I should be back here in less than an hour." He looked around for a place to tie the horses, but there was not a tree within half a mile. "Kenny, do you think you can hang onto these two lead ropes and still give Ron a hand?"

"I think so."

"Good. Here you are. I'll be back in a little while."

The guide pulled himself into the saddle and gave Little Tulip some rein. When they hit the creek bottom, he let her out a little more, and she fell into a smooth, steady lope. He walked her the last quarter-mile to camp, where he watered her before taking her to the hitching rail.

Danny and Ken sat on the porch drinking beer.

"Ron got a nice one," Del called out. "A three-pointer. I'm going back in the pickup." He stripped the saddle and bridle from the mare, brushed her down, and left her drowsing hipshot at the hitching rail.

The guide walked up to the porch to talk to Danny and Ken, who lounged in an attitude that, with the help of a few beers, expressed complete abandonment. Ken's eyelids drooped, and his face held a relaxed smile. "We fixed your chairs," he said, slurring the rough spots.

"Is that right."

"Yeah," Danny said, "these nylon straps were coming loose, so we got a screwdriver and tightened 'em all up." He gave a benign smile. "No charge."

Del smiled. "Well, thank you."

"How's that boy of mine doing?"

"Just fine. He's helping Ron with his deer right now. I'm going back with the pickup to haul it in, and they'll come dusting in behind me."

"Del."

"Yeah, Ken?"

"I really appreciate what you're doing for that kid. It'll mean a lot to him, for the rest of his life. This is a big event for him."

"I'm glad, Ken. I want everyone to enjoy their hunt, I really do."

"It means a lot to me, Del."

"Good. I'm glad everything is working out."

The guide turned to go, and Ken said, "Are you going to leave the mare tied up?"

"For the time being."

"You want me to put her in the corral in a little while?"

"If you want to. I'd appreciate it."

"I will."

Del looked at Danny. "I don't know if I have anything else to fix. Thanks for fixing the chairs."

Danny smiled and gave him a thumbs up.

Del backed the pickup around and drove past the ranch house. When he waved, his hunters saluted him with their beer cans. It must be nice, he thought, to have your hunting done and your deer hanging, to sit in a tuned-up lawn chair and squint at the setting sun.

He shifted into third gear. Things were working out pretty well. Half of his hunters already had their deer, he'd get back in plenty of time to put dinner together, and meanwhile the boys could have a pony ride back to camp.

Later in the evening, after a dinner of hamburgers, pork and beans, and green salad, Danny went out back with Ron to skin the deer by lantern light. Kenny sat at the table drinking his second beer while his dad worked on what might be his eighth or tenth. The Beckers were drinking whiskey and Seven-Up as they scratched out a map of the country they had studied that day. Del washed dishes and listened with half an ear to Ken's monologues.

"Shit yes, it's been twenty-six years, and I can see those milk bottles just as clear as if one was sitting right here. They had 'Moon Lake' written across the top of the wide part, the body, you know. 'Moon Lake' in dark blue letters. And beneath that, there was a picture of a pretty girl sitting with her butt to us, leaning on her right arm. She was sitting on the edge of a little lake or lagoon, looking across it at a crescent moon. 'Moon Lake.' I can see it clear as day. I got up every morning at three o'clock and delivered those damn things all over town."

Len looked up from his map. "You delivered milk?"

"Yeah. My first year out of high school. I had my own route, my own customers, my own accounts. I delivered it in these glass bottles, with a label in dark blue letters painted right on the bottle. 'Moon Lake.' Then after about a year they went from bottles to cartons, and they had stacks and stacks of those worthless bottles. I used to take them out to Walnut Creek, which was way the hell out in the boonies then, and shoot 'em up with a twenty-two. I bet I shot a couple of thousand of 'em. And you know what?"

"What?" Len went along.

"I haven't seen one of the sons-of-bitches for over twenty years."

"Those old milk bottles are worth something now," Chick declared. "People use them for wine carafes. They're probably worth ten dollars each."

"At least," Len said. "That's what you get your ice water in when you go to one of those restaurants with a high h.p.q."

"What's that?" Kenny asked.

"Hanging plant quotient. You know, the kind of place with a lot of hanging plants and ceiling fans and brass fixtures." Len smiled. "You see a lot of those old milk bottles in those kind of places. Classy, you know, in a down-home way."

"Shit," Ken muttered. "I bet I busted enough of them to furnish all my steak houses with carafes, and then some. And every damn one of 'em is shot to smithereens. I bet I destroyed two thousand of 'em."

"Well, they're gone now," Len said, "but I'll keep an eye out for them, and if I see one, I'll let you know. I have your card. You say the brand is 'Blue Moon'?"

"No, 'Moon Lake.' There's a moon, and a lake, and a pretty girl with her cute little ass poked at you. And it's all in blue."

"I'll keep an eye out for that one."

"Do that, if you would. 'Moon Lake.' But they're probably gone, every last one of 'em."

* * * * *

As Del settled into his sleeping bag later that night, he had a clear image of a girl sitting by a lake, looking at a crescent moon, shining her blue moon of a pretty butt at the customer. Del understood how Ken probably felt, to have been so casual with all those bottles, which seemed so common, and then to realize they were all gone for good. Even if Ken could never get one back, it must make a very good memory.

Chapter Fifteen

Del was up and awake at five in the morning, making short work of his preliminaries. He tossed hay to the horses, gave them a quick look-over, and went into the cabin.

The night before, he had settled accounts and exchanged best wishes with the Iowa bricklayers. They would want to get up at a leisurely hour and then hit the road. Meanwhile, Del and Kenny would want an early start, as they had a long ride before the morning hunt. Ken had offered to hang around camp and cook a pot of beans, and the Beckers had seemed content to be left to their own plans. Del had breakfast to cook for himself and three hunters, and while the bacon was frying, he put together some snacks for Kenny and himself.

The Becker brothers had gone to sleep early, unbothered by the pop of beer cans and the slap of cards, so they were alert as soon as they rolled out of their bunks. Kenny, who had stayed up to watch his dad and the bricklayers play cutthroat cribbage, was groggy and not so quick to get going. Breakfast was a quiet, business-like event, and the morning was still night-dark when Del and Kenny went out to saddle the horses.

The guide went about his work with quick and efficient motions as the young man held the flashlight. Del had explained the night before that they would take all three horses, with the hope that they would need the extra packhorse down in the bottom where Del was going to take them. Len and Chick set out on their hunt while Del was halfway through saddling the second horse. When the guide had all three rigged and ready, he transferred his saddle bags and the rolled-up panniers to Spud, the extra horse. He and Kenny secured their rifles in the scabbards, snugged their front cinches, and mounted up.

The plan was to hunt beyond the big drainage they had hunted the day before. They would ride to the northwest corner of that basin and leave the horses at the top. From there they would drop off the other side, down to a water hole and meadow that was more than a mile from the nearest road. If they killed a deer there, they would welcome the help of horses.

The party moved at a brisk walk, sending up clouds of breath on the chilly morning air. Daybreak made its slow appearance, greying the rocks and grass and sagebrush. When the riders arrived at their stopping place, the sky in the east was beginning to pink upwards into a thin layer of clouds. Kenny, shivering, held the horses as Del hitched them to the corner brace of a four-strand barbed-wire fence. The sun was not yet showing when they began to work their way down the draw.

Neither of them had said a word since they left camp. The guide led the way down the ridge until it ended, giving way to a larger draw flanked on either side by longer ridges. As he side-stepped down the side of their ridge, he paused at a cutbank and pointed. About a foot and a half below the level of the grass, an old thigh bone of a cow or perhaps a buffalo stuck out from the grey-black clay. Kenny raised his eyebrows and nodded. Del moved on with the young man following.

Del was sidehilling up the next ridge when he heard a distant shot rumbling from Len and Chick's direction. He turned to Kenny and, tossing his head in that direction, smiled. The young man nodded and smiled back. They waited, facing each other on the hillside. After about a minute, they heard two more shots together, followed by a brief silence and then a fourth shot. They waited another minute or so without hearing any more shots, and they resumed their soft-stepping hike.

Down in the bottom, the land widened into a grassy meadow that sloped to a waterhole. The water level had receded, leaving a dark periphery on three sides. On the fourth side, the waterhole was framed by a grassed-over ridge that someone long ago had bermed with a bulldozer. Beyond the little ridge, the land fell away again along a dry creek bed, as one could guess from the leafy treetops beyond. The guide led his hunter to a vantage spot in front of a low-spreading juniper. They hunkered down behind a low screen of sagebrush.

The spot was just as Del had left it the year before. They sat with their butts on a cattle trail and their backs against square-sided rocks. Kenny leaned to his left, away from Del, and picked up an empty brass casing, well weathered. He handed it to Del, who read the caliber imprint around the dented primer. It was a .270 Winchester, Remington-Peters manufactured. He held up two fingers and whispered, "Two years ago."

Kenny nodded. He pointed to the bolt of his own rifle and raised his eyebrows in a question. Del nodded, and the young man worked a shell into the chamber and set the safety.

Del exhaled and relaxed. Some people were better than others at this type of hunting. Some could sit nearly motionless for hours, while others couldn't sit five minutes without shifting and scratching and rustling, clearing the throat or wanting to light up a cigarette. Kenny was somewhere in the middle of the two extremes, shifting his gun or his posture every fifteen to twenty minutes. He was not a compulsive throat clearer, though, and that made the waiting more tolerable for Del.

After they had sat for about an hour and the sun had spread full daylight on their scene, Del began to doze off. In a semi-conscious state, he became aware of movement on his left, and he came awake to see Kenny with the rifle up. The guide sat up straighter to see the cause of his hunter's interest. A coyote had slinked up to the waterhole, which was between a hundred and fifty and two hundred yards away. Kenny was watching it through his scope, with his finger outside the trigger guard. The coyote dipped out of sight, down to the water level. A few seconds later he came trotting into sight again with his tail streaming out behind him. He ran along the base of the man-made ridge, ducked to his right, and went up over and out of sight. Kenny lowered his rifle and let out a silent yawn.

They sat for nearly another hour with no further incident, each of them bobbing his head and yawning from time to time. Then, without any prelude or ceremony, a procession of deer came mincing in from the left. They must have come down the big draw, Del thought. As he watched, he saw three, four, five, six does and yearlings, a forked horn buck in the rear, and a buck with some pretty good antlers crowding in the middle.

He was wide awake now, and his heart was thumping, but he had the presence to lay his hand on Kenny's arm. The boy nodded and paid attention without moving his rifle. The deer milled around the waterhole two or three at a time while the others browsed on the short grass. The big buck, which looked like a four-pointer, moved among the others and bullied them for a while without offering a clear shot. At last he stepped away from the herd and put his head down to browse, giving three quarters of a broadside. Kenny brought his rifle up, and one of the does flicked her ears and stared at him. The buck was bringing his head up and around for a look when Kenny touched off a shot that made a violent crash in the stillness of the morning. The buck gave a lurch and charged straight up and over the ridge as the other deer scattered and zig-zagged. In an instant the scene was empty, quiet again but not the same.

"Shit!" Kenny muttered. "I had a good steady aim right on him."

"I think you hit him," Del said.

"I had to have hit him, but he took off like a sonofabitch."

"Well, let's wait a few minutes, and we'll go take a look see."

"Damn, I'll be pissed off royal if I missed him!" Kenny's hands were shaking as he coaxed the spent casing out of the rifle and closed the bolt on an empty chamber.

"I think you hit him," Del said. "They can run fifty or a hundred yards easy and then keel over. If you didn't nail him that good, we'll give him time to stop and bleed, and maybe get stiff and sore."

"Damn, I hope I got him."

"I think you did. But let's wait a few minutes, and then we'll see if we can pick him up."

"O.K." The young man sat back against his rock and laid the rifle across his lap.

"Count to five hundred. Slow. Then we'll go."

Kenny let out a heavy breath. "O.K."

"Take your time."

On the little ridge, they found a drop of blood on the dry grass. Del pointed at it with his rifle barrel. Down the other side as they approached the creek, Del pointed out another speck, this time on a yellow leaf that had caught in the grass. The new sign gave them a bearing, and they followed the presumed route to the creek bed. As they came to the first cottonwood, half out of leaf, they found the buck lying on his side in the shade. He was stretched out as if he had plopped over in mid-stride, with his hind legs straight out and his front legs crossed. He was dead beyond question.

Kenny exhaled long and low. "Sonofabitch. I got him, sure enough."

"Yep, you sure did." Del noticed a fly already at the corner of the buck's eye, which was clouded milky blue. The mouth was cracked open, and Del imagined the tongue was hanging out of the other side. "What do you think of him?"

"I can't believe it. It's my first deer, ever. Sonofabitch. He's a good one, isn't he?"

"He sure is. I think he's a little bigger than the other three we've brought in so far. His rack is, that's for sure." The guide pulled the head around so Kenny could get a look.

"Do you think I should mount him?"

"That's up to you and your dad."

"But what do you think? I mean, is it that much of a—you know, is it that good?"

"It's a bigger deer than a lot of people get in a lifetime, and it's a good symmetrical four-point with a good spread. But in truth, the tips are sort of blunt, where he didn't get them polished up and pointed yet. And that ear doesn't look all that classy—it looks like he lost a piece of it some time back."

"Then you don't think I should."

"I'm not saying that. But for pure looks, Ron's had nicer features and prettier horns, especially out on the tips. But you see," the guide said, stroking the tips with his free left hand, "a taxidermist can put a point on these and stain them, and he can even give you—well, sell you—a whole new cape."

"What do you mean by cape?"

"The hide, from the shoulders on up to the tips of the ears. When he mounts one of these, he'll skin the head and then mount the hide and horns on a styrofoam cast, put in glass eyes and a rubber nose, and there you are. When someone messes up a cape, the taxidermist has to come up with a new one."

"Oh. That's what you meant the other night about cutting the throat."

"Right. But in your case, he could do it as a way of replacing that ragged ear."

"That all sounds kind of phony to me. I'd want to keep him as he was when I got him."

"As much as you could, anyway."

"Well, yeah. I understand you don't just chop off the head and stick it on the wall."

"No. You're going to have some degree of . . . fakeness, I guess, one way or the other."

"Hell. I'd rather have one that looked nice and came that way."

"Well, you think it over. We'll field dress him, and then I'll go up and get the horses. You can give it some thought. If you don't want to have him stuffed, there's no need for us to haul the head and hide up out of here."

Kenny looked at him wide-eyed, in apparent disbelief.

"Oh, we'd take the horns in one piece so you could mount them on a nice plaque. I just mean the part that we'd throw out in camp anyway."

"Oh."

Del dropped the head and ran his hand down to the spot where the bullet had gone in. He poked the tip of his little finger into the wet spot, and it came out moist with blood. "Good shot. You got him right through the boiler." A quick association with that phrase stopped him for a second. He said, "Go ahead and fill out your tag, and we'll get this guy cleaned out."

Amidst the smell of blood and dust and fallen leaf, the field dressing went smoothly enough. Kenny held up a leg and maneuvered the carcass while Del reached in with hands that worked almost by themselves. The hands knew where they

173

were, the slippery right hand never slipping with the knife, the trusting left hand always knowing what the right hand was doing. As he worked, the guide explained each step in the operation, even though Kenny had seen enough of this, just the day before, to know how to do it himself.

When the job was done, Del straightened up and observed his sticky forearms. "If we'd thought to bring a canteen, I could wash off."

"Boy, I could sure go for a drink."

"Get a little cotton mouth, did you?"

"I sure did. And my stomach got a real jolt, too. Is that what they call buck fever?"

"One kind of it. The other kinds are worse, when a guy can't pull the trigger or when he loses his judgment. You had the good kind."

Kenny held his hand out and studied the spread fingers. "I'm not shaking any more. But I'm thirsty."

Del didn't mention it, but the young man wasn't swearing like a high school kid any more, either.

"I'll be back with the horses and water in no time at all," he said. "You keep an eye on him, and don't let him go anywhere."

"O.K." Kenny smiled. "I'll do that."

* * * * *

When Del returned with the horses, Kenny took a long drink of water and announced that he wouldn't have the head mounted. That was fine, Del told him; they would skin it one way or the other. This way, he didn't have to be quite so careful.

With the help of Spud and a rope, they got the buck hanging, rear hocks upward, from a cottonwood branch. Del did the skinning without any incident and, as was his style, laid the horns, head and hide out on the grass. He went to his saddlebags, which he had transferred to Little Tulip, and took out a leather case.

"They call this a Wyoming Saw," he said. "That's the brand name." He spoke as he unfolded the case and took out the parts. "It breaks down so you can pack it. When you put it together, it looks like a snub-nosed hack saw." The guide had the saw assembled in less than a minute. Without pausing, he split the pelvis and the front of the rib cage, then moved around to the back. "O.K., now, if I can get you to stand around here and put your hands on his hams to steady him, I'll try to cut straight down the spine."

For the next several minutes, Del worked the saw, *zhinka-zhinka*, pausing every two or three minutes to rest his arm. He stopped once for a slug of water. When he finished, he had two handsome halves swaying in the autumn shade. He stepped back and dragged his shirt sleeve across his forehead, pushing his hat back.

After another drink of water, he unrolled the set of panniers and draped it over Spud's saddle. He checked the cinches and the breast collar on the saddle, and he tightened the belly straps on the panniers. "We're going to put one half in each side," he said, "but we have to quarter him first." A few strokes of the saw dropped the right front quarter into Kenny's arms. Del took the quarter and hefted it chest high. "We pack it fleshy side in, bony side out. Load the left side first."

Spud sidestepped until Del got a hand on the saddle horn, then slipped the front quarter into the pouch. Next they got the other front quarter stowed into the right side, and with a length of twine, Del snugged the shanks against the horse's withers. Then came the hind quarters, one in each side, and Del tied them across. When he had snugged down the flaps between the protruding shanks and tied the pack across with the rope, the loading was done.

"Now for the horns." The guide set the blade of the Wyoming saw behind the antlers and sawed downward, in front of the ears and through the eye socket. Then he pulled the saw out and applied it to the front of the skull plate, where the nose ridge began, and he sawed through to meet his first cut. He stepped on one ear, the good one, and twisted the antlers until the set came free. With a twig he dislodged the portion of brain from inside the skull plate. "All ready," he said, holding out the antlers as they would look on the wall. Kenny nodded and smiled, and Del could see that he was satisfied with his decision not to mount the head.

They tied the antlers on top of Spud's load, gathered up their gear, and stowed it. They paused to eat a trail bar, the kind with peanuts and chocolate chips, and had a full drink of water. Kenny mounted first and edged Whisker out into the late morning sun. With Spud's lead rope in one hand and Little Tulip's reins in another, Del paused for a last look around. The hide and the gut pile would bring good times to the coyotes and magpies. In another year or two, someone might find the plundered skull somewhere down the creek bed. And up the slope a ways, where a cattle trail was flanked by two square rocks and a juniper on one side and sagebrush on the other, regardless of whether anyone ever saw it, a shiny .30-06 casing would lose its lustre and assume the mouse-grey color of its neighbor. Del put his left foot into the stirrup, brought his hands together on the saddle horn, and climbed aboard. With the packhorse at their side, Del and Little Tulip moved out of the shade and into the fragile, warming October sun.

Chapter Sixteen

Del and his young hunter rode into camp at about one o'clock, and as they hung up the deer quarters, Kenny told his dad about the hunt. He stopped at the point where he had decided not to save the head.

"I just thought of something, Del."

"What's that?" The guide was starting to take Spud to the hitching rail, and he stopped.

"We forgot to get a picture."

"Oh, hell. We sure did." Del turned to the father. "I'm sorry, Ken."

"Not much we can do now." Ken turned to his son. "It's too bad you didn't get a picture. It would have been a nice memory, and something to show your mom."

"I'll tell you one thing," Kenny said, "I've got it on videotape here." He tapped the side of his skull.

"That's the best place," his father answered. "You can lose a photograph or damage it, but nothing can take away that memory. It should stay with you for a lifetime. Of course, you've got the horns, and they're a hell of a nice set." He clapped the boy on the shoulder and gave him a wink. "Shall we check to see if the old man knows how to cook a pot of beans?"

"I'll be right with you," Del said, leading Spud away. In a matter of a few minutes he had stripped the horses and had left them to roll in the corral dust. When he went inside the ranch house, Ken had set out bread, butter, and three bowls of beans. They were waiting for Del, who made short work of washing his hands and sitting down.

"Well," said the guide as he buttered a slice of bread, "what news of Len and Chick? Have they been back?"

"Oh, hell, yes. I forgot to say anything, I got so caught up with you guys' stories. Yeah, they came back in about eleven. Chick said he shot at a big one and missed it. He wasn't real happy about it."

"We heard four shots pretty early," Kenny put in.

"That's what he said. Four clean misses."

"That's too bad," Del said. "I wonder if I ought to go out there. Are they back on the same ridge?"

"That's the impression I had."

The guide put away a mounded spoonful of beans. "I kind of have the feeling I've been neglecting them, but I also get the feeling they don't mind being on their own."

"Me too," Ken said. "If Chick isn't happy, it's because he made some bad shots." After a few minutes, Ken rose from his chair and went to the stove. He returned with the bean pot. "You guys look like you're ready for seconds."

"You cook a good pot of beans," Del said. "I'll hate to see you go."

"Did you really cook these yourself, Dad?"

"Sure did. But don't tell your mom. She'll make me cook at home."

"She'll want to know we didn't go to one of those resorts with the camp whores and hired hunters."

179

Ken laughed. "We got a picture of me. I'm covered. You're the one that needs an alibi."

The young man smiled and shoved his spoon into the second serving of beans. "I think she'll believe me."

Del spoke up. "Well, I hope you stay through tonight before you start back. Get rested up good, and let the meat cool overnight."

"We hate to leave at all, Del, but that's our plan. Get a good start in the morning. But we'll be back, uh, Kenny?"

"I hope so." He looked at Del.

"I hope so, too. I start booking in late winter, early spring, as soon as folks start making plans."

"If it's not too early," Ken said, "count us in."

"You're on my list."

After lunch, with the dirty dishes in a neat stack to be washed after supper, the guide sat on the front porch with his two happy hunters. The sun was shining, but a slight breeze brought enough of a chill that they all wore jackets.

"This is a different kind of weather," Ken said, "to be cooler in the afternoon than it was in the morning."

"That's the way it is here," Del answered. "You never know whether you're going to—" He broke off his sentence as he heard the roll and rumble of a rifle shot. "Sounds like Len and Chick."

They listened for a long two minutes, but no more shots followed. They went back to talking about the weather.

Kenny got up and took a handful of carrots to the horses, leaving Del with a mild apprehension that Ken was going to become effusive again, but the father kept it short. "It's a great time in a boy's life." He cleared his throat and said, louder, "It might be chilly, but I'm about ready for a beer. How about you, Del?"

"Slippin' over the yard-arm."

They were finishing their second slow beer when Len came hiking into the yard. He was cheerful but a little winded from walking fast. He told the story of how Chick had gotten on the trail of the buck he'd missed that morning. "He had a feeling that he might have hit it after all, and the more he thought about it, the more he had to go back and find out. At last he jumped it out of some tall sagebrush at the end of the ridge, and he shot it in the base of the neck."

"Nice deer?" Ken asked.

"Oh, yeah. Four-pointer with eye guards, and a little good luck hook on one side. The right side."

"Did he hit him earlier?" Ken asked again.

"Yes, he had, but not very serious. Sort of nicked him on the right front foreleg."

"From the sounds of it," Del said, "we can fetch it with the pickup."

Len nodded. "Let me get a drink of water and take a leak, and I'll be ready to go."

Del hauled the deer back to camp, leaving the Beckers to hunt until dusk. They came into the cabin out of a chilly, darkening evening and set their rifles side by side in the rack.

"Nice and warm in here," Len said.

"Yep," Chick added. "Smells good, too. You got my deer put away all right?"

Del, frying two skillets of chicken, was adjusting the burners of the stove. He turned and looked up. "Sure did. It took me and my two helpers, all three of us, but we got him hung up."

"Well, I sure thank you. I think I'm going to sit here and have a beer in front of this nice fire, and then I'll go check him."

"I don't think he's going very far," Ken said, moving his chair to make room.

Len handed a can of beer to his brother. *"Salud,"* he said, and sat down.

As the guide got dinner ready and set the table, the four hunters lounged in front of the fire drinking beer and sharing stories. It was a relaxed setting with everybody happy—three of them happy because they'd gotten their deer and the fourth one happy because he had the opportunity to hunt some more. It was not Del's job to be happy or otherwise, but the job was better when everyone was cheerful and not hangdog, pushy, or surly.

When Chick mentioned that he would skin his deer after supper, Del reflected that everyone but Kenny had taken care of his own animal, and Kenny would do so next year. That made the job better, too, when the hunters took more of a part in the total process rather than ride around in the pickup and pull the trigger. They were still paying guests, but they weren't paying for the privilege of cooking beans or dressing their own game. They just did those things because that was what a hunting trip entailed. Del had known of dude ranches where paying guests, dressed up in ginghams and denims bought for the excursion, paid handsome fees so that they could have a hand in the adventure of cooking chuckwagon flapjacks and saddling a horse. This way was all right. It was better to be bunkhouse cook and horse wrangler than chuck-wagon impresario.

After supper, the Beckers went out to skin Chick's animal. Del washed the dishes and cleaned up the kitchen area while the Kerrs sorted out their gear for the trip home. When Len and Chick came back in, the other three were staring at the fire. Ken came out of his trance and proposed a game of poker, dealer's choice.

Len and Chick, being good sports as they were, accepted. Del joined in also, with the comment that he didn't want to stay up too late. The brothers seconded him, making it clear that they were both going out in the morning. Ken no doubt felt that a poker game was an imperative part of a hunting trip, but he was willing to compromise and shut the game down in "an hour or so" if the others wanted to cash in. He spread a blanket on the table, then counted out chips at penny, nickel, and dime values.

They cut low card for first deal, and Len dealt a hand of five-card stud. Chick won the first pot, a small one. When it was Del's turn, he dealt a hand of five-card draw, open on guts. Chick won that pot, too. The deal went to Ken, who said, "Let's play seven stud. And to make it interesting, let's make the whore wild."

"The queen of spades?" Len clarified.

"Yep. The old dark-haired bitch."

Del winced but said nothing.

Chick took a drink of beer and nodded at Kenny, saying, "O.K., queen of spades is wild."

Ken turned out to be the type of player who rattled on with table talk, in part to relieve the silence and in part, Del imagined, to assure the others that a prosperous businessman could still be a good old boy. When he wasn't providing a commentary on the cards and the betting, he proposed toasts. They drank a sip of canned beer to Chick's deer, cooling in the lean-to. A few hands later, they drank to Len's deer, waiting somewhere in the dark hills. Then it was Kenny's deer, his first, and a special toast for Spud.

"I was sure glad he was there," Kenny said.

"He's a damn good horse," Ken said. "Even if he farts a lot."

Kenny sputtered his beer, turning the spray toward the fire. "He does do that."

"All horses fart a lot," Ken said. "Isn't that right, Del?"

"Uh-huh. They got a lot of wind in 'em."

"My deal," Len said. "Let's have another hand of five-card stud."

"I like that game," Chick returned.

"I guess you should," Ken said, pretending to growl. "I think you've won it every time it was dealt."

"Somebody's got to." Chick smiled as he peeked at his hole card.

"There's a cowboy," Ken announced as the king of clubs fell face up. "And a nine. And a seven. And a dirty little deuce for Del. And another nine for the dealer. Say, Chick, do you think you always win this game because you're under the gun?"

"Might be. But then again," he said as he widened his eyes in mock surprise, "maybe there's something in the cards for me tonight." He tossed a blue chip into the pot. "I open."

Ken called, Del went along for the ride, Kenny folded, and Len called and raised. Chick called the raise. Del folded and stood up to take a walk in the moonlight, then paused. Ken called. The next round of cards brought a second king to Chick, a stray jack to Ken, and an eight for Len the dealer. Chick bet the limit, only a dime but enough to make Ken fold. The dealer looked at his hole card and flipped his cards to the center, and his brother raked in the little pile of chips.

"Deal me out for this hand," Del said. "I'll be right back."

Outside, in the bracing cold air, he smiled. He would be out of chips in another hand or two, and he could leave Ken for the amusement of the Beckers, who were going to have a good time taking the blue chips one or two at a time. Del yawned and stretched, then walked inside.

Ken was announcing, "Let's have another game of seven stud, with the old whore wild. I'm dealing you in, Del."

Del didn't feel that he had to lose his three-dollar stack of chips evenly around the table, but he was glad to see things go that way. "I hate to leave you playing four-handed," he said when the hand was ended, "but this old hoss has got to get some sleep."

"Can't sleep on your feet, uh?" Ken cut the deck.

"Not like I used to. Good night, all. See you at breakfast."

"Good night, Del," the four hunters said in unison.

In his tent, the guide laid out a change of clothes for the next morning. The Beckers were going to hunt their same ridge in the morning, and if that didn't turn up what they needed, they would all take an afternoon horseback hunt. The morning would be less hurried than the past two, and at the most, Del would have one more animal to take care of before he hunted for himself.

He wound his alarm and turned out the lantern. The boys inside could gamble and drink and raise hell all night if they wanted, but he was going to get some sleep. He heard the horses moving in the corral, and at one point he heard someone go out the back door of the cabin and then back in.

He didn't know he had been asleep until he woke up. There had been some noise other than the wind and the horses and the cabin. Sitting straight up, he paid close attention. It wasn't a sound but the absence of sound. That was it. He was pretty sure that a car engine shutting off had awakened him. Peeking out the window flap, he saw a light-colored passenger car parked behind the pickups. He slipped on his pants and a coat, pulled on his hiking boots, and left them unlaced. He heard a car door close, the snug quiet close of a late-model car door. He emerged from the tent to see a woman in a white jacket walking down the driveway. The crescent moon did not shed much light, but he recognized the shape and the walk. He didn't need any light to know that the car would have Nebraska license plates and that the lawyer from Omaha was not in it.

Chapter Seventeen

As Del walked from his tent, he noticed with relief that the lights were off in the cabin. When he came within soft speaking distance, he said, "Hello. Nice of you to drop by."

"Glad I could make it," she said, tossing her head in the moonlight.

When he was an arm's length from her, he stopped. He could feel himself trembling, which was normal after an unexpected awakening into the chill night. But he was also excited by the mere sense of the woman. "The hunters are asleep in the cabin," he said, softer than before. "Let's go to my tent." He brushed away a flickering image of Rita.

He knew that the first move would be easier in the dark, so before going into the tent, he paused. She turned toward him, and he felt she was letting herself be guided by his movements. Time seemed suspended as they wrapped in an embrace, both of them trembling as their lips met and held, released, shifted, held again. Del could feel himself letting go of all restraint, and he knew he was crossing the line. He had a clear awareness that he was doing something irretrievable, that taking her in his arms was something he couldn't undo. It was a bold feeling, the letting go, and he gave himself up to it.

"I had to come and see you," she whispered, caressing the back of his neck.

"I didn't know if I'd ever see you again," he whispered back. "I've been thinking about you all the time."

"After I found out where you were, I tried sitting around my motel room, but I couldn't stay put. I had to come out here."

"How did you find out where I was?"

"I asked at the hardware store where they sell hunting licenses."

"Yeah, they'd know." He kissed her again, pressing the whole length of her upper body against his. When they released, he whispered, "Let's go in."

Once inside, he fired up the propane lantern and unrolled the extra sleeping bag, to work as a blanket. He wrapped it around her where she sat on the bedroll, then sat beside her as he drew the loose end of the cover around his right shoulder.

"Actually," she said, "I drove out this way on the highway this afternoon, and then I went back and took a room."

"I'm glad you found me." He kissed her in a quick motion. "I'm sorry I don't have anything to offer you out here. Everything is inside, with the kitchen."

"Oh, that's O.K. I'm fine."

"Well, um . . . how long are you here for?"

"I've got a room at the Wagon Wheel. I didn't know what your schedule was."

"All of my hunters but one have gotten their deer. I expect he'll fill tomorrow."

"Do you want me to come back when they're gone?"

He stopped rubbing her back and drew her side close to his. "Don't be in a hurry to go. You just got here."

"What I mean is, I ought to be gone when you go to work. But do you want me to come back?"

"Of course I do." Del put his right hand around her waist as they each turned inward. He could feel both of them still shivering, and the embrace steadied them.

When they released again and drew back, she said, "I hope you don't mind my coming out here."

"Not at all. I was dying to see you."

"I mean, it doesn't look good."

He shrugged. "I don't see where any harm will come of it."

"I won't stay long."

They sat for a lengthy moment without speaking until Del said, with some hesitation, "I don't mean to bring up an unpleasant subject, but where's—"

"Vince? Oh, he's out here somewhere. We got into a squabble after we left your camp, and I'm not entirely sure he didn't pick it. He didn't want me to stay, so he sent me home on the plane."

"Why didn't he want you here?"

"I don't know. I've got a sneaky little suspicion that he's got some girlie-friend come out here to be his . . ."

Del nearly filled in the phrase "camp whore," but he thought better of it and said, "Hunting partner?"

"Whatever you'd call it. But I don't know it anyway. It just seemed like he was up to something."

"Did you come out here to check up on him?"

"No, I came out here to see you." Her voice took on the petulant tone of someone speaking about an ex-boyfriend. "I don't want him to know I've been here."

"Do you know where he is?"

"He said the Medicine Bow National Forest."

"That could be anywhere. It spreads all over this part of the state."

"He was going to Laramie when he left me off in Cheyenne."

"Then he's probably out in the Snowy Range somewhere. Good place for him."

"How far is that from here?"

"Half a day's drive." He took her right hand in his. "You came all the way back out here to see me, then?"

"That's right."

"Why?"

"Because I knew you wanted me to. And I wanted to."

She turned to him, and with her left hand on his right elbow, she drew him to her. They kissed again, in long and luscious abandon, before they gave up their sitting position and pulled the quilt-like sleeping bag over them.

* * * * *

The clanging hammer of the alarm banged against the twin bells, stirring Del into consciousness. Thick-headed and cotton-mouthed, he sat up to stifle the alarm. He thought of Rita and, as he had done the night before, he blocked it out. Sylvia mumbled from beneath the covers.

"Time for you to get up?"

"Yeah," the guide said, "I've got to get goin' on the day here." Between the few extra drinks he'd had with the boys and the loss of sleep he'd had with the woman, he didn't feel very peppy. But he had a job to do, so he rolled out of the warm bedding and put on his cold clothes. "I'll be right back," he whispered into her ear.

Inside again, having tended to himself and to the horses, he took a long drink of water from the quart bottle. When he lit the lantern, Sylvia sat up and rubbed her eyes. "I guess I'd better get up and get going, too." As she reached for her clothes where they lay between the bedding and the side wall of the tent, it occurred to Del that even her back was pretty and shapely. He wanted to shuck his clothes and get back under the covers, but he just sat there with a half-smile as she put on her bra. Then he pulled her to him and kissed her breasts through the lacy white fabric.

She smiled as she sat back and pulled on her sweater. "How does my hair look?" she asked, smoothing it.

"Fine."

"I guess it doesn't matter. I'm going straight back to my room anyway."

"I'll think about you, sleeping in till noon, while I'm trying to keep my eyes open."

She leaned over and kissed him. "Poor baby. You can catch up later." She patted his cheek and turned back to finish dressing.

After shutting off the lantern and zipping up the tent, he walked her to her car. They paused at the open door. "I wouldn't be surprised if these fellows are gone by this evening," he said.

"All of them?"

"There's only one hunter left who needs to fill a tag. The two guys in that Blazer will pull out this morning, and there's just the other two fellas, two brothers, in the Ford pickup, and one of them got his deer yesterday."

"Oh, O.K. I guess you said that last night."

"Sort of."

"When should I come back? Or should I?"

"Of course you should. This will be a nice place to spend a little time, away from everything and all." Despite his twinge of guilt, it seemed like the only way. He could feel the urge.

"Uh-huh. You think tonight? Too bad I can't call."

"Sometimes it would be handy to have a phone. But yeah, I think this evening would be O.K. Come on out, say, after supper time, and if I'm still busy, I guess I'm still busy."

"Are you going to smell like chicken again?"

"Huh?"

"I could smell fried chicken on you last night."

"Oh, I'm sorry."

"I liked it." She kissed him and settled into her car, and he snugged the door behind her. As the engine churned into life, she lowered the power window. "See you this evening," she said, waving a wiggling left hand as she slipped the car into gear.

Del watched the car drive away in the quiet darkness. No lights appeared yet in the cabin, so that was good. He looked at the tent, faint but visible in the dark. Well, he thought, you never know what will happen or what's coming next. Raising his eyebrows, he turned and went into the house.

As soon as he turned on the lantern, Chick and Len stirred. When Del had the coffee going, he walked over to ask whether the Kerrs wanted to be awakened early.

"I don't think so," Chick said, looking up from lacing his boots.

"No," Len added, "they want to sleep in."

"O.K." Del went back to the kitchen area and cooked breakfast for three. The meal went on, with little comment and no questions. When the Beckers had shoved their plates aside, Del filled the coffee cups again. The three men sipped coffee for several minutes before anyone spoke.

"I think I'll hang around camp this morning," Del said. Both hunters nodded. "You think there might be another decent-sized buck out where you've been?"

"I kind of think so," Len said. "I just hope it doesn't take the rest of the season."

"I think we can turn up something," Chick said. "If not, we can try that place you mentioned."

Del yawned. "I think I might even catch a little snooze while you're out."

Chick tipped up his coffee cup as Len nodded, yawning himself. The two of them got up, put on caps, coats, and gloves, and stepped out into the dark chilly morning.

Del turned out the lantern, noticing that the morning was beginning to turn grey. Making his way to the bunk that had been Danny's, he lay on his back and used his coat for a blanket. He did not fall into a comfortable sleep but rather drifted in and out of a dream state. Whether he was half-awake or half-asleep, his hazy mind replayed and overlaid the details of dressing Kenny's deer and of becoming intimate with Sylvia. It was all one continuous action with no beginning or end, the uncovering of her sleek, firm body and then the nuzzling and mingling and blending. In his dream, he went about it in a methodical way, as he floated in a soft glow of pleasure.

Grey light was spreading in the ranch house when he awoke, shivering, to discover that his coat had fallen to the floor. Pulling the coat back over him, he lay still with his hands on his chest. As he rubbed his chin on his right shoulder, he realized he needed a shave, which meant he would have to heat water. He remembered that the dishpan had dirty plates in it and the Kerrs hadn't had breakfast yet. Fending off a feeling of weariness, he told himself there would be time for everything to be done in its right order.

When he opened his eyes again, the room lay in light, not yet full daylight but clear. The guide turned and sat up on the edge of the bunk, feeling better rested but still thick and dull. Standing up, he walked light-footed to the kitchen area and put on a new pot of coffee.

Del heard the father speak to the son, and a cot creaked. Looking over, Del saw Ken sitting up and moving his head back and forth. The son rolled over to turn his back to his father, who spoke again. "Let's get up now. Del's waiting to put our breakfast on the table."

Showing signs of being hung over, father and son put away a full breakfast, finishing off with the last of Del's cinnamon rolls. The guide poured more coffee, then sat down to listen to Ken's account of the poker game. The father seemed to be perking up, but his son, who did not seem to have much to say in the company of older men anyway, was even more taciturn than usual. Before Ken had finished his narration, the son stood up and announced his intention to go see the horses.

"I think he's still a little under the weather," Ken said.

"How late did you stay up?"

"Till about midnight. Say, that reminds me. I thought I heard a car pull in here after everyone went to sleep."

"You probably did. A friend of mine dropped by for a little while, to check in on me."

"Oh." Ken raised his cup, blew steam across the surface of the coffee, and said, "Uh-huh." He took a swallow and said, "That Chick has got to be the luckiest sonofabitch."

"Huh?"

"I think he won every hand that he and his brother dealt, and half the rest."

"Oh."

"But we had a good time."

"Good. No one got hurt."

"Nah. I think I lost four dollars at the most. Kenny lost three and a little bit of change. That's not much of a hurt."

The Kerrs were packed up and on the road by 9:30, and Del had the dishes done by 10:00. He decided to leave the shaving and clean-up until later, after he had done whatever dirty work he would have to do.

Len and Chick were back for an early lunch, ready to try a horseback hunt. They didn't seem inclined to loaf around for the middle part of the day, so Del set out a quick lunch for them all. Assuring them that he could get the horses ready by himself, he left them to relax with their Pepsis.

It seemed like business now, not much in the way of ritual and adventure. The Beckers had hunted hard for two and a half days, and now they seemed not to want to detain or retain the guide for another day. Len had gotten his trophy the year before, and he would no doubt like to take another one on this trip, but the general tone of the present moment was that he wanted to get some meat on the ground.

When they had cut across the basin and crossed south along the top for a mile and a half, the guide led them off the rim to the left. Leaving them to hunt the two ridges downslope, he took the horses and rode out to the far point of his ride, where he would loiter.

He sat in the narrow shade of a cedar tree and held the lead ropes in his hand. Around him, the afternoon seemed dry and flat. His own senses were dulled, not yet regenerated, and the sun had not slipped far enough westward to set the hillside into shadows and relief. The charm of solitude and simplicity seemed to have wisped away.

As he sat there, he had an unpleasant awareness of himself, of his own body smell. Beneath that, in his nostrils and hanging in the back of his throat, there hung the lingering odor of horse sweat. He spit on the dry grass at his feet.

At the same time that he felt disenchanted with the world of things he sat amidst, he could link that feeling with another. At some point along the way, he had been taken with the idea of getting close to Sylvia. He could think back now, and he could remember all the little sparks that made him want her.

He could also recall at what points he began to think about her instead of Rita when he was out on his own with the horses. Sylvia had crowded into his daydreams—or, more fairly, he had brought her in, just as he had brought her into the tent.

He had let himself want something from outside his world, something exotic, and he had gotten what he wanted. It had been rich to mingle and tumble with the woman he had fantasized about, but now that the fantasy had become reality, the unknown had become known. The suspense—the mystery of wondering what it would be like—was gone. In its place was his new knowledge, plus the feeling that he should be pleased with having had the experience. But that was not a free feeling either, because he knew he was also satisfied, in a smug, cold-blooded sort of way, at having gotten around on Vince.

It was not a good way to feel, but there were ways to rationalize being with another man's wife. He could give the woman something her husband couldn't, some level of understanding or compatibility, minus the domination. In a hazy sort of way, Vince had almost pushed her towards it. At this point, it seemed as if Vince might even have wanted something to hold against his wife—maybe not the act itself but the temptation—something to balance out whatever he might be up to. Del told himself that if she hadn't had her fling with him, it would have been with someone else. Just as well be him. Yes, that was the way a guy rationalized it, just a little cold-blooded.

Del pushed away his thoughts of Vince and let himself be pleased, in a warm-blooded, tingly sort of way, at the prospect of further intimacy with Sylvia. Now that he had come that far, he felt he might as well indulge himself some more, to make the best of the opportunity. He recalled the magic of her compliant body, the yielding as he slipped her black panties off of her firm hips. The desire came back strong, and as much as anything, he wanted more of what he had already enjoyed.

At the same time, he knew it would not be all raw adventure. The woman would return, as he wanted her to, but when she came, she would bring attachments. He could feel it. She would bring the complications of their own affairs, and that in turn would revive a sense of all that he had tried to get away from—the unsought connections and linkages brought on by computer networks, eight-lane freeways, lawyers and lawsuits. It was returning, that feeling of entanglement he had not freed himself from until the last wheelbarrow had been hauled away. It would not all come back, but life was going to be sticky again in ways he could not yet know. And he would know that he should have known better. He had a glimpsed memory of a Budweiser light swaying over a man on the floor, and he felt as if he had been brought back into its shadow.

Still, his sense of the dangers did not keep him from wanting to see her again. He wanted more, as if a greater proportion of pleasure would make the risk worthwhile.

Chapter Eighteen

When it was time to move on with the horses, Del had thought it over enough to satisfy himself on one account. It wasn't the woman's fault. He had wanted the encounter, had let his want be known in sub-surface ways, had had it come to his doorstep, wanted a second round of it so he wouldn't want any more, and had himself to thank for what might come after that. With a wry smile he shook his head and formed the actual words in his mind. *What the hell did you expect?*

The road he followed, like most of the others on this part of the spread, was grassed over in the middle. Sagebrush grew to the edge and often in the center. It was an easy trail for the horses, and the guide did not have to pay much attention. He was brought back to awareness, however, when Little Tulip whipped clear around to the left, tightening the lead ropes across his ribs. As Whisker and Spud gave resistance, he passed the ropes behind his back to his left hand, then pulled Little Tulip around and set her back on course. She argued with him again and again, turning one way and then the other as the other two horses milled. It was a job in itself just to keep the ropes and horses straight.

He brought them to a standstill. "O.K., damn it, we're going down that trail, and that's that," he said, patting his mare on the neck. He took them in a wide, fifteen-yard circle and goaded Little Tulip back onto the trail. She did not like it, but she did as she was told. Sixty or seventy yards later, he smelled the skunk. Patting the mare on the neck again, he said, "Sorry, girl. I should have listened to you. You knew." The smell was not very strong, so they pushed through it soon enough, and after another fifty yards, the horses were stepping normal again.

They followed the road on down to the bottom, where they turned left to trail along the dry creek bed north. Shadows were beginning to lengthen on the west side, where Del kept an eye out for his hunters. By and by he saw an orange hunting cap against a rock outcropping, and when the cap rose up, it proved to be on Chick's head. Smiling, the hunter sauntered down to the creek bed. As he shouldered his rifle, he asked, "See anything?"

"Nope. Just smelled a skunk. How about you?"

"I pushed out a little bunch of does was all, but Len saw a big buck head north, and he went after it."

"Big one, uh?"

"Yeah. He said he saw the rack go up and over the ridge, and it looked pretty impressive when it was skylined."

"Uh-huh."

"What do you think?" Chick asked.

"How long ago did he set out after it?" Del asked back.

"Maybe half an hour."

"We might as well poke along behind him." Del sorted out Whisker's lead rope. "Here, you can climb aboard if you want."

They rode side by side in the creek bed, occasionally moving to the left bank or the right when travel was easier. Twice they paused in the shadow of a cutbank to enjoy the gathering coolness. During their second stop, they each took a drink of water, smiled and nodded, all without a word. Len was half an hour ahead of them on foot, stalking a deer. He would have moved quickly at first, but if he had slowed to a creeping crawl, they didn't want to blunder onto his hunt and spoil it. So they took their time, poking along and then pausing.

Del saw an old sardine can, bent and rusty, lying in the gravel. As the horses plodded past it, he realized that he had seen very little rubbish on this ranch. He stopped, dismounted, picked up the can, and, showing it to Chick, tucked it into his saddlebags. Chick smiled and nodded.

In a long, lone moment, the shot came, rippling through the cool ravines. The riders stopped to wait for more shots, and after a couple of minutes, they turned upslope. The shot had come from higher up as well as farther north, and they would have a better view if they rode across the ridges than if they stayed in the bottom.

By the time they found Len, he had laid out the buck and opened the abdomen. He looked up at Del and Chick as they rode downslope, and he returned to his work. Blood was spilling out of the cavity as Len's hands worked on the intestines.

Drawing closer, Del saw what Chick did, that the buck was only a three-pointer. The single tines were long, while the forked tines were short and high up. It was a shapely rack, but not a trophy.

Chick dismounted and waved at the head. "Is this the same one you went after?"

201

"I'm not sure. I thought I saw a better set of horns the first time, but it might have been the way they crisscrossed."

"Could be."

"I didn't have a lot of time to decide. I came up behind him and saw him from the back as he was going up this ridge to cross it. I saw it was less than I'd expected, but it was good enough for me."

"He's just fine," Chick said. He handed his reins to Del, who had also dismounted, and he took the deer's free back leg and lifted it, to give Len more working room. "Is his bladder full?"

"Not bad," Len answered.

"Is he fat?"

"Seems like it, from what I've seen so far."

"You don't think he changed head-dresses, to talk you out of it."

"No, I don't think so. I think he looked better when I first saw him." Len shifted in his crouch and reached farther into the entrails.

"He's just fine," Chick said again.

"Oh, yeah."

"Where'd you hit him?"

"In the back of the neck, right at the shoulders. Split the hide wide open, and he went down like a sack of potatoes."

"I bet."

Len drew out the bladder and colon, slashed the colon free from the intestine, and threw the offal aside. "Got that part out clean." He stood up to straighten his back. "What do you think, Del? What would be the best way to pack him out?"

"We're kind of in the middle of it all here," the guide answered, "but I think we can get Spud to drag him up to the top. That's probably the closest road." He turned to Chick. "What would you think of going back and getting my pickup, and meeting us up on the road?"

"Sure."

"Before you go, though, let me get a picture here, of the two of you."

Len wiggled his bloody fingers and said, smiling, "Won't make as good a picture as Chick's, but that's O.K."

When Del had tied up the horses and gotten the picture taken, he took over as assistant field dresser.

The work went smoothly. After Len dressed the deer, Del laced up the belly as he had done on Ken's deer. Then he checked the cinches and breast collar on Spud, got him hitched to the burden, and started him on the long upward pull. When they reached the top, Del untied the rope and coiled it.

As they waited on the roadside, Len picked burrs from the dead deer. "These deer don't have fleas as bad as the coastal blacktail," he said.

"Is that right?"

"Yeah, those deer are always lousy with fleas. And ticks."

"You'll get some of that here."

"Yeah, but not so bad. Out there in the coast range, some guys carry a can of bug spray."

"I've seen that," the guide said, "but I don't care for it."

"Me neither." Len began to rub some of the dried blood from his hands. "We'll probably go in for a shower and a room tonight, get set up for an early start back tomorrow."

Del nodded. "You'll help me get rid of some pork chops first, won't you?"

"Oh, yeah, as long as we can get to the meat locker before it closes."

"It stays open pretty late during the season. You plan on hanging the two carcasses overnight?"

"That's what we figured. Skin this one when we get back to camp, cool 'em both in a meat locker, and drive straight back."

Del nodded. "Sounds like a good plan. You think you'll be out this way again next year?"

"We're thinking of trying the western part of the state, maybe hunt deer and elk back-to-back."

"You'd get into some different kind of country there."

"That's what we're thinking. You expect Ken and his boy to come back?"

"I think so. They were pretty pleased with the way things went."

"Oh, everyone was. We are, I know. The two guys from Iowa seemed satisfied."

"I don't expect them back right away."

"Probably not," Len agreed. "I got the impression that was something they could do maybe every four or five years."

"Yeah, they told me that before they came."

They sat for a while without speaking until Len made conversation. "Do you have more deer hunters coming, or do you have some time off now until the elk?"

"I have a little time off. I might hunt on my own."

"Here?"

"Yeah."

"Well, I hope we didn't get 'em all."

"Sometimes it seems that way after the first couple of days of the season, but there's more of 'em here."

"Oh, yeah. You'll see that when the season is over."

"I should do all right for myself in the meanwhile."

"Oh, yeah. If anyone can, you ought to. No reason for you to do without." Len drew his brows together. "Is that Chick already?"

"Sounds like it," Del said, "just coming up the other side. He'll be a while yet."

* * * * *

Back in camp, Del brushed the horses down and looked them over, gave them their evening bait of grain, and tossed hay into the bunk. He fixed a pork chop dinner while Chick packed the Beckers' gear and Len skinned his buck. The evening meal was not hurried, but the hunters ate with a sense of purpose and were on the road by eight o'clock.

As Del heard their vehicle rumble away, he dipped a finger into the large basin of water that he had set on the stove. With a smaller basin, he dipped out enough for a shave, and when he had finished with the razor, there were tiny bubbles forming on the inside bottom of the larger basin. The water was hot, too hot for direct use, so he took it off the stove and diluted it with cold water. He made a quick trip to the tent for clean clothes, and then he stripped for a complete sponge bath. The fireplace cast a comfortable glow as he dried and dressed.

By the time Del had heated more water, tidied the cabin, and done the dishes, it was after nine. He fidgeted. He thought about bringing the bedding in from the tent so they could sleep by the fire, but he decided to let that wait.

Going outside, he walked to the road that led from the highway. The evening was quiet and still, and he saw no headlights. He took carrots to the horses and checked the road again. There was no reason she wouldn't come. She was just giving him time. He felt himself wishing both ways, that she would come and that she wouldn't. With his pocket flashlight he checked the lean-to, making sure it was cleared out. He checked the saddles and tack he had stored in the horse trailer, checked to see how much hay and grain he had, and looked down the road again. Back with the horses, he flashed his light at the grain trough, where carrot niblets had fallen but would not stay long.

The night sky was beginning to cloud over, and he wondered whether it would bring a late cold rain or an early snow. It was the third of October, and the weather could go either way. Thinking of how he might use up the time between now and elk season, he remembered Rita. This time he didn't block her out. A lurch of fear ran through his stomach. Although he didn't have a standing obligation to check in with her, he had told her he'd be back when he had all the deer killed. Well, he still had his own to hunt. It might take a couple of days. She knew he was busy, and she should be happy to see him when he got back. He could be done with this other thing in the meanwhile, have it wrapped up and put away, and get himself back in line.

It smelled more like rain than snow. The fresh air opened his nose and reminded him of the smell of the skunk from earlier in the day. He shook his head. A man can't smell danger, he thought; he'll put his nose in it as square as a dog in a skunk's ass.

He smelled at the cool, damp evening as he looked at the sky. What few stars were not yet covered were dim. He pointed his flashlight upward, and the light seemed to go nowhere. He looked down the road again to see a pair of headlights. A surge ran through him, a tingle that told him he was on the verge of something bold again.

When she stepped free of the car, she showed him a bottle of chilled white wine and two plastic wine glasses. "Can we put this on ice?" she asked.

"Sure. Let's go inside. I've got a fire going."

"Are your hunters all gone?"

"They sure are. The last ones left after supper." He put his arm around her waist and walked her towards the cabin.

She turned her head toward him and sniffed. "You smell clean."

"I am. Squeaky clean." He ushered her through the doorway, and it was not until he had the wine poured and the bottle on ice that he took her into his arms and met her lips with his.

At length they separated and turned to their wine glasses, saluted with them, and took a sip.

"It's nice in here," she said, looking around.

"It is. I thought maybe we'd want to stay inside. The weather seems to be turning cold out there."

"That sounds good."

"Let me put down a couple of these mattresses," he said, turning to the cots, "and then I'll go out and get some covers."

When they were situated on the floor, reclined in the firelight and sipping wine, she said, "You seem tense, Del."

"Do I?"

"Yes, you do."

"It's nothing." He thought he sounded stupid, and he felt that way, too. He knew he should be doing something other than just sitting back.

"Did you want me to come?"

"Of course I wanted you to."

"Well, I wanted to. I told you that."

"I'm glad."

"Glad of what?"

"That you came. That you wanted to."

"Are you nervous?"

"Not exactly."

She set her wine glass on the floor, took his, and set it beside hers. After a long, quiet embrace she said, "Talk to me."

"What about?"

"About what's on your mind."

"I'm not really sure."

"Do you not want to . . . um . . ."

"Yes, I do. I guess the thing that's bothering me is—"

"Is—?"

"Is why you came."

"To be with you." She brushed him with a kiss.

"Yes, I know that, but why did you want to do that?"

"You mean my motive?"

"Yeah."

"Well, it's because I was attracted to you. There was something between us. We both felt it, both wanted to follow up on it, like we said last night."

"Nothing else?"

Sylvia paused. "Like what?"

Del hesitated and then asked, "You didn't come out here to spy on old what's-his-name, did you?"

She drew back. "Vince? My goodness, no. Not at all. I certainly want to stay clear of *him* on this trip."

"Then you're not doing it out of any kind of revenge."

"You mean to spite him?"

"I guess that's what I mean."

"No, I don't want to spite him, not to his face or behind his back." She paused, and thought showed on her face. "But I will tell you he's involved in why I wanted to know you better."

"How's that?"

She laid her hand on his forearm. "You're one of the few people I've met that can put him in his place."

"You mean about not having him hunt with me any more?"

"Mainly that, but in little ways, too. You handle Vince. And he doesn't like it."

"But you do."

"To be handled, or to see him be handled?"

Del shrugged. "Either."

She kissed him. "Both."

He felt the boldness coming back. "Then it wasn't just my warm-hearted generosity in giving you my antelope permit."

"That was a nice thing to do. It was a tender, generous thing. It meant a lot to me." She paused. "No, to answer your question again, I'm not doing this to spite Vince."

Del let out a breath. "That makes me feel better."

She kissed him. "This is just between you and me. Something we both wanted to know more about."

"That's what I was hoping. I just wanted to make sure," he said. He returned her kiss, then moved his right hand up from her waist to the swell of her breast. As she nestled her head on his upper chest and shoulder, he knew he was not sure in any complete way. But he also knew it was good enough for the time being.

Chapter Nineteen

Daylight straggled grey and cold upon a drizzly morning. The rain had not fallen hard enough to be audible, but Del could feel and smell the weather from where he lay in the bedding with Sylvia. He glanced at the fire and decided he should build it up. After doing that, he went to the window and saw the heavy dampness that had fallen and was still falling, quiet as snow and wet as rain. It certainly wouldn't hurt, he thought, to let things clear off before he tried hunting. He crawled back under the covers, glad he had chosen not to stay in the tent.

By mid-morning, the guide had a pot of coffee thumping on the stove, and his guest was combing her pretty blonde hair in front of his shaving mirror. Del took the basin of warm water, now that she was finished with it, and he emptied it out of the back door. He turned off the burner beneath the coffee-pot, and as the coffee settled, he rummaged through the tableware and took out two mugs.

"You take your coffee black, don't you?" he called out.

"Yes." She stopped combing and smiled at him.

Setting the coffee in front of her, he sat across the table from her. "What would you like for breakfast?"

"Oh, the usual," she said. "Strawberry crepes and a small dish of plain yogurt."

"I do have yogurt," he answered.

"I remember, even though we didn't eat any."

John D. Nesbitt

"Same stuff. It's in the little half-pint cartons with fruit in the bottom."

She wrinkled her nose. "I don't really care for that kind."

"Actually," he said, "I don't have many takers for it."

"I would be happy with just a bowl of cold cereal."

"O.K.," he said. "That would suit me, too."

As they ate their cereal, they seemed each to fall into a separate pool of thought. For his part, Del was immersed with a sense of the woman who sat across from him, who had been intimate with him through two nights and a morning, who no longer held an aura of magic and mystery but whose being, now familiar to him, gave him a feeling of rich and renewable sensation. Desired and obtained, she was still desirable, a sensuous goddess of this island in the sea. He wasn't in a hurry to run her off.

When they had finished their cereal and were sipping more coffee, he said, "It's pretty nice out here, once the crowds have gone home."

"Yes," she said, "it's a very nice retreat." She looked around the room. "People actually used to live here, didn't they?"

"Oh, yeah. Years back."

"That's funny."

"How is it funny?"

"I don't mean funny *ha-ha*, but funny like strange or quaint."

"Oh."

"It's like when you go on vacation and see people who live in funny, out-of-the-way places or in funny ways, and it seems like they're that way just when you're there. Then later, a month or a year later, you think of them and it's hard to believe that they live like that all the time. You're back living your normal life, and they're, um, living their story-book life."

"You think that living off by yourself like this, away from it all, is that way?"

"Not exactly. But it's hard to imagine that a place like this, with no electricity or running water, and not really in a forest or the mountains, would be much of a place to live in year-round."

"Well, people did live here."

"Oh, and it's nice to visit. Your hunters probably loved it. I do too."

"Uh-huh."

"What do you mean, 'uh-huh'?"

"Just that."

"Come on now."

"Well, it seems like you think of your life in Omaha as being normal, but this kind of life as being . . . well, something we take out and put on show for the tourist season."

"This part of it is, isn't it? I mean, people don't live like *this* all the time. It's set up, isn't it?"

"I think it's something we fall into pretty easily, from time to time, without thinking about how deliberate it is."

"When you say 'from time to time,' don't you mean the tourist season?"

"I think it's more of a way of life than that. In the spring and summer I take people on pack trips. In the fall I guide hunters. In between times I scout the country, and in between all of that I pick up ranch work. A lot of the time I end up sleeping on the ground, cooking outside—and it's not always fun."

She paused before answering. "Well, I guess you do more of it than I thought, but isn't it still sort of . . . unrealistic? I mean, people out here have satellite dishes. I see them. And I'm sure they have all the other home entertainment services, along with microwave ovens and air-conditioning and home computers."

"Lots of folks do. But I can't say that I have much of the high-tech stuff. I try to stay away from it."

"I can see that, and you seem to do it honestly, the way you, I guess, avoid barriers between you and what I imagine we'd call the natural world. But you go back to the modern world, don't you?"

"Yeah, I guess so. The place I start from and go back to has electricity, a TV, a stereo—but I slip out of it and get back in touch with this other stuff without really working at it."

"But you always go back to it."

"By degrees, I guess you'd say."

She got up to poke a log into the center of the fire, and instead of sitting back down, she stood behind him, draping her arms on his chest. He felt the light pressure of her breasts against his back.

"I'm enjoying this," she said. "Let me ask you some other questions."

"Shoot."

"Do you have—let me see—a chain saw?"

"Yes."

"An electric meat grinder?"

"Yes."

"An ice-maker on your refrigerator?"

"No."

"Of course not. And no ice-crusher either."

"No."

"Electric blanket?"

"No."

"Thermostat heat?"

"Some." He turned his head to kiss her. "My turn."

"O.K."

"You came to see me, right?"

"Right."

"Because you wanted to find out."

"Yes."

"And because I'm different from . . . your typical Omaha fella."

"Yes. That, too."

"Am I real?"

She poked him in the chest. "Sure feels like it to me."

"Am I real the rest of the time, when you're not here?"

"Yes. You were, and you still will be."

"Then what I am, and what I do, at least part of what attracts you, is real, not just—"

"Cultivated. Right."

"Then deer hunting must be real, and cowboying."

She laughed. "Yes it is, and you are too, but it still seems escapist to me."

"Then what about you? Aren't you on a sort of safari, too?"

"Oh, for sure." She kissed him. "But I've got a great guide." She sat in his lap and ran the back of her index finger along his cheekbone. "Still, won't you admit that a lot of what you do is escapism?"

He pursed his lips, then said, "Yeah, and I'll do it for as long as I can get away with it."

She put her arms around his neck, pushed the tip of her nose against his, and said, "Me, too."

* * * * *

The drizzly weather began to let up in the early afternoon, but the sky remained grey and overcast. Del knew there had been enough moisture to make the trails gummy and sloppy for vehicle travel, and Sylvia did not seem excited at the prospect of a horseback ride. He understood that she had come to see him, not to avail herself of the outdoor adventures. She said she'd like to try it some time but it looked pretty clammy out there.

Del also understood that she planned to leave the next morning, go back to her room at the Wagon Wheel to clean up and check out, and then drive to Omaha. He took the day as it came to him, then, as a day unto itself, detached from what he had been doing and from what he would be doing next.

That evening, as they lay together in front of the fire in the relaxed afterglow of a session of intimacy, Sylvia said, "I don't know exactly how to say this without sounding trite."

"I'm listening."

"Well, I leave in the morning."

"Uh-huh."

"I go back to my normal life, and you stay with yours here."

"Sounds pretty likely."

"I guess the words I was avoiding are, what is going to become of us, Del?"

"I don't see myself moving to Omaha."

"No."

"Or you moving here."

"No."

"And I don't expect you to come hunt antelope."

She laughed. "No, we covered that question a while back."

He laughed with her and then shrugged. "Then I'm not sure."

"Del?"

"Yeah?"

"Would you want to see me again?"

"Of course," he said, knowing that his answer might have been too quick.

"Are you sure?"

"Well, yes, I *am* sure." Yet as he said it, he knew he was saying what was easiest at the moment.

"What we've had together has been very fine, Del. It's been more than just a safari or adventure. I wouldn't want to think that we couldn't see each other again if we wanted to."

"I guess we could."

217

"Would you want to?"

"Yes, I would."

"I would, too."

He paused and said, "Of course there'd be other things to take into consideration."

"You mean Vince, don't you?"

"Yes, I do."

"I don't know about Vince. We haven't gotten along very well for the last year. I thought that coming on this trip with him might help our relationship, but I think he just wanted a vacation, and when he wasn't getting what he wanted, he sent me home."

"Do you really think he has himself a . . . companion?"

"Oh, I don't know. Maybe I just want to think that. But I'm pretty sure he's got one some place."

"Either way, whether he does or he doesn't, I'm a little gun-shy about another man's wife."

"You weren't when I drove out here the first night."

He waited to frame his answer. "I know. I wasn't as concerned about principles at the time."

"You mean that in principle you don't want to get involved with another man's wife."

He nodded. "That's a clear way of putting it."

"But that in practice, you don't mind."

He was silent for a long moment before saying, "I think I'd have to agree with you on that."

"And now that you've had the practice, you want to go back to the principle."

Her phrasing stung him. It was a hard point to deny. "You make me feel like I'm being cross-examined," he said.

"I'm sorry," she said, relaxing on his shoulder. "Maybe I was being too pushy. I just wanted to know if we would see one another again if we wanted to—that is, if I wanted to, I guess. I wondered if you'd try to keep me at a distance. But then again, maybe neither of us will want it."

"It's hard to tell which way it will go," he answered, "but I don't see myself wanting to slam the door on it as soon as you get into your car tomorrow."

"I didn't want it to be that way either," she said, as she nestled closer.

Del kissed her on the forehead. This was a good way to be, on friendly terms, even if it was talk for the time being. Being amiable seemed imperative to the way things were between them—they needed to agree that they had a good understanding. The agreeing would make things easier.

Chapter Twenty

In the morning when Sylvia was gone again, the charm was gone as well. When she was around, Del wanted her to be there. He wanted to be compatible; he wanted to run the risks of keeping up their acquaintance and finding out more about what clicked between them. During her visit, he had been in a mood, a sort of spell that had allowed him to flow along. He could see he had taken the easy way instead of breaking things off when he had the chance. He had felt free from the world that lay beyond the ranch and the nearby plains. Now with her gone, he felt the world closing in on him again. It was not a good feeling to have the sense that consequences might come, the sense that if they did, they would be of his making.

One thing she had said returned to nag him. She liked the way he had handled Vince. Vince the master. Yes, Vince had liked the way Del handled the other two hunters, had liked Del's mastery until it came his way. Now, as Del squared with himself, he had to admit he had enjoyed handling Vince and he had enjoyed where it had gotten him. But it wasn't a free and open adventure all the way—it had the attachment of a power struggle, a game to see who could be the master. The game was a small part of it, but a part nevertheless, and not pleasant to recognize. It had seemed like a strong thing to do, but really, he had weakened to the pull of it all—attracting the woman, overcoming the other man, winning the woman from him.

The sun was shining as he saddled Little Tulip and started out on the trail. It was late in the morning to be setting out on a serious hunt, but he wanted to be in the sage and cedar, away from the buildings. As he rode along the trail, the world materialized around him and became tangible. He realized that if things came to their worst pass again, he would have jeopardized all of this—his relation to the world that had taken him back. It was a clean world of dirt and water, plant and beast, where he had recently felt free. As for the interlude with Sylvia—it had not been freedom but a flash in the pan that looked like the real thing. He had let her in and crowded Rita out.

He knew that even if he continued the affair—a risky campaign at best—he couldn't bring her into his world and have her take it on its terms. She was of a different world and would stay that way, coming to this place only on safari if at all. He knew that, just as he knew he wouldn't leave this place for her. Theirs had been a pretty picnic, and with a little luck they might be able to keep it that way.

His thoughts turned back to Rita and to the same question. Could he really have her and all of this, too? Rita was not a barefoot nature girl herself, but Del knew her well enough to know that she was compatible with the way he got by. Although she didn't hunt and didn't ride much, she understood those things as a way of life rather than as a pageant. She preferred to stay in town because the winters were not so rough and the summers were not so dusty; she had gotten used to central heating and soft water. Like a great many people who lived in town, she had grown up on a farm and knew the rhythms of the country. She still knew by heart the things that a person didn't forget—when the snakes came out, when the last cutting of hay came in, when the chokecherries were ripe on Horseshoe Creek, when the wild geese flew.

Little Tulip stopped. Three antelope flashed tawny bright in the morning sun and wheeled away to the southeast. This was the same place he had seen antelope on the first morning of deer season, just four days earlier, when they had reminded him of Sylvia. He patted the mare's neck and said, "Good eye, girl," then touched his heels to her flanks.

Yes, Rita was all right. She knew what he was about, knew it by feel. Not that that was the only important thing about a woman, how easily she accepted a man's ways, but that was the main issue now as he clip-clopped along, hoping to kill his deer and get back to town as he'd told her he would. She was a good woman, and he wouldn't want to lose her, not over something that was here and gone. He had rationalized that he and Rita did not have a spoken agreement not to see anyone else, but now he admitted to himself that he had done wrong by her. He told himself that maybe this episode would make him appreciate her more, but he saw where that idea was coming from, too. He wanted things both ways, and he didn't regret the fling with Sylvia—not yet.

He hunted through the middle part of the day, lunching on leftovers and trying to keep women out of his mind. Somewhere along three in the afternoon, the idea hit him that Rita might know he had company. Uneasiness settled into him like a certainty. Sylvia had asked at the hardware store and had taken a room at the Wagon Wheel. The word could have gotten to Rita by the time Sylvia had stepped out of her car in the moonlight. A chill went through him. That would be bad. Rita was no fool, and she wouldn't let Del walk all over her—that was the way she might see it, and with good reason.

If the golden goddess had lost her glow, and if the change had brought him to the feeling that he was on the verge of losing Rita, he couldn't patch things up merely by telling her that he had come to his senses. No, if he was in trouble it was his fault, and he would not be in control of whatever mending he might hope for.

The late afternoon hunt seemed also to have lost some of its enchantment. Knowing where the deer might be, Del sneaked and peeked in his favorite draws and hidey-holes until he came upon a medium-sized forked horn buck. With the decision already made that he was hunting to fill his tag as soon as possible, he drew down on the deer and killed it. The field-dressing, the fetching of the pickup, the return to camp, and the skinning made up a smooth succession of workman-like tasks.

It was late in the evening when he had finished his work, tended to the horses, cleaned himself up, and made another meal of leftovers. He fidgeted, now sitting in a chair by the fire, now getting up to tidy or pack some part of the camp kit he wouldn't need in the morning. It was too late to go into town this evening and check on how things were with Rita. He would stay tonight, move his gear and critters tomorrow, and face the music when he and Rita had finished their day's work.

He decided to sleep inside, where it would be warmer. Before he turned in, he went to check the horses. All three were munching hay. Their forms stood out sharply in the clear night, and their warm smell drifted in the chilling air. Tomorrow would have them back at the home place again, to loaf for a few days until the elk season started. Spud would stay with him for the interval, hogging the feed as always. Del climbed into the corral and patted Spud, then Whisker. He scratched Little Tulip around the base of her ears, and he said out loud, "You're all right. All of you."

He went inside and went to bed. The last clear thought he had was of something he had forgotten to explain to Kenny Kerr, that it was always better to cut through a deer hide from the inside out. But that was O.K. The Kerrs would be back next year, and he'd tell him then.

* * * * *

His deer was cold and firm in the morning. Del left it hanging in the lean-to as he struck camp and loaded the truck. When he was ready to go, he took down the deer. The carcass rode to town in the front seat, dry and cool in the muslin bag. Del thought he would eat well this winter, even if it was always alone.

When he had finished his second trip, he tended to such details as hauling the garbage and filling the propane bottles. In his usual routine he would go to the bank on this day, but when the image of Rita presented itself, he decided to let that chore wait until the next day. When he drove past the Wagon

Wheel, he was relieved to see that the car with Nebraska plates was not there. He thought Sylvia should be back in Omaha by now.

Del called Rita at a time when he knew she would be done with dinner. When she answered the phone, he put on a cheerful voice. "Hello, Rita?"

Her tone was non-committal. "I was wondering when you would call."

"I just finished hauling everything back today. Got the last deer killed yesterday afternoon. Mine."

"Uh-huh."

"You don't sound happy."

"I'm not sure if I'm supposed to."

"Oh."

"What am I supposed to say?"

"You could ask me if I got a nice deer."

"Did you?"

"Not really. Just so-so."

"Oh." She was quiet for a long moment, and then she said, "All of your out-of-staters have gone back, have they?"

"Um, yes. I have a little time now before the elk hunters get here. I thought I'd give you a call."

"Did you figure I'd just be sittin' around waitin' for you to call?"

"Well . . . no."

"What do you think?"

"About what?"

"About anything. The weather."

"I don't know what to think." Del pursed his lips.

225

John D. Nesbitt

"I know what I think."

"What's that?"

"I think you got a lot of damn nerve, that's what I think."

"Oh. Sounds like word got around here well enough."

"What in the hell would you think? You know how this town is. You run out of toilet paper, and you'd just as well put it on the front page."

"I know. I'm sorry." He paused and said, "I wasn't expecting her to show up."

"Don't make things worse, Del."

"What do you mean?"

"Don't try to tell me that everything would be all right if you'd known ahead of time and kept it all on the *q.t.*"

"That's not what I meant."

"What did you mean?"

"I meant . . . that I didn't have anything planned. It just happened. I wasn't expecting to stand you up."

"You didn't stand me up. You got back about as soon as I expected, as far as that goes."

"Hmmh."

"No, you didn't stand me up. You just made me look like a fool, on top of everything else."

"I'm sorry."

"Sorry. You feel sorry and I feel . . . I don't know. I guess I feel . . . cheap."

"I don't think you should feel that way."

"How should I feel? You put me on a par with . . ."

"With what?"

226

"With . . . some little thing with hot pants for the Marlboro man."

"That's not exactly how it was."

"I don't want any details."

"I'm sorry."

"You know who you sound like?"

"Who?"

"Jewel. When he'd go chippie around, he'd come back and apologize up and down. Said he'd just had a case of the dumb-ass, and now he felt like pure hell."

"I'm sorry."

"Don't say that."

"What do you want me to do?"

"Call back in a couple of days, Del."

"I'll do that." Del set the receiver in its cradle and looked at the wall clock. It was a little after eight, and the evening loomed long and empty ahead of him. He didn't want to sit by the phone all night, wondering if Rita or the elk hunters would call, so he made sure the answering machine was working before he left for the bar.

* * * * *

Sitting in the Silver Spur was easy work, once he got over the feeling that everyone knew what he had been up to and what he had gotten himself into. At first it seemed as if everyone looked at him knowingly, but as the evening wore on, he lost the self-consciousness and took on the easy air of a man who was at liberty to drink in the middle of the week.

227

There might be some folks in the bar who knew some part of his recent story, but there were few of them who would be bothered by it. He made an honest living, paid his own way, bought rounds when it came to him, and minded his own business. He had a nodding acquaintance with the cattle buyers and tractor salesmen who frequented the Silver Spur, and he was on conversational terms with the fraternity of feedlot cowboys, horseshoers, truck drivers, backhoe opera-tors, and mechanics who kept the cash register ringing and who in turn minded their own business. It was easy to make talk with them, to answer that the hunting season was going well, to ask how affairs prospered in the world of horse hooves or diesel engines.

As he dropped in and out of conversation with the other men, Del was troubled by thoughts of Vince. Justify it as he might—that Vince was an overbearing lord, that Sylvia had made the actual overture, that it would have happened with someone else if it hadn't happened with him—he could not escape the knowledge that he'd done the man wrong. He hadn't felt that way with the first guy, the guy he had punched all the way out. Back then, it had seemed like bad business, unwise actions with a bad outcome. Now, with the outcome yet to be seen, he felt actual remorse at having done a wrong, regardless of how much the other man seemed to deserve it.

By and by, Del found himself held in a conversation with a man he had not met before, a short man with a dark beard, a full head of dark hair, and a pair of beady eyes. He worked for the highway department and was recently divorced, said he didn't give a damn if he ever got attached to a woman again.

He was glad to be single, glad to be shut of that day-in and day-out routine. His work took him all over the state. You had to be careful who you went home with these days—you could die just as miserable as the queers and the junkies. Most people didn't drive worth a damn when they had quite a bit to drink, but he was a good driver even when he was snockered. Had to be—it was his work. One thing that helped was knowing how to drive with your fingertips. Really. You had a lot more control then, and it was easier to keep your attention focused. It made a difference. There was nothing wrong with getting something strange every time you went out. Hell, he'd probably gotten laid in every town in the state. But the things you could catch these days took a lot of the fun out of it. Chasing women wasn't what it used to be. If a guy really wanted to place some smart money he'd take San Francisco for the Super Bowl. It ought to be easy to get takers with all these Bronco Fans. It's hard to believe they're advertising condoms right on the damn teevee. Hell, it wasn't that long ago that a guy had to ask for them at the prescription counter. Now they were out on display and advertised like chapstick.

When the man slid off his bar stool for a trip to the men's room, Del made his getaway. The clock behind the bar showed a few minutes past midnight. Del walked out into the cool air, climbed into his pickup, and got it going. When he was out of town, he experimented with the technique of driving with just his fingertips. His control didn't seem improved, and furthermore, he doubted whether the man with the beady eyes would be picky at all if he could only talk a woman into leaving the bar with him.

229

When he parked the pickup and went into the house, the red light was flashing on his answering machine. All night long as he had sat in the bar, he had nourished the hope that Rita might show up, but of course she hadn't. Now he had a call waiting on the tape. He pushed the replay button, and when the message began, the voice was not Rita's at all. It belonged to the lawyer from Omaha, and it was not friendly.

"Del, this is Vince Furtino calling. I wanted to tell you in person that I think you're a low-down sonofabitch, but I'll leave you this message anyway. I'm not done with you, Del. People don't get away with the kind of dirt you pulled on me. You're a sniveling two-faced sonofabitch, and you'd better be looking over your shoulder from now on. That's all I've got to say for right now."

Vince's was the only message on the machine.

Chapter Twenty-One

On the day after the truculent phone message, Del went about getting things ready for the next excursion and thinking about the work ahead. The elk hunters would be returnees, four fellows from Wisconsin. They were in their early fifties, and they all went to the same church. That was something Del had learned right away, even though their religion and their church activities didn't figure into the conversations very much after that. Del couldn't remember which religion theirs was, except that it wasn't Lutheran. He remembered the first time he'd met them, two years earlier, when they pulled into his camp in their Jeep Wagoneer. When they got out of the vehicle, they all had blaze-orange hats and coats, standard regalia for Wisconsin. Del's first impression was that they looked like a squad of umpires.

It had been their first year out to the high country and elk hunting. They were staying in a motel in Saratoga and hunting on their own, and after seeing Del's camp, they decided they would like to book him for the next season. So they came out the next year, stayed the full seventeen days, and didn't fire a shot. They went home happy nevertheless, and shortly after New Year they called Del to make reservations for this season.

They did not like to walk long distances, so they drove to a spot near to where they would hunt, and they would do as they did when they hunted Wisconsin whitetail—walk a ways, sit for a while, walk a ways further, sit some more. They were not all that taken with horseback riding, but each of them went on a couple of horseback hunts, as if in obligation to the general spirit of guided hunts as detailed in the hunting magazines. The cold weather didn't seem to bother them, nor did they seem to mind hunting day after day without ever getting a shot. For the most part, they employed Del to run the camp and to take care of whatever meat they might bring down. Sometimes they followed his advice on where to hunt, and sometimes they followed their own notions—all with equal success.

Overall they were an even-tempered bunch, not very interesting or exciting, but easy enough to get along with. And as full-term paying guests, they were of appreciable value to the guide. He would have liked to go back to packing into wilderness areas for elk, but for the past few years, his work had kept him in areas accessible by vehicle. That was all right; it was what his clients wanted, and as long as he had an agreeable arrangement with them, it was fine. It would still be a welcome retreat, he told himself, to go to the high country and stay there for a couple of weeks, busying himself with the daily chores of cooking meals, washing dishes, gathering firewood, tending to the horses, and guiding the hunters as they felt the need. Business was business, and he would try to go back to keeping it that way.

Even though the elk hunting camp would be within half a mile of a well-traveled National Forest road, he imagined it as an isolated refuge far from the telephone line and highway that linked him with Vince, Sylvia, and the complications he had let himself into. He wondered whether the lawyer had stayed in Wyoming and gotten his knowledge long distance, or whether he had gone back to Omaha and expressed his contempt from there.

All that day as Del was getting things ready for the elk hunt, he had the urge to call Sylvia for the state of affairs as she saw it. He wanted to call, but not knowing her number at work, he would have to call before or after work hours, at a time when the indignant husband might answer the phone. Del decided to wait until elk season was over. Maybe the interval would let things settle and cool, and then, if he still felt the need, he could take his chances at calling her.

The elk expedition might also be good for letting Rita's smoldering resentment burn out. Maybe she would even take to missing him before he got back. He smiled at his own optimism. He had barely finished offending her the night before, and here he was sketching out her forgiveness. She might just tell him to go to hell and stay there.

* * * * *

Two days after his first call, he coaxed himself into calling again. He told himself Rita had suggested it. He dialed her number, and when she answered, he said, "Hello, Rita. This is Del."

"I know your voice, Del."

"How are you today?"

"I'm all right. How about yourself?"

"Well enough. I'm getting ready to take out my next bunch of hunters."

"Elk hunters," she said, in a tone that said she knew things about him.

"That's right. Same four that hunted with me last year. The four guys from Wisconsin."

"When do you meet up with them?"

"Not until Wednesday. I'll take my camp and set it up, and I'll take one horse. Then I'll come back for groceries and the other two horses, and I'll meet them in Laramie on Wednesday morning."

"Uh-huh."

Rita didn't seem talkative, so Del talked some more. "They'll drive out from Wisconsin and stay overnight in Laramie. I can meet them there and convoy them up to camp."

"Uh-huh."

"They stayed the full season last year. I wouldn't be surprised if they did it again."

"You just leave the horse there by itself?"

"Yeah. I'll take my gelding, Whisker, on the first trip. He does real well by himself. I'll rig a rope corral in a little stand of trees there, and I'll leave him plenty of hay and water. He'll do fine."

"He won't get shot for an elk."

"Season won't be open yet. I tie orange ribbons all over the tree branches anyway, and my whole camp set-up should be obvious, too."

"Oh. Where was the blonde from?"

"Um . . . Omaha."

234

"I knew that. I mean where did you know her from?"

"She and her husband hunted antelope with me."

"I thought you knew better than that."

"I should have. I usually do."

"Did they come out this year?"

"Yes. They were part of that first group I had."

"You didn't tell me about them."

"I will. Actually, they make a pretty interesting story."

"No doubt."

"I meant the hunting."

"That's all I expected you to mean."

"Anyway . . ."

"Anyway . . ."

"I was wondering if you'd like to go out for dinner or something in the next couple of days."

"It's nice of you to ask, Del."

"But . . ."

"But I think I'd just as soon wait."

"Oh."

"I appreciate you asking, but I'd rather wait."

"Until I get back?"

"Something like that. Put a little time between . . . one thing and another."

"O.K."

"Del, I'm having a hard time with this."

"I understand."

"Maybe you do."

"Is there something else you wanted to say, or something you wanted to ask?"

"Does it seem like it?" Her voice sounded neutral, neither resentful nor encouraging.

"I don't know, but if there's something to face up to now, I'd just as soon do it."

"Del," she said, and her voice quavered as if she were starting to cry. "Damn it, why do you do something like that?"

"I don't know."

"Just a case of the dumb ass?"

"Not just, but it's dumb enough. Actually, I've thought about it a little bit. I guess I did it because I wanted to."

"You wanted to."

"Well, I guess you want things in different ways."

"*You* do."

"When I say you, I mean me. It's like a little bug inside, working against what you know is best. It's like wanting what you can't have, or what you're not supposed to have, or what's not good for you. But you want it, and you want to get away with it."

"Ego."

"Well, selfish. Yeah. The want-to crowds out the ought-to."

"And you still want to be with her?"

"No, not really."

"You didn't think about how any of it might come back on you?"

"You don't think about that part soon enough, I imagine."

"*You* don't."

"No, I didn't. But now I do. I realize I've jeopardized things with you."

"Do you really?"

"I imagine you're pretty down on me."

"I don't know if you know how much."

"I guess quite a bit."

"Del, right now when I think about you, I think about a man who chippies around and gets in trouble for it. This woman has a husband, doesn't she?"

"Yes, she does."

"Well, what about him?"

"He's mad."

"Of course he is."

"He's a jerk, too. He pissed me off before anything ever happened."

"There are women that piss me off, too, but I don't take their husbands to bed."

"I can tell I'm just making this worse. I wasn't trying to make it into his fault. And you said you didn't want details."

"And I don't. I just wanted to know why you do something like that and whether you think about the consequences."

"Well, I guess we covered that. It was better than not talking about it at all."

"Maybe I didn't sound very nice."

"You did earlier, but this was probably better."

"If you say so."

"I guess that's probably about it for right now, then."

"I suppose. I've got things to do, and you've got another hunt to go on."

"Yeah, like I said earlier. And don't worry about the horse. He does just fine by himself."

"I'm sure he will. You be careful, now."

"I'll be thinking about you, Rita. Tell Mickey I said hi."

"I will."

"I'll call you when I get back."

"Take care, Del."

He let out a heavy breath as he hung up the receiver. All was not lost. It could have been a lot worse. He thought of Rita, sitting on her couch with a troubled look on her face. He realized it was more serious than hurting her feelings and making her mad, although he had done that, too. He could be making both their lives miserable, spoiling what they could have between them. He thought of Mickey. There was a lot there, with Rita. He was glad not to have lost it and all that went with it—not yet. He told himself he would be careful.

* * * * *

Whisker was a quiet, obedient horse. He was solid and dependable but not remarkable—not endearing like Little Tulip and not amusing like Spud. Just a good horse, he loaded into the trailer with no trouble, and he traveled well.

When Del unloaded him at camp, he stood tied to the end of the horse trailer and watched as Del set up the corral and the two tents. He munched the granola bar that the guide gave him, and he watched with a placid stare as the pickup and trailer rolled away. Del kept an eye on the rear-view mirror until the road turned.

* * * * *

That night, back in his own bed at the home corral, Del thought of Whisker standing hipshot and complacent in the cold mountain night. Then he thought of the others, people, fixed like stickpins here and there on the map. Rita was in town, close but out of reach. Sylvia was in Omaha, sleeping near a telephone if she was not up late arguing with Vince. The lawyer, in turn, might be there or here or somewhere in between, a pinhead moving on the map. The Wisconsin hunters would be checked into their motel in Laramie by now, camped on the interstate that led west to the Kerrs, east to the Furtinos. Wherever Vince was, he was probably not making people happy around him.

Del awoke long before the alarm was to go off, and he lay in the cool darkness to sort out his dreams. In one, Sylvia was renewing their debate from the hunting cabin, asking if he had a microwave oven. In another dream, unconnected with the first one in any way Del could recall, Vince appeared. He had merged identities with the man who worked with the highway department, and he was trying to talk Del into playing shuffleboard for money. That was funny. There wasn't a bar in town that had a shuffleboard. Del almost laughed in the early morning stillness. Vince and his counterpart got around a lot more than he did, so they would know where the shuffleboards were.

Del was on the road by seven that morning, the beginning of a cold, grey day. The weather forecasts, which were frequent and variable this time of the year, predicted snow for the mountains. That was all right. He had the tents and the corral set up already, so all they had to do was get there. A bad storm could shut down travel, but there was no sense worrying about that in advance.

The sky was starting to spit snow when he pulled into Laramie, and the gasoline nozzle was winter cold as he gassed up the pickup. The weather was always colder in Laramie. As he drove from the gas station to the motel, he saw young people walking to classes at the university. Long wool coats were in style this year with the college girls. He smiled. Omaha probably had rugged winters too, but he couldn't imagine Sylvia as anything but a foreigner here. The isolation, the altitude, the piercing frigid winds of the mountain plains—it all brought out a hardy cheerfulness in the young men and women who, having gathered from the far-flung corners of the state, partied outside in the dead of winter and laughed when their cars wouldn't start.

The elk hunters were packed and ready to go, and after a round of hand-shaking, they got into the Jeep Wagoneer and followed Del out of town. The road to Centennial and over the mountain was still reported to be open, so he held to his original plan and headed west out of Laramie. Snow was falling heavily enough to melt on the windshield and be slushed aside by the wipers, but it wasn't piling up on the ground. Not far from the highway, he saw a herd of antelope moving one step at a time, grazing as the snow fell around them.

When he arrived in Centennial, he pulled into the parking lot of the steak house on the left side of the highway. He wanted to take a look at the horses and get some coffee for himself. His hunters had parked next to him, and two of them went to use the rest room. He opened the upper side door of the trailer and poked his nose in to see the horses. The sweet smell of hay, horse breath, and sweat rushed his nostrils, and Spud snuffled. Everything looked all right, so Del closed the peep door. As he was latching it, he heard a voice he recognized.

"I thought I might find you somewhere out here."

The guide turned and looked into the hard-set face of the lawyer from Omaha. The man was not wearing his glasses, and his eyes looked cold as slate.

"Hello, Vince," Del said. "Are you hunting elk in this country?"

"I might be. Maybe I'm just scouting for two-faced sons-of-bitches."

"Then I take it you think you found one."

"You take it right."

Del told himself to keep cool. "What's on your mind, Vince?"

"What in the hell do you think?"

"What I mean is," Del said, taking a deliberate breath to keep from firing up, "what do you have in mind when you come looking for me?"

"As much as I need to tell you is, I know where you are, and I know a little bit about you."

"Is that right."

"Yes, that's right. For one thing, I've had half a notion to drop a hint to a game warden about that little cover-up you did for that twirpy insurance agent."

241

John D. Nesbitt

"They weren't the only ones who violated a law."

"No, you did, too."

"I meant you, Vince."

"We had permits to cover what we shot. That other guy didn't, you helped him cover up, and then took the extra money he gave you. That's not very becoming conduct for a licensed guide."

Del was aware of the two hunters returning to the Wagoneer. A glance told him that the windows were down and all four hunters could pick up the conversation. He looked at the thumb and first two fingers of his left hand, which had picked up road grit from the door latch on the horse trailer. With his thumb, he rubbed the grit across his fingertips, and then he settled his gaze on the lawyer. "That's not a fair way to re-tell it, and you know it."

Vince had his mouth turned down in an expression of disdain. "Fair? Where do you get off talking about being fair?"

"Well, go ahead and turn me in, then, if that's what you need to make you feel better." Del looked at his fingertips again and then returned to the lawyer.

"No, I'm not going to. I could, but I won't."

"O.K." Del sensed that Vince had more cards to play. "So you have that to hold over me."

"That's not all I know about you."

"I'd imagine you know more."

Vince raised his eyebrows. "Uh-huh. Like a little barroom fight you got into a while back. With a Mr. Bentley."

"That's really none of your business, Vince. But, yeah, it's public record. I've got nothing to hide about it. I hit a man. He

242

died. I paid for it. I lost my ass when it was all done." Del cut the air sideways with his flat right hand, as if to say, "That's that."

"Maybe it wasn't my business, but it is now. You got into that jackpot because you were screwing the guy's wife. You don't like me saying that, do you? Well, you were. Yeah, you paid for it, but you didn't learn much."

Del was taking deep breaths, trying to maintain his composure. He could tell that Vince felt he had the upper hand, felt he had Del on the run. There was not going to be an easy way out of this. "Go ahead, Vince," he said, with his palms open. "You've got the dirt that there is about me, and you want to rub it in a little more, is that it?"

Vince sneered. "I'm not going to do anything with it. It's just a nice thing to know, to help me understand you a little better."

"Well, good for you."

"It helps me understand you. I don't feel threatened or intimidated, once I know what a fool you are."

"Is that right."

"Yep. A hot-blooded fool."

Del was shaking. He clenched his teeth and told himself not to let it get to him; he deserved to have to listen to some of this. Taking a deep breath, he said, "Don't you be a fool, Vince, any more than you have been."

The lawyer smiled and shook his head in a light, slow motion. "Don't worry about me, Del. Worry about yourself."

Del frowned at him without speaking back.

"Worry about yourself and how poorly you learn."

"Hmmh."

"You should have known better than to screw my wife."

The action happened by itself. Del's fist came up and found its mark, smashing solid against the man's cheekbone and sliding across his damp face where snowflakes had collected and melted in his beard. Time hung suspended for a moment in which all the world fell away and there was only this, a man needing to be hit and the need taking care of itself. Then the man was on the ground and the world came back, a world of cold wet falling snow, a gritty horse trailer, a Jeep Wagoneer with four paying clients who had listened and watched, a tingling right fist that had done what it should never do, and the man on the wet ground fingering his left jaw.

With cold, controlled hatred in his eyes, the man on the ground looked up at the man who had hit him. "You should have known better than that, too," he said. "You don't learn a damn thing, do you?"

Chapter Twenty-Two

On the first evening in camp, Del served hamburgers, bean with bacon soup, and fried potatoes. The bigger of the two tents served as a sleeping area for the four hunters and as a kitchen area where Del cooked and served meals. There wasn't a great deal of room to move around in, and sometimes the air became close and thick, but overall the arrangement was a good one. The tent walls did a halfway decent job of holding the heat that was generated by two propane lanterns and the cook stove, so that the place was warm when the hunters went to bed and again when they got up for breakfast. When the weather turned really cold, Del would use a propane heater. For the present, the interior of the tent was comfortable.

The hunters, who had been puttering around with their duffel bags and sleeping gear, sat in the close-crowded camp chairs and made cheerful talk as they ate their meal. Del felt they were being courteous in light of the incident in Centennial, and he imagined how Roger must have felt as he sat in camp with people who knew what he had done and who made obvious efforts to talk around it.

This evening the main topic of discussion was whether propane camping equipment was superior to white gas equipment. Harry, the man who more or less assumed the role of group leader, advocated propane. Del assumed that Harry grew a beard every year at about this time, for Del had never known him to have a beard that was in full growth. It was a thick but not handsome salt-and-pepper beard that needed trimming along the neck and under the ears. Harry's eyelids drooped over the outer corners of his eyes, and that feature, coupled with his tendency to poke and probe the emerging beard with his right index finger, gave him the air of being worldly wise and not yet weary. When he spoke of the virtues of propane, he did so with quiet authority. After explaining that propane burned cleaner, was not as messy to handle, came in containers already pressurized, and could run several appliances off of one tank as well as off of separate canisters, he rested his case.

He gave the impression that anyone who disagreed with him could be assumed to be a fool, but that opposing points of view were welcome nevertheless. The man who defended white gas and thereby represented the opposing platform in the debate was named Bob. His face was clean shaven and probably always had been. He wore thick bifocals and had a square-shaped mouth with lips the color of drained liver. In spite of his expression, he was a friendly, conversational man who seemed always to be waterproofing a pair of boots, dismantling the bolt of his rifle, laying out the inventory of his day pack, or sharpening a knife that had not had a chance to go dull. This evening he was studying the literature that accompanied a one-burner white gas stove that he had bought at a great bargain in Laramie. "From an economical point of view," he said, "a fellow can get an incredibly greater amount of heat and light from white gas. Just look at this chart."

"Keep the chart," Harry said. "I believe that you'll get more fuel and energy per penny. But I've had propane for years, and I'll stay that way."

"Well, I've had them too," Bob returned, "and I got tired of always having to carry an extra bottle or canister. You never know when you're about to run out. With white gas you can shake the damn thing, and you can fill up when you want to and not run out of fuel in the middle of a job." He held his prize in his left palm as he plinked his right forefingernail on the fuel reservoir.

Harry scratched the neck area of his beard. "Well, that's just fine. But it's sloppy and smelly, not to mention dangerous, to be gurgling white gas out of a can. I hope you don't have any intentions of doing it in here."

"I wouldn't mind firing it up in the evening," Bob answered, "but if it makes you feel better, I'll fill it outside." He smiled at the other two hunters and at Del, as if he had just won a minor point. He unzipped the tent flap and stepped out into the cold, snowy night.

"I wish he'd just leave that stupid stove alone," Harry said. "But I guess this is the only way to settle it."

Phil, who had been drinking coffee and looking over the hunting regulations, said, "Oh, you know how Bob is. Once he gets a notion he won't let go. Huh, Leonard?"

Leonard was reading a novel about the Korean War, a paperback novel which he held up to the light with his right hand. "Nah," he said, "he's not doing any harm. Let him play with his little toy."

With his left hand, he turned a page, and then he resumed plucking his mustache.

Del was finishing the dishes when Bob came back inside.

"Ready to go," he said, holding the stove up as if it were a pie or a cake.

"Cold out there?" Phil asked.

"Yeah. Not bad, though."

"Still snowing?"

"About the same. Say, Del, how about if I set this stove on the table here?"

"Sure."

"I'd like to try it out, maybe heat a little water for hot chocolate."

"Sure. I'll get this dishpan out of the way." Del put on a hat and coat, then stepped outside to fling the dishwater. Snow was falling in its quiet, soft way, as it gathered to form a blanket on the ground and on the vehicles. Del liked the looks of it. Fresh snow, in addition to moving the animals around, made it easy to read recent traffic, be it animal or human. When the snow melted, the soft ground itself would be readable. As he thought of the frosted mountains all around him, it occurred to him that somewhere out there, maybe not far at all, there lurked a sullen man—a man out of spirit with the shaggy elk that huddled in the timber, out of spirit with the hopeful hunters who would take to the timber in the morning, reading tracks and leaving their own.

Del frowned. The lawyer was arrogant and vindictive, no doubt about that, but he had his justification. Del nodded his head in recognition of the truth, gave the dishpan another shake, and went back into the tent.

As soon as he stood inside, the effects of the white gas stove burned his eyes and nostrils. "Boy," he said, "that little stove puts out some strong fumes."

"That's what I tried to tell him," Harry said, "but he wants to heat his little pan of water."

Leonard put down his book. "I would bet," he said, as if he was used to being heeded, "I would bet that if you read that literature carefully, there would be something in there about not running that thing in a closed area."

Bob gave him a scowl. "Well, I'll shut the damn thing off."

"You'd better take it outside, too," Leonard answered. "Those things smell the worst when you've just shut them off."

Phil was folding up the hunting regulations. "That's okay, Bob. You've got plenty of time to try it out when the weather clears. We'll be here for a while."

"I guess," he muttered, setting the saucepan aside and picking up the stove. Phil unzipped the tent flap for him, and he stepped outside.

Harry looked at his watch. "Hmh. Nine o'clock. Just about time for a nightcap. Phil, if you push me my valise over here, I bet I can find us some brandy. Del, I'd bet you could go for a little nip."

"I think you're right." Del felt that he was getting an invitation to say something like "It's been a long day," but instead of saying anything he took five clear plastic glasses from the camp kit and set them on the table.

Harry poured a generous two fingers of brandy into each glass and handed out the drinks as he poured them.

Bob came back into the tent and accepted his. "Thanks, Harry."

"You're welcome." When each man had a glass in his hand, Harry proposed the toast. "Here's to a good season."

Del raised his glass in salute with the others as they all said, "Here!"

Harry took a sip, puckered and licked his lips, and said, "I think it's going to be a good season."

When the ceremony of the nightcap reached its end, Del rounded up the glasses and gave them a quick rinse. He knew from the year before that each man would take his turn instituting the nightcap, following a rotation that would bring the brandy bottle out of Harry's valise in four nights from now. Knowing also that the nightcap was the ritual closing out of the evening, he stood up to leave. "I've got a little checking up to do," he said. "I'm going out on an errand for a while, so if you hear the pickup come and go, don't think anything of it."

Harry stared at him. "You're not scouting elk at this time of night, are you?"

"Nah. I've got other things to check on, too."

"Oh. Um-hmh. O.K. See you in the morning."

Del didn't like to make the drive so soon after getting settled in camp, especially while snow was still falling, but he knew he had to talk to Sylvia before he bumped into Vince again, and he had a better chance of reaching her at night than in the daytime. Saratoga would be a little closer than Centennial, so he drove there in less than hour to find a pay phone.

Sylvia answered, sounding sleepy.

"Hello, Sylvia. This is Del."

"Del. Just a minute. O.K. I've got a light on now. I wasn't expecting you to call. I thought you'd be off in the mountains by now."

"I am. But something came up, and I thought I should give you a call."

"I'm glad you did. What is it that came up?"

"I saw Vince."

"Oh."

"He wasn't very nice."

"I wouldn't think so. What did he do?"

"He told me he did some checking up on my past. He dug up some dirt about me."

"That sounds like Vince."

"Anyway, he threw that in my face, and he said he had half a mind to turn me in for helping Roger and Mel cover up that violation."

"Anything else?"

"I hit him."

"You did? Why?" She sounded as if he'd reported something more preposterous, like buying a home computer.

"He went a little too far. Didn't shut up soon enough."

"Vince isn't much for settling things with his fists," she said, still with a tone of surprise.

251

"Well, he didn't. It wasn't much of a fight. Just one punch, from me to him."

"Where did you see him?"

"In a little town called Centennial, up in the mountains out of Laramie."

"I thought he might try to find you when he went back out there."

"He was home, then?"

"Oh, yes. He was here when I got back from visiting you. He had been calling at all hours of the day and night, and there was no answer, so he came back to find out what was going on."

"So you more or less had a conversation about what you'd been up to."

"You might say he browbeat it out of me."

"He must have called from there."

"Huh?"

"He called a few days back, and he left me an unfriendly message on my answering machine."

"You have one of those?"

"For all the good it seems to be doing me."

"Del?"

"Yeah?"

"I think he wants to get even. He doesn't like to lose."

"I'd believe that. I've got a feeling I haven't seen the last of him."

"Where are you calling from?"

"A town not too far from where I've got my camp set up."

"Then you've started with a new group of hunters."

"That's right. Season opens in the morning."

"The fifteenth. That's what Vince said."

"Then he's hunting elk here?"

"As far as I know."

"Well, I wouldn't be surprised to see him again."

"Del, be careful."

"Oh, I won't hurt him."

"I meant be careful for yourself."

"Oh, I will."

"Del?"

"Yes?"

"Do you mind if I ask what kind of dirt he got on you?"

"No, I don't mind. He didn't tell you?"

"We didn't talk much."

"Well, he's liable to drag it out sooner or later, so you might as well hear it from me." He heard her let out a heavy breath on her end of the line. Then he said, "Ready for it?"

"Yes. Go ahead."

"I hit a man and he died. Not exactly because I hit him, but kind of. What I mean is, I didn't kill him."

"Del, that's terrible."

"It's not anything I'm proud of. But it happened, and you'd just as well hear it from me."

"Why did you hit him?"

"He and his wife were separated, and she had been seeing me."

"Oh." She was silent for a moment. "I don't mean for you to take this the wrong way. I don't want to sound too judg-mental, but I didn't think that would be a habit of yours, to solve things with your fists. I know it's a way of life with some people, but I just haven't known people who—"

"No, I don't make a habit of it. Vince is the first guy I've hit since I got in trouble."

"You were involved with the man's wife?"

"Well, yeah." He had already said as much, but he realized she was putting things in her terms.

"Excuse me for asking this, Del, but I have to."

"Go ahead."

"Were you in prison?"

He laughed. "No, but it was a long fight in court that ruined my life for a couple of years. Between that and losing every dime I'd ever worked for, I paid. At least I feel I do. Vince knows what that does to a guy, and I could tell he just loved throwing it in my face."

She gave a heavy sigh.

"Go ahead," he said.

"Well, I don't know . . ."

"Go ahead."

"I know this sounds trite, and probably rude, but it seems like you should have known better the second time."

"You mean for getting involved with you?" He realized as he said it that he was using her word.

"Well, that too, I guess. But I meant hitting Vince. You should have . . . well, I'm not going to tell you what you should or shouldn't do. But I'm sorry things have developed the way they have, and it's too bad you felt you had to hit him."

"I didn't have to, but I did. And I'm sorry it happened, too."

"What do you think is next, Del?"

"I don't know, but I think Vince will try some other little stunt to get even. I don't think he's done with me."

"I doubt that he is. He doesn't quit easily, and he doesn't like to lose."

"That's the impression I'm getting."

"I guess that leaves us on hold," she said.

"You and me?"

"Well, yes."

"I guess so."

"Will you call me, or do you want me to wait to call you?"

Del paused to think. "I'll call you. I'll call you if he pulls something else, and if he doesn't, I'll call you when the elk hunting season is over."

"When will that be?"

"In a little over two weeks."

"Oh. O.K. I'll try not to get impatient for you to call, then."

"I'll call one way or the other."

"I'll look forward to your call." When he was silent for a moment, she said, "Was there something else, Del?"

"There was one thing I was wondering. Did Vince get his deer?"

"Yes, he did."

"Well, good for him."

"He seemed pleased—with that, at least." After a brief pause, she said, "Del, be careful."

"I will. And I'll call you back."

Snow continued to fall as he drove back to camp. The conversation with Sylvia gave him a few things to think about, besides her not asking him whether he had gotten his deer. For one thing, she seemed offended by the act of one man hitting another. Maybe it was something fundamental with her, that lifting a fist was one thing a man should not do to another. Harassment, ridicule, torment—those were the civilized weapons. Then again, maybe it was just the angle she needed, just the thing to help her ease out of the entanglement. Maybe up until now she had been like he was—half-wanting to get out but not wanting to be the one to do it without a reason. Now she could become disenchanted, and she would have a peg to hang it on.

He smiled as he thought of Rita. She knew about the old trouble he'd been in, but she didn't seem to have an ingrained objection to the spirit in him that brought the fist up and around. She might even have wished it had been one of her ex-husbands. At any rate, in that respect she took him for what he was, a man with a vulnerable spot. What was bothering her now was the other part, the knowledge that he was not immune to a case of the dumb-ass. He had fooled around and had gotten himself into a mess. That was something she didn't accept and something he couldn't expect her to.

He drove on in the falling snow, returning again and again to the awareness that now there was a barrier between him and Sylvia. It was no longer a philosophical dialogue about microwave ovens and cordless telephones. He could see the break coming more easily than he could before. Flexing his right hand inside its insulated leather glove, he knew that he was not altogether sorry for hitting Vince.

Chapter Twenty-Three

By the time the coffee was plunking and the hunters were stirring, the dark morning outside echoed with the bang and rattle of vehicles on frozen roads. The pre-dawn traffic was worst on opening morning.

"Sheesh," Bob said. "This is as bad as the public hunting places at home."

"It's all right," Harry amended. "They'll get the elk moving around."

"They're probably stirred up enough already," Phil said, wheezing as he crammed his right foot into its felt-lined boot. "There's been deer hunters in here for the past two weeks, keeping things all worked up."

"I don't mind all the other hunters," Harry maintained. "This is big country, and the hunters get spread out. It's not like back home, where there's a guy on every rock."

Bob blew his nose. "I still like to be by myself."

"No one's crowding you," Harry answered.

Del had gathered, the night before, that there had already been substantial discussion on who could fill whose tag. Bob, who had applied separately from the other three, had gotten an "any elk" permit, while the others were all restricted to shooting antlered elk. Some hunters would party hunt from the beginning, agreeing that whoever had a chance to shoot a cow elk should take it. Although party hunting was against the law, Del knew it was a common practice, and it was more accepted in elk hunting than in antelope. Bob was not above party hunting himself, provided that he got to hoard his privilege until the second week. The agreement was that if he hadn't killed his elk after a week, he would offer his permit for the party plan. Meanwhile, the others would hunt bull elk and make remarks like Harry's.

Having been through the topic the year before, Del saw no need to bring it up this year, especially in view of the unethical portrait Vince had sketched the day before. In the eyes of the present company he had killed a man, helped a client cover up a game violation, bedded another client's wife, and punched out the husband for complaining. In addition, even though Vince hadn't mentioned it, he had let someone else party hunt on his antelope permit. So he held his tongue on the subject of ethics.

Phil changed the subject. "What's the weather like, Del?"

"Looks like overcast, but it's not snowing anymore."

"I like hunting in snow," Bob announced. "Makes it easier to read anything recent."

Harry smiled. "I'm ready for it." Del looked up from scrambling eggs, and Harry explained. "I bought one of those insulated cushions."

"Oh, one of those miniature bean bags, sort of. Those are supposed to work pretty good."

"They do. And I can use it hunting deer later on."

"Harry got the best kind," Bob said, almost in a sneer. "You can get them in all orange, all camouflage, or half and half like his. Is yours a Hot Seat, a Heater Seater, or a Thermo Seat, Harry?"

"It's a Hot Seat, Bob, and if you're real nice, I'll let you use it after I kill my elk and sit around in camp waiting for the rest of you to fill out."

For a fleeting moment, Del wished they would all fill out today and go home. Rather than phrase the complete thought, he said, "Let's hope everyone fills."

Day broke slow and grey as the hunters set out, each on foot for the opening morning hunt. They wished each other good luck and trudged away through quiet snow. Del, who carried a rifle and a license, planned to spend the first few hours scouting for sign. When he knew where the elk were moving, he would have a better chance of taking his hunters to them. It would be good for business if at least some of them killed elk.

He set out on foot and moved at a steady pace, covering ground twice as fast as he would if he were hunting for himself. Following the big ridge that ran north from camp, he noted where elk tracks moved east across the saddles in the ridge. The back side of the ridge dropped off sharp into thick timber, deadfall, and snowdrift—a favored retreat for elk, and a tough place for packing one out, even with horses.

The first shots had come a few minutes after daybreak, and rifle fire continued off and on through the morning. By ten o'clock, Del was glad to realize that none of the trails had been marked by blood-melted snow. The escape of crippled animals was the one thing that made hunting look bad even to hunters.

Pausing at a tall, spreading pine tree, he dug out a snack bar and a pint flask of water. Looking around for a place to sit, he found a rock and turned it over to expose a dry side. He felt warm and loose inside his woolen shell, and the water felt clean as it went to his center. As he was tossing the crumbs into his mouth, he was startled by a rifle shot right below him in the timber. He sat forward with his rifle ready in case an animal made a move, but no sounds followed. He had heard just one shot, nothing before or after. After a while, he felt cool and rested again, so he went on his way.

Before he reached the end of the ridge where it fell away to the creek bottom, he went down the back side. He followed an elk trail through a patch of timber where the deadfall was not so bad, and he ended up in a bottom that was at least two uphill miles from any road. Lots of elk had been through the bottom already this morning, and some of them had lingered long enough to leave droppings. Del found the old logging road he was looking for, a road that had not been good in its best days and was now overgrown with ten-foot pine trees. He decided to follow the road up and out, to make sure it was still passable for pack horses. Slinging the rifle on his shoulder and thumbing the strap, he started his return march. His boots squeaked and crunched in the soft snow, but he was not noisy as he moved through the soft, cold, quiet world of grey stumps, rotting slash from bygone logging, patches of new timber, stands of old timber, and tall mountains reaching up on every side. It was big country, all right. Elk and men vanished into timber, maybe to meet and maybe to follow separate winding paths.

He made it back to camp by 11:30. Phil and Leonard sat inside the tent, boots off, drinking coffee from the thermos.

"See anything?" Phil asked.

"Lots of tracks. How about you?"

"Same. Lots of tracks, but no hoof and horn."

"Where did you go?" Leonard asked.

"I took this ridge north of camp and then dropped off the back side before I got to the end. It would be a good hunt for one or two guys if they wanted to try it. Did you see many hunters?"

"I saw quite a few," Leonard answered.

"I saw a couple," Phil said. "How was it where you went?"

"Didn't look like anyone had been down there. It wouldn't be a good place to kill one if a guy didn't have a horse to pack it out."

"You think someone ought to try it?"

"Sooner or later. I can take someone down on horseback, or I can explain how to get there. There's an old logging road that goes down into it."

"I think Harry went down that way last year," Leonard said. "He might want to try it again. He seems to like horse-back riding the best."

"We'll see how he and Bob did," Phil said. "I heard a lot of shots. Maybe one of them killed one."

"That would be nice," Del added, setting a pan of water on the stove. "We'll get some warm water going in case anyone wants to clean up. I'll make some more coffee, too."

Harry came in at a little after noon. "I saw a cow and a calf," he said. "They stood in front of me for two full minutes. Never saw me. Fifty yards away. I could have shot her a hundred times." He set his rifle and cushion on his cot, took off his coat and set it, folded, on his pillow, and sat in one of the camp chairs. "Quite a few shots. What did the rest of you see?"

His two companions gave their reports, followed by Del's account. Harry nodded as he fixed a sandwich. "Might be worth a try."

It was almost one o'clock when Bob came in, glowing through dried flecks of blood on his cheeks and glasses.

"You look like you got some meat on the ground," Del said.

"I sure did." Bob pulled off his gloves to expose a pair of dry, crimson hands.

"Cow or bull?" Harry asked, picking his teeth.

"Cow."

"Dry, or did she have a calf with her?"

"She was dry and by herself. Lots of fat on her."

"Where did you shoot her?" Del asked.

"Right here in the ribs," Bob answered, making a chicken wing with his left arm.

"No, I mean whereabouts?"

"Oh. Over there." He pointed to the west.

"Up high? Down low?"

"About halfway down the other side of the ridge that has the clearcut on it."

"In the timber or in aspens?"

"In some fairly open timber. She was grazing on grass in there, and I sneaked up on her and shot her at seventy yards."

"Good deal," Del said. "You got her field-dressed and tagged, I take it."

"Oh, yeah."

"Are you close enough to the road that we can drag her to the pickup?"

"Oh, yeah, I think so."

"Not a lot of down timber or thick aspens?"

"No, I walked out to the road and came back that way. There's a little uphill, but not bad."

"Well, go ahead and help yourself to some lunch and catch a little rest, and then we'll go get her." Del turned to the other hunters. "This would work better as a three-man job," he said. "If one of you wouldn't mind going with Bob and me, maybe the other two could go on that hunt I described, if you want to."

"I'll help drag the old cow," Phil said.

"Fine with me," Leonard answered. "I'll go with Harry on the horses. Sound all right with you, Harry?"

"Sure. I went down there last year, and I've been looking forward to trying it again."

"Sounds fine," Del said, as he set a basin of warm water on the table for Bob. "Take your time, Bob. I'll get the horses saddled for these two, and we'll still have plenty of time to go pick up your elk. Harry, I'll saddle Little Tulip for you and Spud for you, Leonard."

Harry nodded as he poured himself a cup of coffee from the pot. "Coffee, Bob?"

"Thanks."

"I'm glad you got an elk, Bob."

"Thanks, Harry. I am, too."

The day was still overcast but had been warming little by little since morning, and the sun broke through as the guide saddled the horses. Snow had already melted on the pickup cab, forming shiny, clear icicles over the grill, on the fender lip, and even on the side-view mirrors. The water-clean icicles contrasted with yesterday's road ice, which hung like a dirty grey beard on the pickup body behind the front tires.

Phil came outside to watch. "Day's warming up."

"Seems to be."

"Nice that Bob got an elk." Phil kicked at the curtain of road ice, knocking it off in one big chunk.

"Yep. We're off to a good start," Del said.

Phil banged on the pickup fender to shatter off the new little icicles, and Little Tulip sidestepped as Del was drawing up the front cinch. "Sorry," Phil said.

"No problem."

"I'll get the other side later." Phil gave a sheepish smile.

Del smiled back. "That'll be fine."

Snow was beginning to melt in the upper branches of the timber, giving the effect of a mini-rain forest as Bob led Phil and the guide to the site of the kill. The cow lay chocolate brown against the patchy snow. A gray jaybird lifted off the gut pile, carrying a scrap of tallow in its beak. Even the men's footsteps had been muffled in the damp forest floor and melting snow, and as they all paused at the dead elk, the scene was quiet and peaceful. The falling snowmelt made a soft patter until Del spoke.

"That's a nice-looking one, Bob. Looks like you did a neat job with her."

"Thanks."

The guide leaned over and, catching a musky whiff of the elk, pulled the corner of the animal's mouth into a grimace to expose the ivory back tooth. "You want to remember to pull these for souvenirs."

"Uh-huh."

Del laid his rope on the ground, then brought out his knife and a small coil of nylon twine. With Bob holding one hind leg out of the way, he laced up the belly. Then he picked up the rope, shook it out, and stooped to the elk. He tied the front hocks together, drew them up against the body, and snugged the rope around the neck. Next he let out enough slack for one man to pull with, and he tied back to the neck. He tied off a second loop of slack for the next man to pull with, and he left the remaining rope for himself.

Each man took up a loop of rope, and pulling in jerky unison, they made the first two hundred yards with only a few small hang-ups.

When they came to the uphill drag, they paused. Del went ahead to toss logs out of the way, and when he came back, he waited until the men had caught their breath. Now they had to pull uphill, a fitful fifteen or twenty yards at a time with breathers in between, until they reached the road. Del backed the pickup to the carcass, climbed in back, and hauled on the animal while the other two men lifted. When they had the elk aboard, he jumped down. Clanging the tailgate shut, he said, "One down, three to go."

Back at camp, they hung the elk from a pine tree, and Del opened up the pelvis and brisket to make the cooling go faster. He decided he would skin it the next day. Bob had caught his breath by now and seemed to be enjoying his triumph. He snapped a few pictures of his animal, and he had Del snap one of him standing by the hanging carcass.

"I think I have just enough time to go on a little hunt," Phil said.

"Take Harry's cushion," Bob offered.

"That's O.K. I don't intend to sit that long anyway."

For the next hour, Del tidied up around the camp and inside the tent while Bob cleaned his rifle and sharpened his knife. The guide put another pan of water on to heat, and he made a pot of coffee to set on the fire later. Just before dark, he heard the mushy clip-clop of the horses.

When Del stepped out of the tent, the front rider was within speaking distance. "Any luck?" the guide asked.

"Leonard killed one," Harry answered.

"Nice bull?"

"A spike."

"That's good."

"Uh-huh." Harry heaved himself down from the saddle, handed the reins to Del, and went into the tent.

Leonard rode forward on his horse and stepped down.

"Got one, uh?"

"I sure did."

"Down in the bottom?"

"Almost all the way down in there."

"You got him field-dressed and tagged?"

"Sure did."

"Can you get a horse right up to him?"

"Within a few yards."

"I think he'll keep all right where he is. We'll go get him first thing in the morning."

Leonard nodded and said, "O.K." He handed Del the reins.

Del tied Spud to the horse trailer. In the gathering dusk, he could tell that the horses had sweated but not much. He stripped their gear and rubbed them down, then turned them into the rope corral and fed all three.

When the guide went into the tent, he saw that Phil had returned and was stretched out on a cot. Leonard was washing face and forearms in the enamel basin. Harry had told the main part of the story and was now dwelling on the lesser features.

"And then there's the horseback riding itself. With the gun in the scabbard in front of your left knee, the saddle sort of lists to one side, and you have to keep pushing your weight on your right leg. I wouldn't be surprised if this right leg is stiff tomorrow, with all the pressure I had to keep putting on it."

As Del lit the burner beneath the coffee, he frowned at what he had just heard. "I'll be back in a second to start supper," he said. He went out of the tent and crawled through the ropes into the corral. With his pocket flashlight, he inspected Little Tulip, and sure enough, there was a raw welt on either side, right behind the front leg.

Del shook his head and clucked. "Sorry, girl," he muttered. He went to the tack compartment of the horse trailer and brought out the plastic jar of balm. With one arm around Little Tulip's neck, he smeared the cold cream onto the sores. Then he massaged her ears. "Sorry, girl. He didn't know." From an inner pocket, he took out a granola bar, which she put away in half a minute. Del patted her again and turned away.

Back in the tent, the topic had changed.

"Oh, sure," Bob said, "there's lots of ways of dying in the woods. That's a stupid way, but not the only one."

"Any fool should know to keep the knife pointed away from himself. The animal kicks once, and there you are." Phil jerked his thumb at his femoral artery. "And that's the way they found him, just as dead as Bob's elk."

"Or Leonard's," Harry added.

"Or Leonard's," Phil agreed.

"Lots of ways to die in the woods," Bob repeated. "You can fall off an overhang, you can shoot yourself, you can freeze—"

"Fellow from Eau Claire just before we left home," Phil said, "was cutting firewood by himself. He gouged himself with his chain saw, and that was it."

"None of that for me," Harry said. "I want to die in bed with a hard-on when I'm eighty."

"With whose wife?" Leonard chimed in.

"At that point I won't care."

Bob flickered a look at Del, then turned to Harry. "You farm boys are all alike," he said, which must have been a funny line he'd heard somewhere. When the ripple of laughter passed, he said, "Well, what are we just sitting here for? Two of us got an elk today. In my book, that calls for a drink."

269

Chapter Twenty-Four

The hunters grew happy with the cocktail hour. Bob poured generous drinks, first one round and then a second one, using up the equivalent of at least three nights' worth of nightcaps. It was no bother, he insisted; he would get more fire water when he took the meat to town. He said he and Leonard would have their meat aged, cut and wrapped, and frozen by the time they were all ready to go back to Wisconsin.

Harry was optimistic that they might have to leave sooner. Holding his drink up to the lantern light, he smiled. "Yes, I think it's going to be a good season. I'd hate to blitzkrieg this place and leave Del with an icebox full of leftover frankfurters, but it might happen that way."

"Be fine with me," the guide said. "The best thing for me is for everyone to go home happy that they had a good hunt. If everyone fills out, so much the better." He smiled and nodded assurance to the group, who all smiled in return. It seemed to Del as if the amber glow of Canadian Mist had suffused itself among the company. They would all be willing to fill their tags and go home early, just as he, outdoorsman and small-time businessman, would not mind packing up and going home early. The sooner he closed out the season, the sooner he got out of the neighborhood of the one hunter who had not gone home happy.

The hunters did not drink through the evening. Rather, they had an evident limit of two drinks for the cocktail hour. As they finished, they set their empty glasses on the table and waited for supper. When the chicken, mashed potatoes, and gravy hit the table, the men ate with enthusiasm. Then came the apple strudel and a pot of decaffeinated coffee. As Del cleared the table and did the dishes, the men sat around tiddling their coffee cups and picking their teeth, occasionally releasing a sigh or muffling a belch.

When the dirty dishwater had splashed the ground outside and Del had enjoyed his own cup of coffee, Phil ushered in the nightcap. And so the evening closed. Despite its quality of sameness and blandness, the evening seemed to hold for the hunters a spirit of primitive adventure that far outclassed the comforts of the coffee shop and motel room.

Back in his own cold tent, Del lay in his sleeping bundle and listened to the horses just beyond the tent wall. The snow in the corral had melted partway and then re-frozen, so the hooves crunched as the horses shifted and moved in the night. It was a comfort, as Del lay cocooned on this random spot of the cold earth, to have his warm, capable allies so near at hand.

* * * * *

He awoke to a cold morning, hard cold. Before he rolled out of his bed, he previewed the day. He chose not to wear his long johns beneath his jeans. Thermals were fine for slow hunting on foot, but they made a man ride slick in the saddle,

271

with friction like the burn of a loose wool sock. Furthermore, they would sweat his legs in the two long uphill hikes he would have in leading the packhorse. That was the way it would be, with Little Tulip staying in camp, but Del didn't mind the walking. His cold-weather riding boots were all right for hiking.

When he was finished dressing, he dug out a blaze-orange coat from the duffel bag. Moving through the timber on a brown horse, a fellow was well advised to wear plenty of orange.

After breakfast, when Harry and Phil had gone their separate ways, Del saddled the horses. He sent Leonard, riding Spud and leading Whisker, to the place where Del would meet him and leave the pickup.

* * * * *

Day had broken cold and clear as they rode down the old logging road. Crunchy snow lay in heaps and patches wherever yesterday's afternoon sun had cast shadows from trees, rocks, cutbanks, slash, and deadfall. The weathered logs carried a sparkling thin blanket of frost, and the open spots on the trail were hard and frosty. It was a clean morning, and the horses blew clouds of breath.

The two men dismounted when they came to the elk, a frosted mound in the morning shade. Leonard was not as exuberant as Bob had been, but when Del asked if he wanted to keep the hide, he was quick and cheerful to say yes. After snapping a couple of photographs, Del picked out a tree where he could hang and skin the animal. With Spud's help, he got the elk dragged into place, hoisted, and tied off. As he expected, the cold hide came off without much trouble, and the guide recognized the two separate smells of rank elk hide and rich cooling meat. He detached the hide at the neck, then folded it up to keep it moist. Tying it with crisscrossed ropes onto Whisker's saddle, he said, "We'll get the horns and ivories on the second trip." Leonard nodded as he held the lead ropes. With Whisker's bundle secure, the guide draped the panniers onto Spud and tied them down. With his Wyoming Saw, he split the elk lengthwise and cut off the front quarters. With a little sashaying on Spud's part, Del got the quarters loaded and tied across.

The frost was beginning to melt on their second trip down the logging road, and by the time they had Spud loaded with the third and fourth quarters of the elk, mists were rising from the grey logs, now darkened with melting frost. Del was warm and limber; his calf muscles, which had been tight during the first uphill march, had relaxed. He was pleased that the job had gone well. It was the best he had felt since he had helped Kenny with his deer.

Back in camp, he skinned Bob's elk, quartered it and bagged it to match Leonard's, and loaded the meat and hides into the back of the Wagoneer. After lunch, Bob and Leonard would make a trip to the meat locker and would leave the hides with the taxidermist.

Del was scrubbing his hands with snow when Harry came trudging in. He looked worn out as he tossed his coat and hot seat through the tent flap and onto the floor.

"Are you all right, Harry?" the guide asked.

"Oh, yeah. I'm just bushed, that's all."

"Something come on you all of a sudden?"

"Not really. I got myself down in a place where I had to climb up a pretty steep mountainside in knee-deep snow, and I think I got over-heated."

"Have you got sort of a dull headache?"

"Yeah, I do."

"That sun's warmer than it seems. You better take it easy, or you won't make it to eighty."

Harry laughed. "Oh, I'm all right. I'm just not going on any more long walks today." He unslung his rifle and stooped into the tent.

Phil came in at a little after noon. He had seen three elk vanish into a patch of timber, which he wanted to study after lunch. Harry decided he would rest, maybe go out for a stroll before sundown. That left Del free to do more scouting, and he decided he would go out on horseback. He would ride Whisker, as Spud had done the greater share of the morning's work.

* * * * *

Decked out in the bright orange coat and matching cap, he climbed aboard Whisker and left camp in a brisk, swinging walk. They caught the road and followed it as it curved and wound downhill to cross the creek. There he turned left, following the creek as it flowed westward. He crossed the creek several times, Whisker shying from the shady backwaters where ice lay in thin sheets. At one point, the creek flowed through a canyon too narrow for vehicles, and then the country opened up into a wide, watered area where the creek had run a varying course from year to year. Red leafless willows sprouted from the gravel bars, and tall, coarse grass the color of wheat straw grew on the banks. The snow was melting here, giving way in places to a few lingering autumn-red leaves of the wild rose.

Del dismounted and took a drink from his canteen. Slipping the bridle from Whisker, he latched the halter in place. He found a dry spot in the grass and stretched out, leaning on his right elbow and holding the lead rope in that hand. Whisker grazed on the coarse grass, bringing his head close to the man's eye level. Del could see himself, the gun-metal creek, the cold patches of snow, and the warm saffron grass all reflected in the horse's eye. Del closed his own eyes, shutting out the scene as he lay in the warm sun and listened to the casual munch of the browsing horse.

A tug on the lead rope tightened his hand and brought him awake. He was thirsty. He hadn't been asleep for very long, but he had the relaxed feeling that often came in the morning, the feeling that the drag of circumstance had unhooked and slipped away. As Del stood up, stretched, and took a good drink of water, he felt resilient in his arms and legs.

Del led the horse to the creek and watered him, then re-bridled him and swung into the saddle. He had not seen much elk sign down this way, but it was a good afternoon for a ride. He rode relaxed, letting the horse pluck along at his own leisurely rate. Shadows were starting to lengthen into the open spots, and Del could feel the air cooling along the creek bottom. He zipped up the orange coat and patted Whisker on the neck. The horse was warm but not sweating. That was good.

As Del put the canyon behind him, he came back into more timbered country. The elk could be anywhere at this point, but he wasn't sure that this would be a good place to send Harry and Phil in the morning. Maybe Phil would want to go back to the spot he was working on. There hadn't been any shots from that direction. Del thought of taking Harry back into the bottom where Leonard had killed his spike. Elk got pushed into there pretty often. Then again, maybe Harry would just want to go sit on his cushion and wait. Both hunters needed antlered elk. That might take more than—

Whisker jumped and pitched, and as Del heard the echoing crash of a rifle shot, his thoughts came quick and distinct. The horse hadn't just spooked. It had a glistening red trickle on its hip. Someone had taken a shot from up on the left. The orange coat made an easy target. The horse wasn't going to roll over on him. He had to get out the rifle.

Del lay flat on the ground in the shadow of a fallen pine. He peered at Whisker, standing thirty yards away with the reins trailing on the pine needles. The horse stood obediently, it seemed, with blood trickling down the left haunch. No one who hit the horse that high up could have missed seeing the orange. A shot just to spook the pair would have been high and wide, so whoever had shot was shooting at the orange. Del thought, Vince Furtino was playing to win, and he had probably flinched when it came right down to pulling the trigger.

Del leaned his rifle against the log, took off his cap, and squirmed out of the coat. He needed to know where the sniper was, and he needed to get his hands on him. Shooting back wouldn't do any good, even if he hit the man. And he couldn't just walk away. Whoever it was—and he was sure it was Vince—was aiming to hit. The guide peeked over the log and scanned the area. To the left of the trail as he and Whisker had followed it, the land rose up in a rocky, timbered mountainside. Vince was up somewhere in the rocks, jabbing heel prints in the shaded snow and waiting for his target to come back into sight.

Del looked again at the horse, standing as still as he might in a snowstorm. Maybe Vince wasn't shooting to kill, but he had hit the horse, and that alone made Del want to punish the man. Reasoning with himself, he knew there was no way he could come out of this and look justified if he used his rifle. He thought of Rita and the camp they had had that summer. There was too much at stake to make a bad move now.

Del thought it out. He would have to try to circle around through the timber, and at some point he would have to make a rush across open ground. Knowing that Vince didn't like to lose, he still wondered if, deep down, the lawyer had the nerve to shoot him, man to man, at close range. Del might have to find out, if he was going to get his hands on the man before dark.

Del shook his head in disgust as he wrapped his rifle in the coat. *This is stupid*, he thought. He crawled along the

277

fallen pine until he came to cover, and he slipped into the timber. As he walked lightfooted, he was thankful for the damp, quiet floor under foot. He could not see the open hillside from the cover he had to stay in, and he would not know if the other man were to walk right down the open area or even cross over to this very timber to sneak down. Del crept to the edge of the cover and scanned the opening.

He saw a nest of rocks where the mountainside made a sharp incline, and he imagined it was a good spot to hunt from. He watched the rocks for several minutes, hoping to catch some glint or movement. None appeared. Del could not see if any of the surrounding snow patches had footprints. As he gazed, a jaybird swooped to land in the rocks, then picked up flight again and lit in a pine. The guide smiled and dropped back into the timber, deciding to work uphill another hundred and fifty yards or so, just above the rocks, and from there he would make his rush.

At the timber's edge above the nest of rocks, he paused. So far it had been like hunting, moving in silence, unseen, with the added advantage of not having a rifle barrel to drag through the branches. Now it was changed. His hands were sweating, and his guts were churning. He told himself he wasn't dead certain there was a man in those rocks, and if there was, he didn't know whether it was Vince. Nor did he know whether the man would shoot again. Del thought back at what had just happened, and he nodded his head. He knew it was Vince, and the sonofabitch had shot at him and hit his horse. Taking his gloves off and tucking them inside his wool shirt, he buttoned up. He doubled his fist once in the chilling air, released, and took off in gulping downhill strides.

Del braked with his feet as he came to the cove of rocks. Several details came into view at once. He saw an orange cap and vest, with a flash of brass, lying on a low slab of rock. He caught a quick glance of the lawyer jumping up and moving sideways for cover. Del charged ahead, stepped around a boulder, and came face to face with Vince Furtino. Bare-headed and dark-bearded, the lawyer was holding a rifle across his body. Still moving forward, Del punched the man square on the jaw and sent him backward through a crevice. The dark face dropped out of sight, and Del heard a clattering, scrambling sound. Del came to a rest at a large screening jag of rock. He exhaled twice, then drew in a chestful of fresh air. Beyond his own breathing, he thought he heard the lawyer gasping.

"Vince?" he called out.

"Don't shoot me, you sonofabitch. I'm hurt."

Del didn't answer. He glanced back at the sniper's nest and saw the orange cap and vest. Inside the cap lay eight or ten loose cartridges. He turned again to the crevice where Vince had slipped. As Del stood and listened, he heard Vince groan.

"I don't have a gun, Vince," he called out.

"I couldn't shoot you if I wanted to," the lawyer called back. The voice was pained but bitter. Del stood silent for a long moment. Vince spoke again, the pain sounding clearer than the contempt. "I'm hurt. I need help."

Del worked his way toward the crevice, noting the skid mark in the slush, and edged around the rocks to peer down the slope. Vince was lying against a clump of sagebrush. Del's stomach lurched. The lawyer's dark blue parka, unzipped, was sticking out on his left side, and his two hands were clutched on his rifle barrel, holding the stock away from him. He had to have fallen full force on the tip of the barrel.

"What happened?" Del asked.

"This rifle barrel gouged the hell out of my side. It went in through my shirt. On top of that, I caught my foot between the rocks, and I think I broke my ankle."

Del's mouth was cotton. "I don't know if I should move you," he said.

"I need a drink of water."

"I'll go get some." Del hustled down to the horse, grabbed the canteen and his coat, and hurried back up to Vince.

The lawyer had released his grip on the rifle, and it lay in his lap. He took the canteen. "I need to be moved carefully," he said.

"I know. Are you bleeding?"

"I think it still is."

"I'll go for help as fast as I can." Del picked his words with care. "But my horse is bleeding, so I'm on foot. I'll leave you this for a blanket." Del draped the coat over Vince's front, catching a trace of the lawyer's cologne as he did so. Seeing the rifle butt sticking out from the coat, he paused. "Is that gun loaded?"

"No. I only had one shell in it."

Del frowned. "What the hell were you doing?"

"I don't know." A grimace of pain seized the lawyer's face. "I don't know. You don't know. It was an accident."

"I'll be back as soon as I can," the guide said. "Stay put and stay calm." As he sidestepped down the hill, he thought, that's how Vince decided to do it—one shot, all or nothing, and then he flinched. The loose cartridges were ready in case Del shot back.

Del stopped, looked back up the hill, and nodded as he said beneath his breath, "It was an accident. Now don't die, you sonofabitch."

Chapter Twenty-Five

Del waited until Sylvia answered the phone on the third ring.

Her voice was clear as it came over the line. "Hello?"

Del made it quick and straight, as he had planned. "Hello, Sylvia, this is Del. I'm calling about Vince. He's in the hospital. He had an accident. They think he's going to be all right."

"What happened? How did it happen?"

"He fell in some rocks, and he ran his rifle barrel through his side."

"You mean he impaled himself?"

"Not clean through the middle, but he gouged the flesh on his side. He lost a bit of blood."

"Oh, my God. Del, I feel like I'm getting sick."

"Go ahead and get a hold of yourself. I'll hang on."

Sylvia breathed a few times and said, "Tell me about it. Where are you now?"

"I'm in Laramie, at the hospital where they've got Vince. It's called Ivinson."

"Has he gone into surgery yet? My God, it's nearly midnight. What time did this happen?"

"It happened a little before sundown. He's been into the operating room and out again. They've got him hooked up to monitor machines, and they say he's holding steady."

"Oh, thank God." She paused and said, "Del, is there anything I need to do right now? I mean, information about medical coverage, or—"

"Vince had his card, and he signed himself in. They've been trying to call you, and you should hear from them pretty soon. Maybe I should get off the line in case they're trying to call you now."

"Del, before you hang up, tell me—what happened? What really happened?"

"He had an accident. He fell on his rifle barrel."

"And you were there?"

"I didn't see it."

"You didn't have anything to do with it?"

"Vince can tell you what he wants you to know. He may or may not tell you what he did to bring it about. But I don't have any reason to feel sorry for him."

"That's a pretty cold thing to say, Del. He's been hurt, and he's in the hospital."

"If you hear any resentment in my voice, it's probably not much different from the way he feels. I don't think he enjoyed having to depend on me. But we're both done with it, and I thought I should call you."

A pause followed until Sylvia spoke. "Well, I appreciate your calling, and I appreciate your helping Vince, even if it was against your . . . jungle instinct."

"I don't know who's being cold now, but it probably doesn't matter. I'd better get off the line."

"Del."

"Yes?"

"I imagine I'll be going out there. Vince is going to need my help."

"At the very least, he'll need someone to drive his outfit home for him. I should mention that he broke his ankle as well."

"I'll be there, probably for a few days."

"That should be all right."

"And . . . what I mean to say is, I don't know how much good it would do if we saw each other."

"No, I think we've carried it far enough. You've got a man here who's going to need your help, lovey-dovey or otherwise."

"Ummm . . . I feel I should say something clever in closing."

"That's O.K. We can just close it out. Better that way, all the way around, I think, to call it quits."

"It was very interesting, Del, and I won't forget you."

"Same here. So long, Sylvia."

"Good-bye, Del."

As Del drove across town from the hospital to the Holiday Inn, he felt as if a long, unpleasant job had ended. There would be no reports or investigations to answer to, nothing to go to court about. A gunshot wound would have brought in game wardens and sheriffs, but as it was, a hunter had had a bad fall and was in the hospital. As for himself, Del was pretty sure he was done with the Furtinos, and it was a better feeling than it had been the first time.

In the quiet of the hotel lobby, he punched Rita's number and then his calling card number. It was a couple of minutes past eleven, an hour earlier than it was in Omaha. He wondered where Sylvia had been, and he told himself he couldn't care. The telephone line be-blipped and connected, and the phone rang twice.

Mickey answered. "Hello."

"Hi, Mickey. This is Del. Is your mom there?"

"Yeah. Just a minute."

Del could hear the television as he waited for Rita to get to the phone. When she picked it up and said hello, he said, "Hello, Rita. This is Del. Sorry to call so late."

"That's all right. Is there something wrong?"

"No."

"I wasn't expecting to hear from you so soon. What are you doing at a telephone?"

"I had an errand to run, and I thought I'd call you before I went back to camp."

"Well, that's nice. How are your hunters doing? Kill anything yet?"

"Two of them filled out the first day, which was good, and the other two are still hunting."

"How far into the season are you?"

Del thought. "We've just had two days. Seems like more than that, but that's it. These other two guys might fill any day, or they might stay the full two weeks."

"Like always."

"Yeah. By the way, it looks like I'm done with those people from Omaha."

"Oh. Uh-huh." Rita paused. "Did you get a lot of snow? Looked like it on the weather report."

"We got a pretty good cover on everything, but it's been melting fast."

"You're likely to get some more before too long."

"I guess so. How is it there?"

"Just a couple of inches, and it didn't stay around."

"That's good." Del paused and then gave it a try. "You think you can fit me into your social calendar when I get back?"

"If you're sure you're done with those other people."

"Oh, yeah. Both of 'em. He and I sort of had it out, and that part's done, too."

Rita was quiet for a moment until she said, "So you're on your way to camp, then?"

"Yeah. I just stopped for a quick call."

"Well, you better get back to work. It's late. Call me when you're back in town."

"I will. Tell Mickey I said hello."

"I'll do that. And Del, be careful."

He laughed. "I will."

* * * * *

The hunters' tent was dark when Del pulled into camp. They had no doubt had their nightcap and left the dishes for him. Well, that was all right. He was back on the job, and he would give them nothing else to worry or wonder about.

Frost lay on the horse trailer and on the Wagoneer, and the moon was shining bright as he stepped out of the pickup into the cold night air. He could smell the horses as he went to them, talking in soft tones as he crawled into the corral. Their breath was rich and steamy as he looked them over with his flashlight. Whisker was placid as always and looked as if he would be all right. Little Tulip would be ready to go in a couple of days if he needed her, and in the meanwhile, Spud could earn his oats.

As Del stooped into the chilly tent and got ready to crawl into the cold bedding, his flickering flashlight caught the rifle and orange coat in its beam. He shook his head and let out a wearied sigh.

After winding the hammer-and-bell alarm clock, he clicked off the flashlight and wiggled into the sleeping bag, tucking his pants and shirt along the zippered edge as he nestled into place. Not far from his ear, the horses crunched and shifted on the cold ground outside. Del smiled. Across the cold country two hundred miles as the legendary crow flew, a woman and a boy would be asleep in their beds. He winked at Rita. It was a good life if a fellow could keep from getting a case of the dumb-ass.

About the Author

John D. Nesbitt lives in the plains country of Wyoming, where he teaches English and Spanish at Eastern Wyoming College. His articles, reviews, fiction, and poetry have appeared in numerous magazines and anthologies. He has had more than thirty books published, including short story collections, contemporary novels, and traditional westerns, as well as textbooks for his courses. John has won many awards for his work, including two awards from the Wyoming State Historical Society (for fiction), two awards from Wyoming Writers for encouragement of other writers and service to the organization, two Wyoming Arts Council literary fellowships (one for fiction, one for non-fiction), a Will Rogers Medallion Award for *Dark Prairie* (a frontier mystery) and another for *Thorns on the Rose* (a poetry collection), a Western Writers of America Spur finalist award for his novel *Raven Springs*, and the Spur award itself for his short story "At the End of the Orchard" and for his novels *Trouble at the Redstone* and *Stranger in Thunder Basin*. His recent work includes *Poacher's Moon,* a contemporary novel; *Blue Horse Mesa*, a collection of western stories; and *Field Work*, a retro-noir fiction collection. Visit his website at www.johndnesbitt.com

Visit us at www.speakingvolumes.us

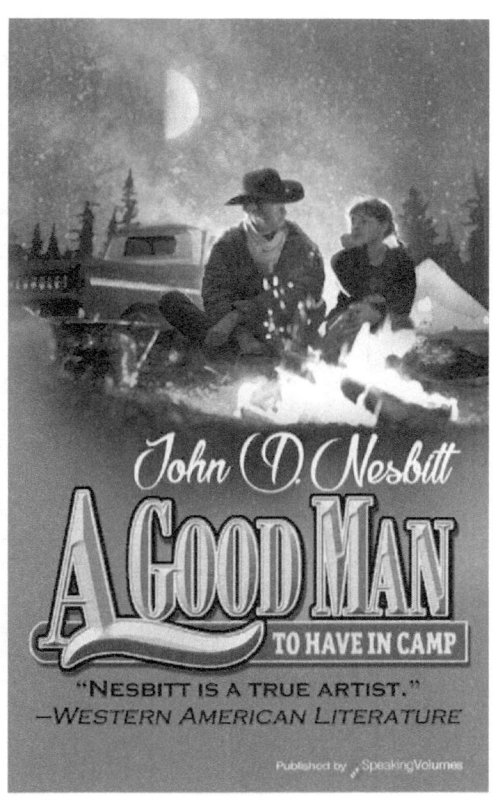

Visit us at www.speakingvolumes.us

Visit us at <u>www.speakingvolumes.us</u>

John D. Nesbitt

ANTELOPE SKY

STORIES OF THE MODERN WEST

"NESBITT IS A TRUE ARTIST."
—WESTERN AMERICAN LITERATURE

Published by SpeakingVolumes

Visit us at www.speakingvolumes.us

Visit us at <u>www.speakingvolumes.us</u>

John D. Nesbitt

WEST OF ROCK RIVER

"NESBITT IS A TRUE ARTIST."
—WESTERN AMERICAN LITERATURE

Published by SpeakingVolumes

Visit us at www.speakingvolumes.us

FOR MORE EXCITING BOOKS, E-BOOKS, AUDIOBOOKS AND MORE

visit us at
www.speakingvolumes.us

Sign up for free and bargain books

Join the Speaking Volumes mailing list

Text

ILOVEBOOKS

to 22828 to get started.

Message and data rates may apply.

www.ingramcontent.com/pod-product-compliance
Lightning Source LLC
Chambersburg PA
CBHW020555260626
47157CB00003B/710